Mirany stood up and lifted the Sphere from the stand.

It was heavy. Solid, maybe. . . . "What is it?"

Kreon shrugged. "An ancient device, full of power. It will need to be read, and doubtless it will show you the way."

"To where?"

He grimaced, a lopsided, humorless smile. "To what you desire. Or is that too dangerous a place to go?"

The Sphere of Secrets

Book Two
of
THE ORACLE PROPHECIES

CATHERINE FISHER

A Greenwillow Book

An Imprint of HarperCollins*Publishers*

Eos is an imprint of HarperCollins Publishers.

The Sphere of Secrets
Copyright © 2005 by Catherine Fisher

The right of Catherine Fisher to be identified as author of this
work has been asserted by her.

Library of Congress Cataloging-in-Publication Data
Fisher, Catherine.
   The sphere of secrets / by Catherine Fisher.
      p. cm.
      "Greenwillow Books."
   "The second book of the Oracle Prophecies trilogy."
   Summary: Together with Alexos, Seth, Oblek, and a fallen silver star,
Mirany is forced to continue the battle against the evil general Argelin.
   ISBN-10: 0-06-057160-8 — ISBN-13: 978-0-06-057160-3
   [1. Fantasy.] I. Title.
PZ7.F4995Sp 2005   2004042436
[Fic]—dc22

Typography by R.H.
❖
First Eos edition, 2006
First published in 2004 in Great Britain
by Hodder Children's Books as *The Archon*
First published in 2005 in the United States by Greenwillow Books,
an imprint of HarperCollins Publishers

The Sphere of Secrets

The First Offering

OF PEARLS

Last night I became a fish in the sea.

I swam deep, and my body rippled and quivered and the long barbs around my tiny mouth trailed and tickled.

Above me was the moon, huge and white. Below, the shells of oysters, half open, breathing. And inside them, tiny and shining, there were pearls, in which I saw the glimmer of my reflection.

Deep in the waters, beauty is made from pain.

This is something gods should study.

She Sees Words on the Moon

So the rumors were true. And *these* were elephants.

Their enormous bodies amazed Mirany. In the evening heat they stood in a great semicircle, twelve beasts, tails swishing, vast ears rippling irritably against flies. On their backs were towers, real towers of wood with gaudy painted doors and windows, within which the dark-skinned merchants sat on jeweled palanquins tasseled with gold.

From her seat before the bridge, on the left side of the Speaker, she watched the animals through the twilight. A huge full moon hung over them, the Rain Queen's perfect mirror, its eerie light shimmering on the emptiness of the desert, the fires on the road, the black ramparts of the City of the Dead. A breeze drifted her mantle against her arm; someone's thin silver bracelets clinked. There was no other sound, except, far below, the endless splash of the sea against rocks.

The central elephant was lumbering forward. Its great feet, heavy with bangles, thudded into the soft sand, the swaying mass of silver chains on its neck and ears and back brilliant in the moonlight. It wore a scarlet harness of tiny bells and immense pearls, the largest dangling between its eyes, a fist-sized, priceless lump.

Behind the mask, Mirany licked sweat from her lips. The eyeholes restricted her view, but she could see the Speaker, Hermia, and the rest of the Nine, the girls sitting rigid as if in terror, their bronze masks smiling calmly as the enormous beast neared. Next to her in the line, Rhetia fidgeted. The tall girl was alert, watching the crowd. Her fingers, light as dust, touched Mirany's wrist. "He's looking at you," she whispered.

On his pale horse, Argelin should have been easy to find. But he sat in shadow, armor gleaming, the bodyguard of sixteen huge men that never left him now, armed and facing outward. Mirany smiled sourly. There were probably others in the crowd. The general was taking no chances. And yes, his helmeted eyes were turned her way. Quite suddenly she felt exposed, unprotected. But she was as safe here as anywhere, these days.

Hermia stood. Hurriedly, Mirany and the rest of the Nine rose with her, and as the elephant came closer over the cooling sand, the smiling masks glinted under their feathers and jeweled headdresses, all color draining in the pearly light.

The great beast reached the bridge, and bowed its head. The smell of it was hot and rank, of dung and perfumes, and Mirany saw the myriad folds and wrinkles of its dusty skin, the sag of its belly as it lowered itself. She drew her breath in. For the elephant was kneeling before the Speaker. It knelt clumsily, and the thud of its great limbs in the sand sent vibrations across the wooden bridge. The rider, hidden behind the vast headdress, flicked a hand and spoke; the elephant lay right down and lifted its trunk; then it made a sound that chilled the night, a terrible brazen roar.

Hermia did not flinch, though one of the Nine—probably Chryse—made a moan of terror. Argelin's horse started nervously. The elephant looked along the crescent of the Nine. Its eye stopped at Mirany.

It recognizes you, the god remarked in her ear.

Recognizes?

As a friend. They are considered very wise, Mirany. Their memories are older than any other beast.

It has such small eyes, she thought, *deep-set and shrewd.* As she answered she seemed almost to be speaking to the animal. *Where have you been for so long? I thought I'd never hear you again.*

Gods have a world to run. I have been busy.

We need you! Things are going wrong.

From the wooden howdah on the elephant, a ladder unraveled and a man climbed down. He was tall and bearded, wearing a robe of white and gold, so stiff with pearls it looked almost rigid. He put his hands together and bowed over them.

"What is it you seek here?" Hermia's voice rang across the desert.

"I seek the wisdom of the Oracle. I seek to hear the words of the god."

"From what land have you traveled?"

The answer was solemn, and measured. "From the east where the sun rises. From the Islands of Pearl and Honey, over the deep sea we bring the gifts and request of the Emperor, the Exalted, the Wise One, to the Bright god of the Oracle."

The masked face nodded. "How have you prepared?"

"By fasting, by lustration, by purification. By three days of meditation. By washing three times in the silver pool."

"What is your name?"

"Jamil, Prince of Askelon, companion of the Peacock Throne."

Hermia raised her manicured hands. Crystals glinted from her fingernails. "The wisdom of the god is infinite," she said. "The day is auspicious, the hour a sacred hour. Enter the precinct of the Mouse Lord."

Formalities over, the Prince turned and beckoned, and two more men, identically dressed, climbed down from the elephants and joined him. Behind them, Argelin's line of soldiers closed up.

The pearl merchants took out jewel-handled swords and thrust them dramatically into the sand; then they walked forward to the bridge. Without a word Hermia swept around and led the Nine and the three strangers on to the Island. They had sailed in a week ago, a fleet of vast caravels that were anchored now in the harbor, all but blocking it. Their wives wore brilliant colors, their children bracelets of pearl. The whole population of the Port had been thronging the wharfs for days, fingering the bales of merchandise, the cloth, foodstuffs, gems, ivories, exotic fruits—bartering, stealing, arguing, tasting. Even on the Island Mirany's sleep had been broken by the bizarre trumpeting of the elephants, terrible and fascinating.

Walking now under the moon, she said in her mind, *Do you already know what they want to ask?*

I know.

And will she give them the right answer?

He laughed, a quiet sound. But all he said was, **The palace is full of such wonders, Mirany, and all for me. Music and silver gaming boards and food—such sweet tastes! And there are tiny fish in the garden pools with snouts and trailing whiskers!**

For an instant the voice was a boy's, full of delight. Mirany shook her head, dismayed. *Listen to me! Don't you know Oblek is missing?*

They had reached the stone doorway. It leaned, to the left of the path, and beyond it in the mothy dark were the steps that led up to the Oracle. The Procession halted and the Speaker turned. "The Bearer-of-the-God will attend me."

Mirany licked her lips and stepped out. For a second she and Hermia looked at each other, and behind the open-mouthed mask the Speaker's glance was a flicker of hatred. Then they were climbing, the three strangers behind them. Everyone else waited on the path. The Oracle was forbidden to them, even to Argelin, though Mirany saw how he watched them, how, just for an instant, Hermia caught his eye.

The steps were ancient, and worn smooth. They wound in a coiling climb through thyme and artemisia and myrtle bushes, and in the darkness small beetles raced across the warm stones, and an owl hooted somewhere over on the Temple roof. Mirany was sweating in the mask, her breathing loud, and behind her the three men toiled in their heavy robes, the last one carrying a box of sandalwood that smelled sweet and attracted clouds of moths.

Are you still with me? Mirany thought.

There was no answer, and she frowned. She had offended him, then. He was touchy, she knew that.

As they came up on to the platform she felt the breeze that always blew up here from the sea. It flapped her light dress and Hermia's robes, and she breathed it gratefully, and saw the black, restless surface of the waves, moon-glittering to the horizon.

Hermia turned. Her voice was breathless and quiet. "Well, Men of the Pearls. This is the Oracle."

They stood together, as if wary. The moonlight made their stiff robes gleam. Prince Jamil's eyes flicked nervously at the stone platform, the ancient tree, the dark, barely visible pit beneath it. He took one step forward.

"Wait," Mirany said nervously. "You must wait for the Speaker to be ready."

Hermia spread her arms wide, and coming behind her, Mirany helped her off with the blue robe that was crusted with the crystals of the Rain Queen. Underneath, Hermia wore a simple white dress, belted at the waist. Her feet were bare. She turned her back to the men and took off the mask.

For a moment then, as Mirany searched for the Flask of Vision in the basket and held it out to her, she felt Hermia's hatred on her like heat, like the glare of some basilisk whose gaze could petrify. As their eyes met she knew it was happening, that terrible turning to stone, the stupid fear coming over her, making her small, nervous, fumbling. And then Hermia had drunk the liquid and put the mask back on, and the beautiful golden face was smiling at her.

She stepped back, cold.

Hermia crossed the platform. Small mists and coils of vapor rose between her and the men. At her feet, almost lost in the darkness, was the Oracle.

It was a pit of darkness. Smoke rose from it, and invisible fumes, and at its lip dark sulfurous crusts formed, faceted with basalt. It led deep into the earth, into the Underworld. It was the mouth the god spoke through. Looking at Hermia kneeling down, bending over it, Mirany smiled a secret smile behind the mask, thinking of the kingdom that lay down there, the place of the god's shadow, furnished with copies of the world's riches. Seth had told her about it.

Thinking of Seth made her frown. She hadn't seen him for weeks. Since he'd been promoted.

It may be he has other things to concern him now. The voice seemed amused.

Mirany snorted. *Apart from himself, you mean?* It wasn't fair. She knew that.

Hermia gasped. The strange weaving movements of her body had stopped; now she flung her head back and screamed, a horrific, savage sound that made even Mirany flinch. The merchants knelt hastily, the one with the box bowing right over, his forehead to the floor.

Convulsed, the Speaker swayed and fell to her knees. Then she cried out, a great wordless cry, a yell of wrath into the darkness. Hands splayed on the hot pavement, head down, she shivered and shuddered.

Very quietly Mirany turned to the men. "You must make your offering now. Don't go too close. Don't move too quickly."

The merchant gave her a glance; then he turned and said something in a curt language to the others. The one with the box opened it hastily; a waft of sandalwood and lavender drifted into the air. The Prince took a gift out and came forward.

He approached the Oracle warily, with exaggerated slowness. As he knelt the pearl-crusted robe buckled in stiff pleats, its rich embroidery scratching the stones, loud in the silence. Moths danced drunkenly in the fumes of the pit.

He held out his hands.

Mirany stared. Balanced on his spread palms was a perfect globe of silver, a polished shimmer of beauty. Lines were incised all over it, devices and symbols and what looked like writing, strange dense letters that she couldn't read, in tiny blocks of text. It was moon-sized, and in the pale light it seemed another orb of the sky, descended into his hands. As he raised it she sensed its weight, that it was solid, priceless.

"For you, Bright Lord. From the ancient treasury of the Emperors, we offer the Sphere of Secrets."

Carefully he lowered his hands into the miasma of the pit, and with a reluctance that Mirany shared, he opened them. The Sphere fell, like a flashing star. Far below they heard it rattle and tinkle. Then there was silence.

Hermia raised her head. She was sweating, her voice harsh, an effort. "What do you ask of the Oracle, Lord Jamil?"

The man sat back on his heels. He spoke quietly. "The Men of the Pearls seek the god's permission to pass through his land. We wish to send an expedition to the Mountains of the Moon."

The Speaker swayed. She murmured words, nonsense. Then she hissed, "For what purpose?"

"There are lodes of silver in the mountains. Long ago, before the time of the Archon Rasselon, there was an arrangement for our people to work them, and carry the metal back on camels to the Port. The work is dangerous, the desert desolate, but we want to attempt this trade again. We will pay any dues the god requires, for his Temple, and his favor."

Silence.

Hermia shivered, curled tight into a ball. She hissed like a snake, and the merchant scrambled up and stepped back. He watched calmly.

Behind her mask, Mirany gave a cold smile. You had to admit, Hermia's act was impressive. Especially if you knew that there was nothing in the Flask of Vision but wine. Mirany knew, because she'd tasted it. Hermia was playing for time now, probably thinking fast of how much to demand. There would be a huge amount in tax for any trading agreement. Harbor dues, bribes. Argelin and the Temple would be rich.

So what's she waiting for?

The god's voice was somber. **Not for my words. And yet she has just seen them. You have all seen them.**

Where?

They were written on the silver globe.

Hermia was ready. Shaking, sweating, its hair uncurling, the gold mask lifted slowly and out of it a voice hissed, distorted, unrecognizable. Its words were forced out, as if in pain, as if from some great depth. "I have heard. I say this. The desert is mine. It is forbidden. Enter it and you will burn in my wrath. For the veins of the earth are sacred, the heights of the moon are holy. None shall tread them but I. The footsteps of men are a disease, and a curse."

Sudden spasms made Hermia's whole body heave and shudder and then collapse; while the devastated merchants scrambled up and stared, Mirany ran forward and wrapped the blue robe over the Speaker. Then she turned, trying to hide her amazement. "The Oracle has spoken. You should go now. The Speaker will need to recover."

The dark bearded man spread his hands wide in appeal. "This is all we are to expect?"

"It seems clear. The god has refused."

"But . . ." He shook his head, controlling his anger with an effort. "We had hoped . . . surely the god will reconsider."

"I don't know." Mirany's voice was cold. All at once she hated herself for even being here, for being part of this. She wanted to blurt out that the god had said no such thing, that it had been only Hermia who answered. But she was in too much danger already. And any hint of trickery might even bring about war.

The merchant stared at her, eyes dark. Then he gave a slight bow, swept around and walked down the steps, his companions close behind him, their backs stiff with hauteur and dismay. When she was quite sure they were gone, Mirany breathed out, in utter relief. She took the mask off and felt the sweat on her face cool in the breeze. Then she turned.

Hermia was sitting up, hair askew, her angular face shadowed by the moon. She had the mask of the Speaker in her hands, its gold discs and ibis feathers tangled, the open mouth gaping and dark.

"Do you want me anymore?" Mirany muttered.

"Want you?" Hermia was hot, and triumphant. "If it were up to me you would have been reburied in the tomb, laws or no laws. Get out. Send Chryse up here."

Mirany didn't move, to her own surprise. "I expected the . . . god to grant their request."

"Did you? Well, the god speaks to me." Hermia looked at her directly. "Not you. You are still only Bearer, Mirany. And not even that for long, because the god will kill you soon, as he always does." She tucked a strand of hair away tidily. "Until that happens, you can put up with hearing me speak. And with knowing your poor little Archon has failed you."

Striding angrily down the steps, her dress brushing the thyme bushes into rank scent and clouds of midges, Mirany raged in despair. "Listen to her! What should I do? Nothing's changed, after all we did. The Oracle is still being betrayed. And why did she turn them down?"

A snake zigzagged across her path; she jumped back

instantly. It looked at her and said, **Maybe others have an interest in the Mountains of the Moon.**

Others? Who?

But the snake had slid into the undergrowth and the night was silent.

Mirany stood still. Far below, the sea lapped the rocks at the cliff base. Cicadas rasped, a night chorus. She folded her arms and breathed deep. There was one thing she could do. If the words of the god were on the silver Sphere, then she would have to read them, even if they lay deep in the dark heart of the earth, in the caves and tunnels of the god's shadow.

It would mean talking to Seth, or finding Oblek.

She scowled. One would be too busy, ordering his hundred scribes about. And the other would be drunk.

She Lives among Spines and Thorns

The sun slanted in early to the Upper House. Already, an hour after dawn, with the Ritual finished and breakfast being served, the heat of it was starting to creep along the shaded terrace, under the awning that flapped in the sea air.

Up in the loggia, Mirany came out of her bedroom door and paused, looking down. There were two voices. Maybe three. One was Rhetia's and she was relieved about that. She walked along the marble corridor, past the beautiful remote statues of past Speakers, and down the steps into the courtyard. Rhetia looked up. The tall girl was wearing a black dress and a necklace of turquoise and silver; Mirany knew it had come from the merchants' stock. Samples of everything had been sent up to the Island, perfumes, jewelry, robes, for all the Nine. It hadn't done the Men of the Pearls much good. As she sat at the table she puzzled again about Hermia's refusal. Why forbid the Mountains of the Moon? No one ever went there. The desert was a furnace, the hills stark and barren. But if there really was silver, maybe Argelin had his own plans for it.

The tables were spread with oranges and figs and soft bread rolls, and the pale watered wine that came from Alenos. Mirany chose an orange and cut into it with a pearl-handled knife. Juice spurted, a ripe sharp scent. Quietly she said to Rhetia, "Where's Chryse?"

"With the Speaker. Where else?"

Mirany nodded. Since the Nine had found out for sure that Chryse—giggly, golden-haired Chryse—was Hermia's spy, since the terrible night of the Shadow, and the coming of the new Archon, a rift had developed in the sacred precinct. Seven against two. No one spoke to Chryse unless they had to. She pouted and threw tantrums and swam alone in the pool and avoided them all. Whether she was ashamed or just didn't care Mirany had no idea. Once she had thought she knew her. That had been a big mistake.

Rhetia glanced toward the other two girls. Her voice was low. "So what did the merchants want?"

"To set up a silver mining operation somewhere in the mountains."

"Nice. I'll bet the Speaker jumped at that."

Mirany swallowed a segment of orange. "No. She turned them down."

The tall girl gave her a sharp glance. "Why?"

"No idea. Unless—"

"Unless Argelin wants to run it himself, yes. Still, it seems odd. Why not get the pearl men to do all the work, provide slaves, camels, ships, and just cream off a profit from the top? No risks for him."

Rhetia was intelligent and arrogantly sure of herself. Mirany always felt small and dull next to her; she was used to it, and it wasn't as bad as when she'd first come here, but still it depressed her. She sensed the tall girl had a sort of grudging respect for her now, after everything that had happened, but they would never be real friends. Not like she'd been with Chryse.

She took some bread. Instantly Rhetia beckoned the servant from behind her chair. "Taste that for the Bearer."

"There's no need," Mirany muttered hopelessly.

"Don't be ridiculous. Give it to her."

The bread was a small roll, soft and fresh. With a bitter hatred of herself for being so weak, Mirany gave it to the servant, a thin dried-up woman called Kamli, probably Rhetia's slave. The woman's hands were calloused and strong; she took the bread calmly, broke a corner off and chewed it. Her eyes met Mirany's; hot, Mirany looked down.

The woman said quietly, "It seems safe, holiness."

She handed the roll back. Mirany took it, miserable. "Thank you," she whispered.

The threat was real, she knew that. Hermia had sworn to destroy her, and even though by law the Nine could be harmed by no one, secret poison would never be proved. For the last few months, especially at first, after her reinstatement, she had hardly dared to eat at all, except for fruit, which was probably safe. She'd got thinner. Oblek had made some sour joke about it and even the Archon had looked up from his latest pet and said, "Mirany, you do look pale."

But putting someone else's life at risk turned her sick. She ate the roll slowly, still wary. It tasted like ashes. How could things be like this! Nothing had changed! Alexos was Archon, yes, but she was in more danger than ever, and Oblek . . . Where was Oblek?

She stood quickly. "I'm going to the Palace."

Rhetia pared an apricot. "Take a litter. And a few guards." Then she said casually, "We could always use him, you know."

"Use him?"

"Prince Jamil." With a swift gesture she waved the slave away, tossed down the fruit, stood, and pulled Mirany aside into a cool white room facing out over the sea. Kicking the door shut she turned, her voice suddenly decisive. "Don't you see? We could explain to him that the Oracle is being abused. You could tell him what the god really says—that Hermia and Argelin are in it together."

"I don't—" Mirany began, aghast, but Rhetia ignored her.

"Our problem is that we have no forces! Argelin's soldiers mean he can do what he wants. There's no leader to stand against him. Now the Emperor is powerful. He has huge armies—cavalry, hoplites, elephants! Think of it, Mirany! They could destroy Argelin, and then Hermia would have no support, and we could force her out. A new Speaker. A *real* Speaker!"

Mirany had backed to the window. Now she said, "You, of course."

"Yes, me! Why not?"

Mirany shook her head. She couldn't believe this. "You'd cause a war? Deliberately—"

"We need to get rid of Argelin. Don't be so prim, Mirany. I doubt there'd be much fighting. Just the threat would be enough."

"You don't know that. People would die!"

Rhetia shrugged. "Slaves. Soldiers. No one important."

Outside, a gull screamed in the blue air, like a cold omen. Mirany clasped her hands together to stop them shaking with anger. She was appalled and very, very scared. "You really believe that, don't you?"

Rhetia was pacing up and down, the black pleated hem of her dress gathering swirls of sandy dust. She seemed consumed with a triumphant excitement, turning her head and fixing Mirany with an irate stare. "Of course I do. Sometimes deaths are necessary. When she was young, my grandmother was a priestess, too, Mirany. Did I ever tell you that? In the Archon Horeb's time. She had an enemy called Alanta, a woman from a good house on the same island. Only one of them could come here, so they fought for the privilege."

"Fought?"

"With shield and spear."

"To the death?"

"Of course to the death!" Rhetia shook her head impatiently. "Sometimes you have to take your life in your hands, Mirany! The gods challenge us, and if we die we die. At least our cause is a good one. You know that more than anyone. And you know things can't stay as they are here for much longer. We have to look out for ourselves or end up choking on some poison. If it takes the threat of war to restore the Oracle, I'll do it. I'm not afraid of that."

Mirany turned and looked out at the sea. The blueness of it seemed deep and safe; she had a sudden desire to plunge into it and swim, anywhere, away from here. Instead she forced herself to turn back. "Listen to me." Her voice was quiet, and firm. "We say nothing to the pearl men—"

"That's utter—"

"*Listen to me!*" Furious now, she came and faced the tall girl. "There'll be no war and no battles and no smashed ships, do you hear me? That's not what the god wants."

"He's told you, I suppose," Rhetia said acidly.

"Yes, he's told me! There are other ways to do this, better ways—"

"We can't wait for the god! *We* have to act. The gods work through us!"

Mirany looked at her strangely. "Not always."

"What?"

"When the Archon was chosen. Who chose him, Rhetia? It wasn't you, because I saw you at the door of the house, and it wasn't Hermia, because you'd drugged her and left her here. So who was it wearing the Speaker's mask? That tall queenly woman in the robe of raindrops? I think you know as well as I do who it was."

Rhetia was silent. They had never talked about what had happened that night; the suspicion that the Rain Queen herself had come from her mystical garden to choose the Archon was almost a thing beyond saying. Now Rhetia seemed to lose some of her strength; there was a chair carved like a bird with open wings, and she went and sat in it, not looking at Mirany at all. After a moment she said, "I don't know what happened. I prayed, and then a sort of darkness came. When I woke up, I was lying there, on the stone platform, and the dawn had broken and everyone had gone. I ran all the way to the City. And yes, there was . . . someone else wearing the Speaker's robes."

For a moment then, they exchanged glances. Mirany said, "I'm going to find the Archon—"

"That little boy! What use is he?"

"I don't know. I don't know what use any of us are. But say nothing, Rhetia, to the merchants or anyone. Wait for me. Let the god do this the way he chooses."

She was halfway out of the door before Rhetia spoke again.

"I won't be poisoned. And I won't keep silent forever. If you're not with me, I'll do something without you. I will be Speaker, Mirany."

As she walked hastily down the terraces of the processional road toward the bridge, Mirany shivered, despite the heat. As if things weren't bad enough! Rhetia had always been ambitious, and she was ruthless. She came from a long line of proud rulers and queens; she'd always resented Hermia and hated Argelin. But war!

Dimly, Mirany realized there was a stone in her sandal and stopped to unlace it. Kneeling on the stone road, the silence of the Island came up around her like a haze, and with it the heat rebounding off the smooth cobbles with a dazzling glare. Sweat broke out on her back. She wished she'd brought something to cover her arms.

The pause calmed her. When she had retied the strap and stood up again, she felt easier, as if some tension had loosened. In her mind she said, *Are you here?*

There was no answer, but as she walked on she felt the god was close, sensed that peculiar awareness of someone other that she was beginning to recognize.

The road was quiet. A few pilgrims to the Temple passed her, all on foot, some barefoot, loaded with offerings. They bowed, and she smiled back. Rhetia always ignored them, and Chryse would giggle behind their backs, but Mirany felt sorry for them, because usually they were desperate for the god's help, their children were sick or their crops had failed. Though the terrible drought had ended with the Archon's coming, the Two Lands were still dry as dust, the fields, as always, irrigated with the barest drips of water. It was well known that only the richer farmers could afford to pay Argelin's taxes on water. His soldiers guarded all wells and oases and even had a guardpost on the dried-up bed of the river Draxis, which had ceased to flow generations ago.

At the bridge she crossed, looking down at the dolphins that always seemed to play there, in the warm shallows. There were two guards at the land end, Temple guards, and she nodded as they bowed to her, and then walked on quickly. She didn't trust any of them.

It was good to be walking, and off the Island. The desert spread out before her, shimmering with heat, rocky and spined with thorny bushes, hissing with insects. A pungent stink of cow dung came from somewhere, though the road was kept scrupulously swept, and away to her left the dark facade of the City of the Dead rose up, the seated silhouettes of the Archons that lined its battlements black against the piercing blue sky. Flicking off mosquitoes, she thought of Seth.

Argelin had been very, very clever. There was no doubt.

Two weeks after the new Archon had been chosen, Seth had been promoted. From fourth assistant archivist to second. He'd been delirious with happiness, and disbelief. And since then he had been so busy with his contracts and lists and plans and invoices that she had barely seen him. Why bother having someone killed when you could work them to death?

The Port wall loomed ahead of her, its gate open. Before that she turned off the main road, down a track lined with myrtle trees. Here on the highest point of the great cliff that tumbled down to the sea, was the Archon's Palace.

A white, gleaming building, its terraces and corridors rose above the drowned volcano. Precious trees grew in its gardens, watered by fountains, an unheard of luxury. As she came in through the gates she saw the fountains were running and splashing, great torrents of water gushing from urns held under the arms of solemn statues, a whole row of them, silent and identical, beautiful young girls. Yellow roses scented the air. Beyond, in the courtyards that skirted the kitchens, the Archon's army of servants worked, the bustle and clatter of pans coming up from below, the smell of garlic making Mirany's mouth water. On the trees lemons grew, almost ripe, and under the olive groves nets were hung to catch the falling fruit. She passed the new aviaries with their thousand colorful birds, parakeets and macaws and hummingbirds and birds of paradise, finches with plumed tails and scarlet beaks—a cacaphony of chirrups and song and fluttering wings. Once the new Archon had come, every ship in the Port had brought him gifts. Because of the rain. And his youth.

Mirany entered the house.

It was cool, the marble floors so smooth that she slipped off her gritty sandals and walked barefoot. The ornamental pool in the atrium had a bench and a pile of pictured scrolls beside it; she dipped her toes in the lukewarm water and padded from room to room, leaving a trail of wet prints.

"Archon?" she called. "Alexos?"

He was only ten, but the god was in him. Everything, all their plans, all their lives, depended on him. And yet Argelin had known how to deal with him, too.

Every room was full. With toys, with carved models of animals that roared and walked and growled, with board games and bats and balls and conjuring tricks and spinning tops. There was a great model of a theater, presented by the actors' guild, with tiny people to make up the audience and a set of actors with removable masks and a whole library of play scripts. In the room at the foot of the stairs she found chests of clothes and expensive fabrics, all strewn about, scattered with the half-eaten rind of a melon. Spilled raisins made a trail through the halls and galleries. Small animals scattered as she came by, a rat, a gerbil, furry things like guinea pigs, whole litters of them. In one room a great reptile slept on a branch in a cage; the cage was heated by underground piping and the creature sat immobile, its scales lurid green, its eye a coned stare. She wasn't even sure it was alive until its tongue darted out and snapped up a fly, an instant of terrifying speed.

There was no one anywhere. Trying another door, she found it jammed; shoving it wide, a table toppled on the other side, spread with fruit, some eaten. Putting her head around, she said, "Archon?"

The room was dim, the windows filmed with silk. Something chirred; a green slither zigzagged across the floor toward her, hissing. Hastily she jumped back and slammed the door.

He had everything a boy could want. The whole Palace was a child's paradise. When the rain had come, the people had been beside themselves with joy; every well in the town had brimmed full, every duct and pipe and barrel had been filled. Next morning there had been queues of people from here right back to the Port, bringing quinces and damsons and precious plums, gold coins and silks, rings and tunics, musical instruments, animals of every species, a million scrolls of tales and stories. And above all, toys. He had all the toys in the world and no one to play with them with. He had stood on the roof in his gold mask and waved his gratitude, a tiny silent figure.

She came to some stairs and looked up. "Alexos! Where are you? It's Mirany."

No one could speak to the Archon, no one see his face. But they had ignored that, she and Seth and Oblek. Oblek had sworn not even death would separate him from the boy, had marched in and sat down and defied any soldier to remove him. Argelin hadn't even tried. Instead, that night, he had started sending the wine.

Casks of it.

Sweet wines and red wines and vintages from Paros. Distilled spirits in amphorae from the ships of merchants, brought from beyond the sea. Honeyed meads and beers brewed from hops.

For the cellar of the Archon.

Oh yes, she thought acidly, climbing the wide marble staircase, Argelin had known just how to deal with them all. He had given them what they wanted. Their secret dreams.

Except her. He didn't know what she wanted.

It would take a god to know that.

She stopped on the fourth step. "Where are you?"

In the jungle chamber, Mirany.

There was a great door to her left, brass, with the sign of the Scorpion embossed on it in copper. She creaked it open and slid in.

It had once been a room. Now it was a forest, carpeted in turf, great trees rising to its ceiling, creepers and branches crowding it. Through the open windows butterflies flew in, attracted by the nectar that dripped from exotic flowers, and flocks of tiny, brilliant birds cheeped and swooped overhead. There were monkeys of all sorts, baboons and tiny gray ones with babies hanging to their bellies, and longtailed lemurs that swung and screeched and somersaulted with a crash through the foliage. And there was Alexos, hanging upside down from his knees, feeding pieces of apple to a chimp as big as himself.

"Mirany!"

"For god's sake," she said in terror. "You'll fall!"

"No. I'm good at it. Watch me with Eno!" He swung, and the small brown monkey that was his favorite jumped onto his back with a chatter, and then the boy was swarming down a rope feet first, then to a branch, then somersaulting down and down to land on the grass at her side, breathless and dishevelled. "See?"

He was taller. His face was red and heated and full of mischief but its beauty was the beauty of the god. In sudden despair she sat down on the withering turf and put her arms around her knees. "Is he back? Has there been any sign of him?"

"No." The boy looked at her, and his happiness faded. He crouched down. "I've had the servants look everywhere."

"In the cellar?"

"We looked there first. He was here two days ago, Mirany, because he had the harp out and was playing it, such sad songs, like he used to sing for me years ago, before I was young. Then we played hide-and-seek and something happened and I never got around to finding him." He frowned. "Poor Oblek. It's all my fault."

"Your fault?"

"Don't you see, it's because he can't make the songs anymore. It makes him sad. I promised him that when I was Archon, we would go on a great quest to find the place that songs come from. But I forgot, Mirany, because there were all these lovely things to play with and the ceremonies and the children to put my hands on and cure, and being carried in a litter and waving at all the people. I forgot about the songs. And I think he may have gone to look for them on his own."

She shook her head. "Not without telling us."

He watched her carefully. "You think Argelin has got him."

"He tried to kill Argelin. Argelin would have been watching this palace. If Oblek stepped outside, they would be waiting for him."

In a scared silence, they watched two lemurs scream over an apricot. Then Alexos stood up. "Mirany, there's something else you have to do. Tonight. You have to go down into the Kingdom of Shadows and speak with my brother."

"Kreon?"

"I dreamed of him. He stood in the dark and held a Sphere in his hands, a Sphere of Secrets, and he said, 'Brother. This is waiting for you. Send for it.'"

Alexos took her fingers, and his hand was cold. "There were mountains all around us, Mirany, in my dream. Ice mountains. Silver mountains. And the Sphere in his hands grew and grew till it filled all the night, and the mountains opened for it to go inside. And there was writing on it. And it was the moon!"

He Gets More Than He Bargained For

"It's from *what*?"

"A unicorn." The trader laid the long, spiral horn in Seth's hands. "Animal like a horse. Lives far in the west. Beyond the ends of the earth."

Seth turned the thing, wondering. "If it lives beyond the ends of the earth, how did you get it?"

The man winked. "One way and another. Things get traded, passed on. See these? They're called thunderstones. Have one in your house and it'll never be hit by lightning. They come from deep in the rocks."

Seth picked one out of the pile. A small coiled animal, made of stone. Its ridges were like the shell of some sea creature. "How much?" he ventured.

"Sixty. The bagful."

"Forty."

"Fifty."

Seth nodded and added it to the list, a few skillful strokes of the stylus. "As for the unicorn's horn, what's it good for?"

"Medicine." The man leaned on the prow of his boat, its siren figurehead drawn high on the rocky beach. "They powder it, the doctors and the sibyls. Deals with all sorts of complaints. Wind, belly gripes, ulcers. Good for women." He winked again. "You know."

Seth didn't know and wasn't sure he wanted to. But he thought he could sell it on and nodded.

"That all?"

"Everything, scribe. Unless—" The trader glanced around at the slaves, saw they were back on board and came so close that Seth could smell his breath. "Unless you want something special."

"Special?"

"Rare. Precious. Not to be found more than once in a lifetime."

Seth sighed. He should have been expecting this. The biggest con. Always left till last. "Don't tell me. The egg of the phoenix. No, a hippogriff that flies. Or dragon's teeth, and if you sow them an army springs up from the soil."

The trader stepped back. His tanned, leathery face, burned almost black, looked sour. "Go on, scribe, make fun of me. You're an educated lad. All that writing and figuring and learning piled up inside you. But maybe there are things even you don't know about. Things from the gods themselves."

Seth nodded with a superior smile. "I'm sure. So what is it?"

The trader wiped his hands on his tunic. For a moment

he seemed absorbed in the task. Then he looked up. "It's a star, master."

"A *star*?"

"That's right." The man faced him solemnly.

"Oh, come on." Seth gave a short laugh. "Do I look that stupid? How did you get it? Prop a ladder against the sky and climb up?"

He didn't have time for this. The cart should have been back at the warehouse an hour ago; the trader had been late, and the goods needed to be under cover before the next duty roster started. If the overseer found out he was bringing smuggled goods into the City, that would be another cut he'd have to pay out of the profits.

The trader ignored the sarcasm. He yelled something to one of the slaves on deck, a few words in some island dialect. The man went below, and the trader turned back. "Three nights ago," he said quietly, "we were out at sea, between the Heclades and the reefs of Scorya. A bit tricky there, so I was steering. A fine night, before the moon rose, all the stars bright, the Hunter, and the Dogs, and the Scorpion. And then there was a flash, a streak of light from the Scorpion's tail, and something scorched down and fell into the sea— splash!—just off the bow."

The slave was trudging up the beach. Irritated, Seth said, "If you're trying to sell me some scrappy chunk of stone . . ."

The trader turned and took a bundle from the slave. "No stone. When we leaned over the side we could see it, shining, far below the waves. Anton dived for it, as he does for pearls. Take a look, scribe. Surely your Archon would want to buy a star."

He was tugging back the folds of the old wrapping. As the cloth fell open his face was lit with a sudden brilliance that made him narrow his eyes; he looked up at Seth in triumph.

Seth stared. He was so astonished that for a fatal moment he even let it show. In the man's hands, deep in the filthy rag, a point of light burned. White and fierce, a glassy crystal, it blazed; he could even see the faint shadow of the trader thrown by it on the sand. Nearby, the slave lingered, as if unable to tear himself away.

Seth breathed out. He licked his lips, said hoarsely, "Is it hot?"

"No. We were afraid it would burn, but it's cool. Take it, scribe."

Carefully, the fragile crystal was placed in his hands. He narrowed his eyes against the light, caught a faint metallic smell, not unpleasant. He shook his head. "The philosophers say the stars are studded in the outermost sphere of the sky."

"Maybe one came loose. What else can it be? It's small enough, as you see." The trader turned, saw the slave, and jerked his head sourly. When the man had gone, he took a shrewd look at Seth's face and said, "Of course, it costs."

Seth looked up. Everything was blurred; rainbow spots of color dazzled him. He flipped the cloth over the brilliance and nodded, arranging the folds. "I had no doubt it would."

They eyed each other. The trader began. "Five hundred staters."

Seth shrugged, elaborately careless. "Out of the question."

"For a star?"

"For ten stars." He put it back in the man's hands. "Besides, what would I do with it?"

They both knew he wanted it.

The trader looked thoughtful. "As I said, the Archon's favor—"

"I'm already a friend of the Archon." Seth tallied the bill rapidly, brought a purse out of his pocket and began to count over coins.

"Lord Argelin—"

"I doubt a star would amuse him."

"The Nine—"

"Are also friends of mine." Tugging the purse strings shut, Seth pocketed it. He gave a shout to the impatient slaves; two of them immediately grabbed the handles of the cart and began to drag it along the steep track up to the road. If they were quick they'd get it back in time.

The trader sighed. "Four hundred, then. As a favor. Though I could get six on the open market."

"Then take it to the Port, and pay Argelin's commission, and the auctioneer's cut, and the taxes. . . ."

They were silent. Until the trader shook his head bitterly. "You're too cocky, son. That will bring you down one day. That and your greed."

Seth shrugged. "My price is two hundred. I've only got your word for what it is."

"You can *see* what it is." Exasperated, the trader glanced at the tide. "All right. All right. Two fifty. Or I try elsewhere."

Seth considered, but it was only a pretense and they both

knew it. "Done." He took the purse out and counted a hundred staters. "Take that. Send a man to the City tomorrow and ask for the Office of Plans. I'm second archivist. He'll get the rest then." Forestalling protest, he held his hand up. "I don't have any more on me. I wasn't expecting stars."

Reluctantly, the trader held out the fragile bundle. As he took it Seth felt a faint tingle of power through the cloth, just as he had in saying "second archivist," in that elaborately off-hand way. They shook hands; the man shouted to his slaves; the boat began to be pushed off the beach. Seth turned and scrambled quickly up the rocks to the track at the top of the low cliff, soft sand slithering under his sandals. At the top he turned; the ship was already afloat, one sail jerking up, a few ropes rattling through hawsers. Slightly breathless, he watched it catch the wind, the white cloth flapping and filling.

Only then did he allow himself to look down at the bundle in his hands. Crouching on the ground, he slipped the loose scarf from his neck, carefully lifted the star from its rags and replaced it in the soft fabric. Its white brilliance astonished him. Alexos would adore it. And when he got tired of it, Seth had no doubt he could sell it on for at least twice the price. A shining star! Making its own light in the dark! He threw the flea-infested rags away and tucked the new tight bundle inside his tunic. It was the bargain of a lifetime! He grinned, rubbing sweat from his hair. And yes, he'd got it cheap.

Standing, he saw the land was already almost dark. Far to the west, over the mountains, the sun was setting, making

the distant peaks pinnacles of gloom, their shadows vast.
Lights were lit in the Port; he could see the expensive houses
up on the very top of the vertical terraces with their kindled
torches blazing. One day he and Pa and Telia would live up
there. They'd already moved out of the potters' quarter. That
was a start.

The cart was too far ahead to hear by now, and the vast
silence of the desert fell suddenly around him. The wind had
dropped, only the faintest breeze creaking stiff branches of
trees dead from thirst. It was three leagues to the Port, and no
one lived out here but the odd goatherd.

Seth walked quickly. The goods would be useful. Most
he would sell to various officials in the City and pocket the
profit. Some Pa could trade in the markets. Altogether he was
counting on a few hundred from this, enough for the rent for
the new house—

He stopped.

Ahead, on the road, someone was coming toward him.
The scuffling run, the loud gasping of a breathless man.

Instantly Seth drew the knife from his boot and stepped
off the track, behind the dark fleshy leaves of a huge agave.
Bandits! There were said to be plenty out in the desert, and if
they'd been watching the trading they'd know he had money.
Cursing himself for sending the slaves off, he licked dry lips
and tried to breathe without shuddering.

The footsteps were fast, and then there was a slither and
a gasp as if the man had fallen and dragged himself hastily
up. Maybe this was someone running from fear. If so, Seth
thought coldly, the best thing to do would be stay hidden and

let him go by. There was no point in getting killed for some stranger.

Slowly he crouched, making himself small. The vast leathery leaves were cold against his hands; the knife seemed brittle and he tried to imagine himself using it, but the thought turned him cold. In the agave grove it was very dark; he sensed that the man had drawn level with him, a rustle among the leaves. Then the shadow stopped, gasping and cursing and bent over. A big man, heavy. From a bag slung on his shoulder he pulled out something that swished; now his head tilted as he drank from it. The sour smell of expensive wine made Seth stare.

Maybe he moved. Made some sound.

The stranger whipped around.

Absolutely still, Seth stopped breathing. And then he realized, with a terrible dread, that he was not hidden. There was light, leaking from somewhere, the faintest silvery radiance, and it was growing, and because of it the man could see him.

The star!

The stranger lunged in, grabbed him with a vast hand and hauled him out. Immediately Seth stabbed with the knife, but a meaty fist twisted it expertly out of his grip and clamped itself over his mouth.

"Shut it, ink boy. It's me, Oblek."

Oblek. The thought was a soaking relief. And in the star radiance, he could see the familiar bald head, the ugly gap-toothed leer. The hand came away; he could breathe. "What are you—"

"Listen. They're after me. Since I came out of the Port. Two, maybe three."

"Thieves?"

"Argelin's heavies."

"Where?"

"Just behind. Thought I was finished, but now . . ." He clapped Seth on the back with a staggering blow. "Grab that stylus parer of yours and get ready. Two of us should see them off."

Seth stepped back, his hands open. "Not me. I'm not in this." He could hear them coming, horses, too, the clank of weapons. More than one.

The musician's small eyes were cold. "Seth—"

"No! Don't you see? I have to think of Pa, and Telia. If anything happened to me—"

"I saved your life once. You owe me." The words were so quiet the approaching rumble almost drowned them.

"Just run!" Seth hissed. "You'll have a chance!"

Oblek didn't move. He looked disgusted. "I hauled you back up that pit in the tomb. I should have let you fall. All you care about is profit, and your own stinking skin. Your father was right."

"My father?"

Oblek spat, and turned. "What he said about you once." He snorted with contempt and looked sidelong. "Get lost. I don't need a weak-kneed boy. I just wish Mirany could see what a useless piece of dung you are."

A shout. Oblek had his knife in one hand, Seth's in the other. He drew himself up.

Furious, Seth stepped back.

"You heard," Oblek growled. "Run away. Bury yourself in parchment and coins."

"You can still escape! Come with me!"

"Why should I?" The big man raised his head and glared at the approaching riders. "What's the point when the songs don't come anymore?"

Two men, with spears, bending low over the saddle. Oblek opened his arms and screamed, an agony of fury, "Here I am, you scum! Come on. Kill me! *Kill me!*"

With a sickening thud one of them struck at him. Seth turned and ran, ducking, breathless into the spiny growth, stumbling into a foxhole and out, never looking back, hating himself. Behind on the road the yells and catcalls of the fight burst out, the clang of metal, a screech of pain. But what chance was there, he thought, almost sobbing with fury, against spears and swords? Oblek was crazy, demented, always had been, from the beginning. Why should he be expected to die as well?

Rounding a scatter of rocks, he fell full length over one and lay with the breath thumped out of him, the tiny hardness that was the star bruising his ribs. Something scuttled over his neck, and slid off. Chest heaving, he rolled over.

The night was quiet.

Far above him were the stars, thousands of them, brilliant over the desert and he could smell smoke, and the crushed spines of tiny aromatic herbs under his body.

Voices. A laugh. The clink of a sheathed sword.

Oblek hadn't lasted long.

Had they killed him, though? Or were they taking him back to Argelin? All in all, that was more likely. The general would want to finish this himself. With his own hands.

As the thought flashed through him, Seth jerked over, scrambled up and ran. He raced heedless through the underbrush and scrub of the desert, keeping low, back toward the Port. There was a place where the road ran right along the edge of the cliff, the treacherous crumbling rim of the drowned volcano that formed the entire bay. They'd have to pass it. That would be the place.

He skidded to a halt just in time; before he knew it there was only sea below him, black, glinting with reflected light. Hurriedly he kicked tinder-dry branches together, hauled a dead branch across the track, picked up another and weighed it in his hands. It crumbled at the edges. Not much of a weapon.

They were coming already. He slid into the shadows on the land side of the path, crouched down, alert, something almost like joy filling him. His hands shook on the worm-ridden wood.

Oblek was alive. The soldiers had him tied and were half dragging him along on a rope behind one of the horses. Whenever he managed to scramble up, they jerked the rope and he fell again. The men laughed. One of them drank from the wine flask.

Seth prayed the musician had some strength left. He couldn't do this alone. *And you*, he thought angrily to the god, *what about you? Can't you help us?*

I have sent you a star. What more do you want?

Not a voice. Just his own mind, thinking. Was this what Mirany meant when she said the god spoke to her? He took a deep breath, rummaged for the tied bundle, tore it open with his teeth. Light spilled out, a thread of it. He stuffed the scarf back over it.

"What was *that*?"

The soldiers slowed. Then the first came on, pacing slowly, the horse flicking its mane, whickering with nerves. As it passed him, Seth swallowed, knew quite definitely he was too terrified ever to move.

Then he leaped out.

The horse sidestepped, shied; he was up and had the soldier by the arm and had dragged him down before the uproar broke out behind him; the soft branch came down on the man's skull with a thud that sickened him, then he spun and whipped out the star.

"Oblek!" he screamed.

The night shattered. Brilliance blazed from his hand; dimly beyond he saw the other horse rear up in panic, heard Oblek yell fiercely. Something struck him on the arm; he turned, slashing wildly. A spear whistled past him, hit a rock, sent a vast clatter of stones and half the path over the cliffside; scrambling back, Seth saw the soldier seconds before the sword flashed out, and could only dive to the side, the star falling out of his hands and rolling to the cliff edge. He scrambled after it, his fingers clutching desperately among rubble and dust; then the man was on him, a staggering weight, and a blow cracked one side of his face. Spitting blood, Seth kicked and yelled, heaved him off, saw his eyes for a second, his raised blade. Then Oblek came from nowhere, grabbed the man, swung him around, punched him in the stomach, and hurled him off the cliff.

After the shrill scream the night was unbelievably quiet.

One horse stood nearby, its reins trailing. The other had run, probably not far. Seth picked himself up unsteadily. "Did I kill him?"

"You couldn't kill a flea." Oblek bent and examined the man Seth had clubbed. "He's coming around." He shoved his arms under the man's shoulders and hauled him to the cliff edge.

"No!" Face numb, Seth could barely manage the words. "Let him be!"

Oblek barely paused. "We can't leave witnesses. They saw you."

"They just saw light! Please, Oblek! I came back for you. You owe me that."

The big man glared at him, a silent disgust. Then he dropped the soldier like a sack on the path. For a second Seth still thought he would roll the man over, but all he did was bend down and rifle his pockets. Taking the sword and a knife and some coins, he stood up. "You'd better be sure of that, ink boy. Because if he did see you, you can say good-bye to your cozy job."

He crossed to the cliff edge then, and picked up the star.

"What in the god's name is this?"

Seth snatched it. "It's mine. Come on. We've got to get out of here." He wrapped the star and shoved it inside his tunic, Oblek's small astonished eyes watching every glimmer.

"It shines."

"I'll explain later. I bought it." He looked up, froze.

The soldier was on his feet.

There was no time to yell. The man shoved; Oblek was thrust forward, arms out, past Seth. He howled as he fell, the rope, still around his waist, snaking over the cliff edge after him, an unraveling too rapid to see, so that Seth fell on it, and grabbed, and the sudden jerk tangled him, burned his hands, whipped him away.

Feetfirst, he plummeted, turning in the air.

Into rocks and spray and horror.

Into the black smack of the sea.

The Second Offering

OF A FALLEN STAR

I don't remember when I first touched water. Billions of eons ago.

I was hot and burning, a child in a fever, and all at once there was this other, this wetness, a cool hand on my forehead.

Possibly I'm not much of a god, because it was the Rain Queen who brought life, dragging it in the train of her dress. Plants grew, oceans swelled. Creatures swam in her folds and crawled from her hems.

Before she came there was no life.

And no death.

He Selects a Dangerous Master

Death was a terrible place. It churned with salt and sand and it roared in his ears. It clutched at him and sank with him, shoved him down, held its great hand over his mouth.

Seth was tangled in it like rope.

Somewhere inside him a bubble was growing, a huge membrane swelling as if it would burst him wide, webbing his open mouth, a scream that could never be screamed. Just as he knew it would kill him, he was hauled up into an explosion of air and darkness and the smell of fish and a gasping vomit.

"Hang on to me, I said!" Oblek's roar was choked and bubbled. Then he yelled, "Can't you swim?"

"*No.*" Seth barely got the word out before swallowing a mouthful of sea. He choked in nose and throat.

"God!" Oblek's bulk maneuvered under him; he gripped frantically on sodden clothes, a fat, slippery arm. The musician's voice was grim with humor. "Didn't teach you that in the City, then? All that learning? All those notes and scribbles?

Not much use now. Any kid in the harbor can swim!"

"Shut up." Seth was terrified. There was nothing below him. Nothing but water, dark and deep and deadly. *Nothing.*

With a huge effort, Oblek's body turned. His feet splashed. He seemed to be lying on his back, a great whale in the water. "Let go a bit," he gasped. "You're strangling me."

Seth couldn't. He dare not. Water lapped against his lips, flooded his ears. Around him it shimmered with faint phosphorescence; he saw things flicker in it, fish, anemones. Something nibbled at his neck.

More splashing. "There," Oblek grunted. "A ship. See it?"

Breathless, Seth managed, "I thought life . . . wasn't worth living?"

The big man seemed to laugh. "Maybe something changed."

Even Seth could see it now, swinging around into his view. A huge ship, so huge it could never be real. A ship of the gods, blazing with light, music drifting from it. A ship to carry the dead.

With a great convulsion of water, Oblek began to swim. Seth gasped, grabbed again; he was tugged along, choking under the sudden wash, into water perfumed with rose and sandalwood, petals floating on its surface. Then the prow was looming over them. In the dark it seemed monstrous, a gaudy woman who sneered, her hair a mass of snakes, her breast wooden, festooned with weed. Torches blazed over her, ladders rattled, a flotilla of row boats clattered and bobbed around her. The roar of her passing sent waves right over Seth's face.

A half-eaten pasty hurtled down and hit the water next to Oblek.

"*Hey!*" the musician roared. "Down here!"

Seth was numb with exhaustion. He knew his hands were slipping. He was saturated with water; his stomach retched it; it blinded his eyes. The yells and calls, splash of ropes, jerk of hands grabbing him seemed oddly distant, things happening far away to somebody else. The sea clung to him, sucked him back, poured out of his clothes. Shivering, he was dragged out, his feet placed on a swaying ladder, rung after rung. Then someone heaved him onto a soft woolen floor that he knelt on and clutched tight, head down, coughing, sick.

His ears popped.

Music soared. Cymbals and drums, a sitar, other brazen sounds. Terror drained out of him, ran through the very pores of his skin. He opened his eyes.

The ship really was vast. The whole deck was roofed with silk; it rippled like a series of pavilions, carpeted with finest rugs, the warm night scented with spices. There were people everywhere.

"What's going on?" he gasped.

"Our High One gives hospitality to your general. Many people come. Rich people. Big party."

The thin sailor who had hauled him up looked uneasily at the mess on the carpet.

Seth almost choked. "Did he say 'general'? *Argelin's here?*"

Oblek was leaning wearily on the rail. He shrugged.

"Out of the frying pan, eh?"

"You're bleeding."

"And you're half drowned. We're in great shape." He turned to the sailor. "We borrow boat. Quick. Yes?"

But they were already attracting attention. The music stopped; there was applause and a crowd of flute girls trooped out from the pavilion, looking hot and thirsty and wearing blue costumes of flimsy silk. Behind them the doors of the upper deck were flung open, and crowds of partygoers wandered after them into the evening air, drinking and laughing and talking and eating, brilliant groups of men in richly woven tunics and fine robes, the women's dresses embroidered and glinting with gems.

Oblek groaned, scratching seaweed off his soaked neck. "Too late."

The bright people dazzled. Their eyes were painted and outlined in kohl; their elaborate wigs glistened with thousands of braided strands. On necks and arms precious stones gleamed. Wide lapis collars of blue and gold reflected the lights; the smell of perfume was overpowering. A red-lipped woman who stared over at Seth wore spiraling gold armlets that snaked from shoulder to elbow. She said something and laughed. Heads turned to look.

He still felt sick, and could barely manage to stand. "We've got to get out of this!" In the lighted pavilion behind, he could see Argelin. The general stood with Prince Jamil's merchants and their wives, his bodyguards at a discreet distance. There were others, too, dignitaries from the City, the Chief Embalmer, the Lord of the Council of Tombs. Seth wondered if the Nine were here, and his heart leaped. Could Mirany get them away?

"Who the hell are you? Where are your invitations?"

This was all they needed. An ephebe, young, in a fresh dress uniform.

Seth glanced at Oblek. "We don't have invitations," he said quietly, keeping his eyes down. "We're just servants."

"Servants are supposed to wait in the boats."

"I fell overboard."

They were surrounded now. A group of grinning young dandies had come to listen, arms around the flute girls. Several were obviously drunk. "Should've swum around the ship all night," one remarked. The others roared.

Seth felt Oblek move closer.

"What about him?"

"He pulled me out."

The ephebe gave Oblek a hard look. Then he asked the question Seth had been dreading.

"Whose servants?"

Argelin's group was coming toward the entrance. Seth licked dry lips. He gave a rapid glance around, at the smirking faces, the brilliant crowd. Then he looked again.

"*His,*" he said quietly.

Everyone turned.

The man at the back was leaning against the ship's rail, a tall, elegant figure, robed in a fine green robe. His fair hair was elaborately tied back; he wore a delicate collar of silver and his manicured hands held a goblet of wine. He drank from it calmly.

"Is that true, my lord?" The ephebe's voice was distinctly more respectful.

Under kohled lashes the tall man glanced at Oblek. Then at Seth. His eyes were strangely long, almond shaped, dangerous as a desert animal's. Seth held the gaze for a tense moment, fingers gripped tight together.

Then the man straightened and came forward. "I'm afraid so, Officer," he said, his voice aristocratic and bored. Folding his arms he snapped, "What happened, *slave*?"

"There was a . . . wave, Master." Seth had to grit his teeth to stop shivering. "I fell in. O-Oblios saved me."

"A waste of his time, I would say." The tall man turned to the ephebe. "I have never had such a worthless slave. Look at him! Soaked, seasick, good for nothing."

"You should sell him, lord." The ephebe had lost interest. He bowed and pushed through the partygoers. Seth breathed out with bitter relief. Now they could get away! But the tall man drank his wine and turned gracefully to the crowd.

"What an excellent idea!" He smiled, his eyes cold. "Maybe I will. Who'll bid me for him? Alia, my dear, make me an offer."

The red-lipped woman giggled. "Two staters."

"Two? Not nearly enough. After all, he's young and pretty."

Seth risked a glance at Oblek. The big man glowered, alert. They both knew the Jackal was playing with them.

He might be some lord, but he was also a tomb thief, the leader of the most notorious gang in the Port. They knew that, but it was Seth's guess no one else here did, and that unspoken threat of betrayal was all he and Oblek had to defend themselves.

"Three!" some old man announced. The flute girls on his arm laughed.

The Jackal gave Seth a sidelong glance. "That may indeed be all he's worth."

Seth stepped forward. "For the god's sake," he murmured. "*Argelin.*"

The general had come out of the pavilion. His smooth face and razored dark beard were clear through the crowd; he wore a bronze breastplate that gleamed. No paint, no jewelry. Instead he surveyed the foppish crowd with cold distaste.

Instantly Seth ducked away.

The crowd bowed; the Jackal stepped back. "My boat is at the stern ladder," he said without looking around. "Get into it. Wait for me."

Seth didn't hesitate. Argelin knew them too well. Oblek was already lost in the crowd; for a hefty man he could move quickly and without fuss when he wanted to. He also seemed to know where the stern ladder was; Seth had no idea.

Argelin was leaving, it seemed. He drew the merchant lord away from the crowd; Seth, scrambling over the side, caught his voice.

". . . for your hospitality, Prince Jamil. As for the pronouncement of the Oracle, what can I say? No man understands the god."

The dark-bearded man nodded gravely. "It was a great disappointment to us. You know that."

"I am sorry for it."

"So you would inform me, then, if there was any gift, any . . . offering that might be made."

"To change the god's mind?" Argelin smiled.

They looked at each other for a long moment.

The Pearl Prince's eyes were dark and steady. "Anything," he said quietly.

Argelin's smile had faded. Now he said, "Thank you. But who am I to have any influence with a god?"

Prince Jamil did not flicker. "You are the general. You're a friend of the Speaker. I'm sure, if *you really wished it*, you could intercede."

For a moment, Argelin's calmness was almost lost. Instead he laughed, a humorless sound. "Your estimate of me is far too generous. I cannot help you."

Seth listened, clinging on like a spider. Argelin turned toward him and he ducked. From the swaying ladder he heard Jamil say, "I have, of course, sent to inform the Emperor of our failure."

Argelin paused, his bronze armor gleaming. "You're not leaving, then?"

"Oh no. Not as yet." The merchant spread polite hands; his red silk robe flowed like flames. "We'll finish trading, buying and selling. My friends and their wives are eager to tour the sights of your great land. The City, the tombs and statues of the Archons. Perhaps even an expedition to the famous Animals in the desert."

Oblek tugged Seth's legs. He kicked him off, impatient. The general's face had darkened.

"Be careful."

"Careful?"

"Of the desert. It's the haunt of thieves and jackals."

"I have many armed servants, General."

Argelin nodded. "Indeed. But it is also waterless and a wilderness. Snakes and scorpions infest it. And did the god not say to you that those who enter it would burn in his wrath?"

The dark-bearded man put his hands together, fingertips to fingertips. His face was grave. "He did. But I had thought, my lord, that no one knew that message but the priestess and my companions."

The silence was charged. A faint flush came to Argelin's face as he realized his mistake, but when he spoke, his voice was almost mocking.

"Good night, Lord Jamil."

Seth was jerked down; breathless he fell into the boat. "Come on!" Oblek growled.

The boat bobbed, almost capsizing with the uneven weight. As Seth grabbed hold of it in terror, he found that it was cushioned, with a gaudy tented roof of mauve silk, the side curtains drawn so no one could see in. Lanterns hung over the side, shiny zigzags reflecting in the sea.

A black man at the oars glared at them. Beside him, armed and astonished, sat the red-haired man Seth remembered only too well. The Fox.

Oblek collapsed onto the frail bench. "Well," he said sourly. "Don't look so pleased to see us."

The slither of a long hooked blade out of its sheath was

his only answer; just then the boat dipped again as the Jackal dropped lightly down and ducked inside.

"Row," he snapped. "Quickly."

Seth grabbed on to the closest thing; it was Oblek's arm. The sudden choppy motion turned his stomach over. He closed his eyes; Oblek laughed and jerked away. "Poor ink boy. Wishes he was at his safe little desk, eh?"

Calmly the Jackal sat and stretched out long legs. Then he leaned forward and considered them both. "I'm afraid this is our night's haul, Fox."

"Nothing else? The jewels?"

"Change of plan. I've told the others. It's all off."

Aghast, the Fox stared. "God's teeth! The planning. Getting the others on. All that work!"

"Wasted." The Jackal's cold eyes watched Seth. "All wasted."

Knife-sharp, the Fox spat. "I've waited for this, chief." He was glaring at Seth in fury. "We'll cut their tongues out, then we'll tie them together and drop them over the side. They can drown in each other's arms."

Oblek leered. "You with me, ugly."

Before the Fox could roar, the Jackal had reached out and caught Seth and hauled him close, face-to-face. "I think that's a very good idea. You betrayed us, scribe, at Sostris's tomb. And what happened to my reward for helping your precious Archon? We had a bargain—you never kept it."

Sweat ran down Seth's back. "Things haven't worked out."

"You surprise me."

"It's true! The Archon's got no power. He's just a boy—"

"And crazy, as I recall. But you seem to have done well enough out of him. This tunic cost a few staters." He flicked at it; at the touch, his face changed. Before Seth could pull away, the thief's quick fingers had darted in and snatched the wrapped packet out. He leaned back, curious. "What's this?"

"Don't open it!"

As soon as the words were out, Seth knew it was the stupidest thing he could have said. The Jackal raised an amused eyebrow at his men. Carefully, he unwrapped the star.

Brilliance shot across his face. He jerked back; the oarsman stopped, swearing in awe.

After a moment, his long eyes bright with the radiance, he asked again, wondering, "What *is* this?"

"A star." Seth was sullen. He knew what was coming, and it came.

The Jackal nodded calmly. "A star."

"It fell out of the sky."

"Did it now. Excellent. It will more than make up for the little enterprise you blundered into tonight." He rewrapped it, hiding the light. "Consider it an advance on your debt."

Seth tried to answer. Instead he squirmed hastily around and was sick over the side, retching uncontrollably outside the purple hangings. The rower grinned and the Fox gave a bark of laughter. Oblek smirked.

"Dear me," the Jackal said mildly. "Perhaps we'd better wait till we get ashore before I tell you what I want from you."

"Us?" Oblek said.

"You. And your Archon and the little priestess."

Seth wiped streaming eyes. His voice was a croak. "We'll pay you, don't worry. Alexos has money."

"I want more than money." The Jackal spoke with perfect clarity. "In order to get his beloved musician back with his ears and fingers still attached, the Archon might consider helping in a little scheme I have in mind."

"What scheme?"

The thief fingered the star, loosing a sliver of silver. He looked sidelong at Seth. "Something is going on," he said softly. "Something strange."

"Strange? Where?"

Over the muted splash of the oars, the Jackal's voice was a whisper. "In the Mountains of the Moon."

She Returns to the Kingdom of Shadow

The City of the Dead brooded over the desert.

As the Archon's litter swayed on the bearers' shoulders Mirany held up a corner of one of the filmy curtains and looked out at the grim black bastions of the towering wall, the great statues of the Archons. Two hundred and sixty-nine of them, every Archon in unbroken line back to the legendary Sargon himself, immense hands on immense knees, staring out to sea. While the Archons kept their everlasting watch it was said that no enemy could defeat the Two Lands. And below, deep in the tombs, their bodies lay, emptied and preserved in gleaming carapaces of gold and lapis, coffined within nine coffins, wrapped and beautiful, nested in by scorpions, eaten by beetles.

Mirany bit her lip. Dropping the curtain she sank back on the red seat, palms flat on each side against the gentle swaying. The *tombs*. She dreaded going down into them again.

Since the terrible night of the Shadow, when she had been buried alive for betrayal of the Oracle, she had never been back to the City. The Island was dangerous, but at least it was bright, its white buildings full of sunlight, its flowers scarlet and scented. The City was a warren of dust and tunnels, a labyrinth of buildings housing clerks and scribes and painters and goldsmiths, millions of slaves, sinister masked embalmers. The peculiar smells of its corridors haunted her sleep. Sometimes now she would wake at night, breathless, desperate for air, would sit up quickly in the fine bed with its delicate hangings, would climb out just to see her dim face in the bronze mirror.

Her hair was growing; it was almost as long as it had been before. But something else had gone—a timid trust she had once had in people, like Chryse, who had betrayed her. And in the Island. She knew now that there was evil even there, that anything could happen, even among the Nine.

The thought made her remember Rhetia, and she rubbed one eye wearily. What could she do about Rhetia?

"Holiness?"

The litter had been lowered so gently she had barely noticed. Now the leading slave had opened the curtain and was looking inside. "We're at the gate of the City."

"Thank you."

She swung her legs out, the man taking her hand briefly, the loosest of touches. Was it allowed for slaves to touch the Nine? She had no real idea. There was still so much she didn't know. Standing, she felt the pleats of her dress swish around her ankles. Above, three huge black blocks of polished marble formed the gate.

"We'll wait for you here, holiness."

Mirany looked at him, alarmed. "That won't be necessary. I'll be going back to the Island from here."

"But you can't walk the road at night." The slave looked appalled. "The Archon said we were to look after you."

The other five were listening, one adjusting the bindings on his hands. In the warm darkness an owl hooted in the desert.

The man was right. And yet Mirany was certain that one of these men, maybe more, would be in Argelin's pay. The general would be told she'd come here. She didn't want him to know any more.

"The City has plenty of litters. I'll arrange for one to take me back to the Island." Her voice was quiet, though she tried to make it commanding, as Rhetia would have done. "There's no need for you to wait. The Archon will understand."

She turned, as if that was the end of the matter, and walked under the gateway. A faint scent of artemisia drifted from the bushes outside. Without looking back, she sensed the men's dismay, then heard their voices, the creak of the empty litter as they swung it up.

They were going.

She allowed herself a tight smile of victory.

On the other side of the gate two guards gave a hasty salute, and then she was striding across the vast plaza that was the central square of the City. At its heart, black against the stars, rose the ziggurat, the stepped pyramid of sacrifice she had climbed only once. Around it, dark facades now, were the houses of mourning, locked and emptied. They would not be used again until Alexos' death. The thought of that gave her a jolt of horror. She told herself it was years away, but there was no way of being sure. The Archon's fate was to be a sacrifice. If it was necessary he would give his life for the people. That was the promise he had made.

Her sandals made a tap-tap on the dusty stones. There were few people around. Dark shapes ran into corners; one darted close in front of her, and she stopped with a stifled gasp, then let out her breath crossly. Cats. The City was infested with them. Oddly big and black, they bred and fought and padded in the buildings and workshops, watched green-eyed in the dark tunnels. Walking on, her heart thudding, she said quietly, "Is that you, Bright One? Are you hiding in cats now?"

There was no answer.

The god was not here. She was quite alone.

The Office of Plans took some finding. The corridors were sparingly lit with dim lamps, but few people were in them this late at night. A woman cleaner Mirany timidly asked insisted on taking her to the place herself, but it was awkward, as she would only walk behind, eyes down, clutching her wooden bucket, muttering at each corner, "Left here, please, holiness. Right, if you please, ma'am. Sorry, down these steps . . ."

Finally, almost bowing to the floor, she groped for a bronze-bound door and edged it open.

"Thank you so much." Mirany slid past, but the woman raised her head and said abruptly, "Holiness, please . . . You know the god, you talk to him, don't you?"

After a second, Mirany nodded. The woman was a slave, probably ignorant as to who was who among the Nine. Perhaps she thought Mirany was the Speaker.

"Then . . . I know it's not my place to ask . . . but it's my son. He's ill. It's a cough, and sores around his mouth. Please ask the god to make him well."

"I will. But you must also ask him yourself."

"Me?" For a second the woman raised astonished eyes. "I'm a slave, holiness. I can't talk to a god."

"You can and should. Does the boy have medicines? A doctor?"

She knew what the answer would be. A quick shake of the head confirmed it.

"Then I'll make sure he gets them. What's your name?"

"Khety."

"Stay here," Mirany said quietly. "Wait. I may need you."

The office was a new place for her. She was astonished at the hundreds of desks. Even at this hour, half of them had scribes huddled over parchment, writing hastily, so intently that some of them barely noticed her swish past. She walked down the airless rows of the cavernous room and wondered how Seth could bear to work here. But then he had no choice. Not everyone could enjoy the luxuries of the Island.

Ink blotched the sandy floor, splashes of rainbow color. In each wall thousands of scrolls were stuffed into pigeonholes, tags hanging. Others were piled in great wheeled baskets. The air was stifling; she breathed particles of parchment, fibers, dust; scraps of gold leaf drifted in the shafts of light. The whispers of styli scratched and scrabbled all around her.

At the far end the overseer sat at a high dais. He looked up and saw her only when she'd almost reached him, and scrambled off his stool in such a panic it fell behind him with a resounding smack.

Every head lifted.

Red-faced, Mirany whispered, "I'm looking for the second assistant archivist. Seth. Is he here?"

The overseer was instantly curious. "No, holiness."

"Do you know where I can find him?"

"His room maybe."

"Where is that?"

"Oh, you can't . . . Forgive me, lady. It wouldn't be right. I'll send someone."

A scribe was dispatched; in minutes he was back, hot. "Not there, holiness."

Mirany had been afraid of this. He was always so busy lately, always up to something! Aware that the men were watching, she tried to look unruffled. "Thank you. It's not important."

"Is he . . . in some trouble?" The overseer glanced fiercely over her shoulder; pens scratched instantly.

"No. I just . . . wanted to speak to him." It was weak, but she couldn't think of a reason. "Thank you." She was saying that too often.

The walk back between the dingy desks seemed endless, but Mirany was thinking hard. She could have asked the overseer where to find Kreon, but that would have caused even more attention, and someone would have passed it on.

Seth had told her that everyone in the City thought Kreon was just a weak-minded slave. It was safest not even to mention him. She had hoped Seth would find him. Now it would have to be her.

Outside, the woman Khety was sitting on the upturned bucket. She scrambled up, anxious.

"Listen," Mirany said firmly. "I want to find a man who works in this part of the City. A caretaker. His name is Kreon."

The woman stared. "That one? Holiness, I know him. A great lanky man all white as paper. He's half crazy."

"Where will I find him?"

"You never know. Here, there. He never goes outside though. It hurts his eyes."

Mirany nodded, impatient. "He must have some place . . ."

Khety shrugged. The whisper that answered was not hers.

Below.

A prickle of sweat touched Mirany's neck. "Below?"

In the tombs, Mirany. Where you spoke to me before. In the shadows.

The slave stared. "You said something, holiness?"

"A light. I need a lamp." There was one on the wall; she took it quickly and checked the oil in the reservoir. Enough for an hour or more. "Where are the nearest stairs down to the tombs?"

"Nearby. But—"

"Show me."

At the end of the next corridor was a bronze gate in the shape of a vast scorpion, floor to ceiling. Khety put her bucket and cloths down and moved apologetically ahead; she opened a grille, a smaller door in the scorpion's thorax. Beyond it was darkness, a faint stirring of warm air.

"The Gate of Kyros, holiness. It goes down to the first levels at least."

Mirany raised the lamp. For a moment both their shadows glimmered, vast and indistinct on the corridor roof. It took Mirany a great effort to say, "Thank you. I'll go on alone from here."

The woman looked relieved, then cunning. "It's all about the god, isn't it. Some of the old women say his shadow wanders the underground halls, that he talks to the dead Archons down there. Once or twice, when I've been working alone, near the stairs, I've heard them. Their voices, muffled and strange. And music."

Music? In a flash Mirany wondered if Oblek was hiding with Kreon; the idea was a vivid relief. "Yes, it's about the god." She turned. "I want you to promise you'll tell no one where I'm going. Understand? And I'll arrange the medicines for your son."

It sounded like blackmail. But the woman just nodded, her face careworn, closed up.

Mirany clambered through the metal grille. The stairs were shallow and broad, well trodden. Without another word she started down them, her shadow at her heels, holding the lamp out, but beyond its small circle the darkness was impenetrable, thick as velvet, muffling all sound.

Down. Down. When she glanced back, even the faint glimmer of the corridor was gone. She was breathing loudly, too loudly; she made herself stop, listen to her heart thudding. There was no need to worry. There was plenty of air; and she could go back up anytime. She was the Bearer-of-the-God, and one of the Nine. She was not going to panic.

Head up, she strode on down. It was as if the earth was rising up around her; the plastered walls became stone, and then soil, and a strong earthy dryness began to must the air. She felt a faint fur of dust on her lips.

At the bottom, the tunnel walls were close; they had once been painted. Rows of wedge-shaped letters ran in blocks; a frieze showed the Rain Queen standing over the desert, water running from her hands and cloak. Below, the great shapes of the Animals waited, mouths wide. The plaster was ancient and much of it was cracked. Lumps had fallen; they crunched under her feet. She made her way cautiously along to a junction of tunnels, and paused. Five mysterious openings gaped before her.

She took two steps farther and stopped.

A draft came out of one of the tunnels, guttering the small lamp flame; Mirany cupped her hand around it, suddenly terrified. Beyond, in the dark, something detached itself from blackness and moved. She whirled toward it instantly.

"Who's there? Is that you?"

The darkness had cool hands. One came around and clamped over her lips, firm and smooth as a snake's skin. The lamp was blown out.

"Quiet, lady," a voice whispered close to her ear. "You're being followed."

The Sun Is Drying Us Out

He drew her back noiselessly. If it hadn't been for his cold hands on her mouth and shoulder, she wouldn't have known anyone was there. The blackness was complete; she had no idea in what direction she was facing.

A tickle in her ear. Words formed out of wisps of draft. "Take my hand."

She could breathe; his fingers came and gripped hers. Then he was leading her into nowhere.

She tried not to stumble, to gasp. At each step she flinched, terrified of walking into the tunnel wall, her hand out in front, groping, though she felt somehow this was a vacuum, a great emptiness in the earth. When the tips of her fingers brushed dusty plaster, the relief was immense, a sudden grounding. In an instant knowledge came back; she knew again what was up and down, what was forward and back.

"This way," the shadow whispered. "Don't be scared."

Kreon moved without hesitation, a creature that stopped and clambered without weight or substance. In the Book of Guidance she had heard scribes read of animal spirits who led the dead Archons along the Way—the Monkey, the Jackal, the Spider—each a guide and a danger. For a disordered second she felt as if one of them had hold of her hand, that she grasped a paw, the jointed pincer of a scorpion.

Then she jolted against him and realized he had stopped.

"From here we can see who's coming behind." He was crouching; his fingers groped for her wrist and drew her gently downward. "I have many spy holes and watching places."

Dust fell. Small stones slithered.

In the wall, a light showed, a faint glimmer of reflected lamplight. She saw a small hole, no bigger than a cherry. His darkness blocked it, then drew back. He seemed to turn to her; she saw his sharp profile, a wry, twisted smile. "Well. Take a look."

She leaned forward, hands among the rubble.

The spy hole looked down into a dim place, one of the tunnels they had just come through. Someone was groping along the tunnel wall, outstretched hand grasping a lamp. The figure was cloaked, but familiar, an overstrong scent of attar of roses rising from the peach-colored robe.

Mirany stared in disbelief. "It *can't* be."

The flames just below her guttered. The figure turned; Mirany saw a pretty, slightly plump face. Delicate blond hair.

"Mirany!" the girl whispered. "Come back! It's me!"

"Is she one of the Nine?" Kreon's voice was a breath.

"Chryse! The one who betrayed me—Hermia's spy. I'd

never have thought she had the nerve to come down here alone."

He seemed to smile. "Her nerve is gone. She's terrified."

That seemed true. Chryse had come to the junction of passages and seemed too scared to venture into any. She sank down. "Oh *Mirany*," she wailed. "Where did you go?"

Mirany drew back. "Don't be fooled by her helpless act. I was, for far too long. What do we do with her?"

"Leave her awhile. I don't want her to see me, or the Sphere. Come quickly."

They didn't go far. Down steps, around a twisting corner, over a pile of rubble into a wider space. When he said, "You can light your lamp now," his voice echoed, as if the roof was far above.

When the tinderbox had finally rasped out a flame and the wick had caught, she put the lamp on the floor and stood back. Yellow light steadied, expanded into radiance.

She saw a painted chamber, every inch of its vast vaulted roof a colored extravaganza of blue and orange, gold and saffron. The Rain Queen had her arms wide, and the arms were wings, and the whole ceiling was her spread cloak. From it hung pearls, thousands of real pearls, pale and creamy, some strung in long chains one below another, reaching down to where Mirany stood, so that she felt as if a shower of rain had been petrified in the air around her, each water drop solid and perfect, hanging, never reaching the ground.

Kreon stood among them, arms folded, his weak eyes watching her. A lanky man, as Khety had said, his skin dead white, his long hair bone bleached, straggly over his shoulders, his tunic patched on one sleeve. She had met him only once before, when he and Alexos had talked to each other in the strange language of the gods. And maybe once in her vision, where the god and his shadow had fought each other before the world began.

"How's my little brother?" His voice was dry.

She swallowed. "Well. Except that Oblek is missing."

"He told me. He and I speak in our dreams. Having a god inside us, we need each other." He looked around and pulled up a wooden stool and sat down, knees huddled up. He gestured for her to do the same.

There was a chair and a table, but no other furniture in the chamber. The wicker creaked as she sat; it was old, and frayed. "Where is this?"

"The tomb of Koltos." He looked around. "Robbed, as you can see. Many centuries ago."

"How did they get in?"

"The same way as we did. There."

In the corner a great hole had been hacked in the wall. Beyond it was darkness. Mirany stared, appalled. "Did they steal everything? Where's the Archon's body?"

"Safe." He watched her closely, his smile secret. "I have places, Mirany, far below. The Fourth Dynasty tombs were made too close to the surface—many have been robbed. But thieves only want treasure. Over the years I have removed the bodies of the Archons, carried them deep into the earth. Don't fear for them. This is my kingdom and I guard it well."

She nodded, thinking of what Seth had told her of the great cavern of copies below the shaft of the Oracle. That reminded her. "We don't have much time. Alexos said you had something for us, and it sounds to me like the Sphere of Secrets. The god told me—"

"I am his shadow, Mirany." He leaned back, his face webbed with drifting pearl shade. "I know about the Sphere."

Between them on the table was a wooden stand, covered in a ragged cloth that looked as if it had been used to wash floors. Putting out a pale hand, he drew it aside. "And yes, I've brought it for you."

The pearl rain tinkled and clinked. On the stand a silver globe reflected it. Mirany stood up and lifted the Sphere from the stand. It was heavy. Solid, maybe. The writing she had glimpsed before was elaborate, cut into the metal, tiny blocks of text, and now she saw them close; the hieroglyphs seemed like those on old scrolls she had seen crumbling in the library on the Island, forgotten and mouse eaten. The lines and devices seemed like a map, linked; the symbols of animals, triangles, three small stars. Looking up she felt the reflection lighting her face. "What is it?"

Kreon shrugged. "An ancient device, full of power. It will need to be read, and doubtless it will show you the way."

"To where?"

He grimaced, a lopsided, humorless smile. "To what you desire. Or is that too dangerous a place to go?"

She sat slowly. "It may be. We all seem to want such different things. Rhetia wants to be Speaker. Oblek wants songs. Seth wants to be rich."

"And you?"

Now it was her turn to shrug, her warm fingers making

cloudy marks on the cold silver. "I don't know. I suppose for everything to be sorted out. For everyone to be happy."

He leaned forward, suddenly tense. "Not even a god could do that. Not without paying a very great price. Mirany, listen to me now. You and Alexos brought the people rain from the Rain Queen's garden, but nothing has changed. We need a more permanent outpouring, as it was before the rivers died. Down here, where the night never ends, I lie awake and listen. I hear the land drying out, Mirany. I hear its rustles and shifts, its dessication, how the roots of the crops shrivel. I hear the slow crack of stones, the jackals gnawing bones that lie in the desert, the soft flesh turning to leather. I hear ants and the scorpions. Sometimes even, I hear people's dreams, how they dissolve, are evaporated, so that when they wake they've forgotten what they were, except the children, who cry. The sun is drying us out, all our life, so that a great thirst is always inside us." He stood up and walked, impatient, the pearls clinking and dragging against him, over his shoulders. "We need water that comes from deep, from the roots of earth, a great river. A deluge."

Abruptly he turned. "Do you know why they call this the Two Lands?"

"No."

"One is the land above, of the living. The other below, of the dead. Those two realms are linked, through the Oracle, but the Oracle is tainted by treason, like a poisoned well, and you need to find another drinking place, Mirany. A well of miracles."

He turned his head, listening. "You must go. Your little

friend is crying. Whatever you do, don't let her see the Sphere." He came and took it from her, wrapping it carefully in the cloth. "The scribe, Seth. He can read all the old letters. He may be able to decipher this, but be careful. He's arrogant and greedy. He's not sure yet who he is."

Mirany took the bundle back. As he held aside the hanging strings of pearls for her, she picked up the lamp and looked back at him. "What about you?" she asked, curious. "Down here, alone in the dark. What is it you desire?"

He stepped back into shadows. "What I already have," he whispered. *"Nothing."*

Chryse screeched and leaped to her feet. The kohl around her eyes was a streaming mess. "Oh Mirany," she sobbed. "Where have you been? It is you, is it?"

"Of course it's me," Mirany snapped, striding out of the dark. She stopped, intensely irritated. "Why are you following me, Chryse? Couldn't Hermia get anyone more competent than you? How did you know where I was?"

"I made an old woman tell me. And I'm not following you." Chryse sniffed. "At least, not for them. I've finished with Hermia. It's just 'Do this, do that.' As if I was a slave, not one of the Nine. None of the others will speak to me. No one likes me anymore."

Mirany walked past her into the dark, trying to remember Kreon's directions. "Are you surprised? You tried to get me killed. They're all afraid they'll be next."

Breathless, Chryse stumbled after her. "Wait, Mirany. Please."

Mirany stopped so suddenly the blond girl nearly fell over.

"I'm waiting."

"I've changed. I'm not like that anymore. I want to be on your side."

"My side?"

"The god's side. You hear him. Hermia doesn't. She makes it up, I know that. So I've decided, Mirany." Her tearstained face was ridiculously determined. For a moment Mirany let the flame light play on the childish blue eyes.

"How can I ever trust you, Chryse?" she whispered.

Chryse dabbed her face. "I knew you'd say that. I'll show you. I've made up my mind. I'm your friend now and I'll show you."

Silent, Mirany walked on and climbed the steps. They seemed endless, and at the top there were the passageways to negotiate, and out in the windy plaza a litter to find, slaves to rouse. So it wasn't until they were being carried toward the bridge that she could bring herself to speak to Chryse again.

"Rhetia won't believe you."

"I don't care a toss about Rhetia." Already smug, Chryse was reapplying her makeup with the help of a small mirror. "Rhetia's not you. I always liked you, Mirany, even when you first came and everyone else laughed at you. We were friends. I just thought you were going against the god, but now that Alexos is Archon, I know you weren't. So it must be all right, mustn't it?" She closed the mirror and looked up, quite satisfied. For a second Mirany was sour with disbelief. And yet it wasn't that simple. It could all be true. Chryse always looked out for herself, and would have no compunctions about changing sides as often as would suit her.

Perhaps doubt showed in her eyes. Chryse smiled and settled her dress. "And now," she said comfortably, "why ever did you go down in those horrible tombs? And when are you going to tell me what's in that bag?"

"I'm not." Mirany's fingers gripped the cloth.

The litter lurched, stopped, then tipped violently to the left. Chryse gasped, grabbing the tassels. There were voices, yelling. Then the curtains were whisked aside and a man looked in. He was well wrapped, only a single eye showing, a gleaming knife in each hand.

Chryse screamed, a piercing terror.

The man shoved a piece of parchment into Mirany's hand, made a mock bow, and said, "Be there." Then he was gone.

Outside, there was panic. The litter was almost dropped; the slaves crowded in. "Holinesses, are you all right?"

"They were bandits—"

"There were ten of them—"

"Twelve—"

Chryse was rigid. "Why didn't they rob us?"

Mirany laid the note down slowly. "Because they've already got something of ours."

"What?"

"Oblek. They've got Oblek."

The Third Offering

OF GOLDEN APPLES

Can a god commit a crime?

Once, long ago, I came to a place where all the dreams of the world were stored.

Dreams of music, of the joys of children, the poems not yet written, old women's hoarded memories. They were all there, lying in heaps around the cave.

Take nothing away, the Rain Queen warned me. She set monsters and many-headed dragons to guard the entrance.

I could not help it. I stole three golden apples.

They were so small!

But I never found the cave again.

It Has Been Centuries
Since I Gazed into Its Depths

"Where is she?" Seth paced the turquoise floor impatiently. He felt trapped in a great jewel; the walls and ceiling were complex facets of blue glass. His own reflections marched toward and away from him, upside down, anxious.

Alexos, feeding the monkey, said mildly, "Running up the stairs. I wish you'd keep still, Seth. It's making Eno giddy."

Seth glared at him. Then the door opened and Mirany stumbled in.

He hadn't seen her for weeks. She never came near the City, and nowadays he rarely left there, because being second assistant archivist meant a lot more work than he'd imagined. She looked different, he realized. Flushed and hot, but more assured. Not the timid girl he'd first met. To his surprise it was he who felt shy. To cover it he made his voice gruff.

"You know about Oblek?"

She looked at him, drew breath, and said, "Yes. Hello, Archon."

"Hello, Mirany. I'm sure Seth doesn't mean to be rude. He's worried." The boy let the monkey drop down and turned to them, his perfect face clouded. "So am I. They won't hurt Oblek, will they? Seth says the Jackal has kidnapped him."

She glanced at Seth. "He's safer with them than wandering around the Port. Look. They sent me this note." She held it out; Seth came and took it, awkwardly. Blue images of himself moved alongside him, over and under him.

The parchment was good quality. The writing was the Jackal's; he recognized it.

WE HAVE THE MUSICIAN. ARGELIN WILL NOT FIND HIM. BE AT THE PALACE OF THE ARCHON AT NOON.

It wasn't signed.

"Well." Mirany crossed to the canopied balcony and sat on the window seat, glancing out at the blue sea and the shimmering white buildings of the Island. "What's been going on?"

"It's very exciting." Alexos came and sprawled on his stomach on the shiny floor, feet in the air. "Seth found Oblek and they had a fight with some soldiers. Then they fell off the cliff."

Her eyes widened, a flash of alarm. "Off a cliff! Were you hurt?"

"No." Seth had caught it though; she still cared what happened to him. He sat in the Archon's chair, leaning back. His voice relaxed; he waved a hand easily. "Oblek was, a bit. We swam, but the currents were strong and dragged us out into the bay. We would have been in trouble if the ship hadn't picked us up."

Mirany looked relieved. "It's a good thing you can swim! Most scribes can't."

He shrugged, red. "I had to keep Oblek up. He was . . . in a bad way."

"Tell her about the Jackal," Alexos said impatiently.

Seth nodded, modest. "The ship was one of the pearl men's fleet, a great caravel. There was a banquet going on aboard—Argelin was there and I was terrified he'd see us. So we pretended to be slaves. Of the Jackal."

"How?" The note of admiration warmed him.

"He's some sort of lord. I think we interrupted a theft he had planned, but he went along with us, though I should have known he'd have his reasons. When we got to the Port his men dragged us through the streets into some cellar. I don't know where—we had sacks over our heads."

Alexos giggled. "I'll bet you looked really silly."

Seth glared and turned back to Mirany. "I thought he was our friend," she said thoughtfully.

"He's a thief, Mirany. Ruthless. He says we owe him for getting Alexos into the ninth house. The cellar was full of his people, cutthroats, smugglers, women. Oblek settled right in. There's plenty of drink and he says they won't hurt him. The Jackal has some scheme—he'll only speak to the Archon, and said to expect him. When I said that no one spoke to the Archon, he laughed. The next thing I knew I was bundled out, dragged down a few streets, and dumped."

Mirany frowned. "You think he's coming here? How?"

"I don't know."

Alexos shook his head. "Argelin has guards all around the building. They'll know."

A knock on the door startled them.

Alexos rolled over. Then he said, "Come in."

The palace steward. Looking terrified. For a second Seth knew the Jackal would walk in behind him with a knife in his back, but the man's words were even more unexpected.

"Lord Argelin is here," he whispered.

Seth jumped up. With a rustle Mirany came in from the balcony; glancing at her he saw she was pale.

"Be careful," she whispered.

Argelin was already in the room. He wore dark bronze armor and a red mantle; his smooth beard was immaculately shaved. A scent of tamarisk drifted around him. He took in Seth and Mirany with one rapid look, then gave a mock bow to Alexos. "My Lord Archon."

Alexos bowed back gravely. "General. This is a big surprise."

"I'm sure."

"Won't you sit down? Fetch a chair, Seth."

Argelin smiled. "I'm not staying. I just came to bring you some unfortunate news."

He waited, so Alexos had to say, "What news?" And then he smiled again, a cold pleasure that chilled Seth.

"The drunken, foul-mouthed musician . . ."

"Oblek?"

"Is dead."

There was an acute silence. Argelin dusted the chair with a glove and sat, leaning forward. "He was found by a patrol out on the cliffs and captured, but a fight ensued. He killed one of my men, and then was thrown over the cliff. No trace of his body has been found, but you know, *Lord Archon*, how the current is out in that bay, how deep and dark the water is."

They were too calm, Mirany thought. They should be more stricken. He might guess.

But Argelin leaned back, as if the shocked stillness satisfied him.

Alexos got up and walked out onto the balcony. Above him the canopy flapped in the hot wind. His back to them, he spoke quietly.

The water has opened her arms to him, then.

Mirany stiffened. Seth saw how she glanced at him, how the turquoise room seemed all at once to be moving around them, as if they were in a bubble, sinking, deep, the waves above them.

Argelin glanced around; a slight frown creased his face. "No loss. He owed his life to the god, after all. The god has taken it."

Alexos turned. With two steps he was across the room and looking straight into Argelin's eyes.

I am the god, Lord General.

For a moment his voice echoed, immensely old, through all the ages of the earth. Then it was a boy's, petulant. "And Oblek was my friend. I liked him."

Argelin stood. "You have two friends left." His dark eyes moved to Mirany. "For the time being. Look after them a little better, Mouse Lord."

At the door he paused and glanced at Seth. But he went out without another word.

Mirany breathed out tension. "He enjoyed that. You could see."

"So did I," said the man leaning inside the balcony.

She gasped; Seth grabbed Alexos, pulled him back.

"It's a sad thing," the Jackal remarked, ducking his head under the canopy as he came in, "that a thief is more feared than a tyrant."

"How did you get in here?"

"Over the roofs, down the terraces." Winding a thin rope around his waist, he put a foot on the chair Argelin had used and slid a narrow blade into his boot. "Your security is lax, mad child. Anyone could get in."

Astonished, they stared at him, but he surveyed the room curiously with his long eyes, noting the crystal walls, the carved balustrade of glass that hung over the gardens below.

"Fascinating. Is this a solid jewel?"

"It's the most secret chamber." Alexos came out from behind Seth. "No one can listen through the walls here."

"And they do that, do they?"

The boy nodded, wide eyed.

The Jackal raised an eyebrow. "There are drawbacks, then, in being a god." He pulled the chair up and sat astride it. "So Argelin thinks the man who tried to murder him is dead. I could show him otherwise."

"What do you want?" Mirany whispered. Despite what Alexos had said, she couldn't help glancing at the door. Seth noticed. He crossed the room, opened the blue crystal panel, and glanced out.

The white loggia stretched empty, all its filmy hangings moving in the breeze.

"No one."

The Jackal had found a jug of water. He poured from it into a chased silver goblet and drank.

Then he said, "What you owe. Without me, you would be dead, girl, and this mad boy would be herding goats and picking lice out of his hair. Remember that."

Alexos came and sat by him calmly. "That's true," he said. "Isn't it, Seth?"

The Jackal took another drink. His grin was amused; his long eyes slid from Alexos to Mirany. Then he said, "Listen. Three months ago, on the day of the second seedsetting, a patrol of Argelin's men were out in the desert, beyond the Oasis of Katra. They saw something dark crawling among the dunes, and when they came up to it, they found it was a man. The burned, dried-out remains of a man. He was barely sane, his skin blackened and flyblown, burrowed by sandworms, his tongue swollen, his eyes blind. They carried him back to the Port, but it was clear he would not live. He was put into a litter and taken to Argelin's headquarters, at dead of night, under heavy guard. No one was told, no reports were made, no forms filled out. A doctor Argelin trusts was sent for. The man's very existence was kept secret."

"So how do you know?" Seth asked suspiciously.

The tomb thief's smile was unruffled. "My people know everything. Go everywhere."

"Even Argelin's guardhouse?"

"Quiet, Seth." Mirany was alert. It annoyed him, but she didn't seem to notice. "Go on."

"Thank you, holiness." The Jackal drank, taking his time. "Well, when he was conscious, the traveler gasped out his story. It seems he was the last survivor of a secret expedition Argelin had sent out months earlier: seventeen men, camels, a wagon. They had left two days after the Choosing of the Archon. Since then nothing had been heard of them. Argelin had probably written the whole thing off."

"Expedition to where?" Mirany said quietly.

There was a suppressed excitement in her voice. *She knows something about this*, Seth thought.

The Jackal obviously thought so, too. He looked at her thoughtfully. "To the Mountains of the Moon, lady."

"For the silver!"

He was silent. Then he said, "Indeed, long ago there were silver mines in those highlands. Before the Archon Rasselon and the great drying up of the rivers. It seems certain that Argelin had plans to try and reopen the trade for himself."

She shook her head. "Not only him. Prince Jamil wants the same."

Outside, the canopy flapped. Warm air moved through the blue jeweled room.

"How do you know?" Seth asked.

"That's what he asked the Oracle. But the god—that is,

Hermia—told him he couldn't enter the desert. Argelin must have told her what to say."

"I'm not surprised." The Jackal's voice was dry. "Because what is hidden in the mountains turns out to be more precious than silver."

"*More* precious?"

"Much more. The survivor gabbled, in his delerium. About great gates, a city, animals that talk. About the Well of Songs."

Mirany turned, her skin prickling. Alexos had lifted his head, was staring at the man in delight, his dark eyes shining. **The Well of Songs! It has been centuries since I gazed into its depths.**

Was it spoken aloud? The Jackal glanced at the door quickly. "The very same. The mystic Well of legend. But what really shocked Argelin to the core was the small bag they found strapped under the man's rags. It contained five tiny lumps of ore. Argelin had it tested. It was gold. Pure, incorruptible, yellow, priceless gold."

Seth was silent. In the blue-faceted room of crystal only the waves could be heard, far below at the foot of the cliffs, and a gull, far out on the water, screaming.

"Gold," Alexos breathed.

The Jackal sipped the water. "Gold, little mad one."

"But he doesn't know where," Mirany said. "Surely the mountains are so vast he could never find it. . . ."

"Surely, holiness, you are wrong." Suddenly the tomb thief had lost all his amusement; his face was tense, his eyes sidelong. "Think of what it means for him. He has to find it, because gold will bring him everything. He will buy mercenaries, artillery, power. He will no longer need the Oracle or the Nine. Argelin will make himself more than General. He will make himself king."

Placing the cup on the table, he sat back and watched them, the mockery coming back into his voice as if he could not keep it out.

"Who knows. He might even decide he can do without the god."

She Sees the Signs in His Face

Mirany gave the steward her best glare. "The Archon is busy," she snapped. "Not to be disturbed."

"But he always wants to see new gifts, lady. A deputation has come from the Guild of Music Box Makers."

She bit her lip. "Thank them for the gifts. Show them somewhere, give them refreshments. They know no one can see the Archon."

The steward bowed, looked harassed, and backed off.

Mirany closed the door and leaned her back against it, breathing out with relief. Her dress was damp with sweat.

The Jackal stepped out of hiding and sheathed the knife. "Very good. I've said before that you're wasted on the Island."

Alexos was cross-legged on the floor, the monkey on his shoulder. "All right," he said as if the interruption had never happened, "so there's gold. But the Well! I remember the Well, Mirany. So high, so remote. Hidden in a cave in the snows of the highest pinnacle. The water is deep and fresh and icy. Whoever drinks of it tastes the god's joy!"

She came and knelt by him. "When did you go there?"

"All the Archons went once. Xamian. Darios. Rasselon went, but he was the last, because he stole the three golden apples from the Rain Queen, and she was so cross that she hid the Well and withdrew the rivers. They shriveled up, all of them, even the great Draxis. Since then, some of the Archons have searched for the Well. None of them found it. . . ."

"You will." The Jackal had come back to the chair. "I intend to get to the gold before Argelin, and there's only one way. You, little crazy one, are to make a great proclamation. That the Archon Alexos will revert to the ancient custom of his predecessors. That he will make the Pilgrimage of Suffering to search for the Well of Songs, and expiate the sin of Rasselon. Unmasked, barefoot, with only a small group of chosen companions." He sat gracefully. "Of which I, needless to say, will be one."

Seth came in from the balcony. "You're the one who's crazy. It's a journey into death! You said yourself only one man survived."

"They did not have the Archon." The thief's strange eyes watched Alexos. "*The Archon who can turn stones into water.*"

Silence.

Until Seth said tightly, "How did you know about that?"

The Jackal laughed his cold laugh. "The musician talks a lot when he's drunk. And believe me, we keep him drunk."

The monkey chattered and ran to Mirany, who picked it up. "This is about more than gold," she said slowly.

"Is it?"

"I think so."

The Jackal looked at her. After a moment he said to Seth, "On the ship. Why did you think I wouldn't give you away?"

"Because I'd talk. And because you enjoy risks."

The tall man stood and strode to the balcony. His back was stiff, his fair hair tied back.

"Astute. A scribe's close scrutiny. Yes, I take risks. Risk is all that keeps me alive." Looking out at the Island, he said, "My family was once among the most exalted here, did you know that?"

"No," Mirany whispered.

"Years ago, before the Council of Fifty was dissolved. Before Argelin came to power, before lists of dissident men were posted on street corners, before wives and children disappeared, before heads adorned the spikes of the Desert Gate. My father was rich, and respected. We had a great house on the cliff top, cool marble floors, fountains. Now sand covers it; bats haunt its ruin."

He turned to Mirany and crouched, so that his face was level with hers, his long hands on her wrists. "I remember how they broke down the doors, how my father was cut down in the courtyard, how my mother screamed, how her sons were dragged away. I remember how the fountains ran red."

She was silenced. His look flickered; something dark came and went in him. But he drew back, and she saw how he breathed in, how his hands were steady.

"I was too young then to be a threat. And by now Argelin has forgotten me. He sees a painted princeling, effete, short of money, a scrounger of invitations to every play and party, with a taste for antiques and pretty women. A man who lives on others, a man without honor. All that I allow him to see." He turned to Alexos. "But below the bright desert lie the tombs. Ghost-haunted, dark, piled high with forbidden treasure. And there's not one thief in the Port who does not fear the Jackal, not one pimp, cutpurse, rogue, or beggar with painted sores who does not know that name. Argelin thinks he rules, but the Underworld is mine. The streets, the opium dens, the hidden store places, the nests of pickpockets. Like the god's shadow, I haunt him silently." His face was edged with blue light. As if he'd said too much, alertness came back to him; he glanced sharply around.

Seth said, "Don't you have enough gold?"

"Not to infiltrate the army. But now I will." Abruptly he walked over to the balcony, glanced over, then up. "Do as I say, Archon. Set up the pilgrimage. We'll find your Well, any well, and I'll gain us enough to bring Argelin crashing down." He glanced over. "I'll be awaiting your proclamation. And remember, so will Oblek."

With a lithe vault he swung himself up onto the blue glass balustrade, feet balanced. "Though he may not want to come back."

Alexos said, "You won't hurt him?"

"Hurt him?" The Jackal tensed, ready. "Why bother? He'll drink himself to death."

Then he jumped.

Mirany gasped, but already the man was gone, hauling himself lightly up the carved cornices of the building, slithering on to the flat roof. She ran over and looked up. A few flakes of dislodged plaster fell on her face. The sky was blue and empty.

"And how does he think," Seth muttered angrily behind her, "that we can find the Well or some seam of gold in a range of mountains thousands of miles long?"

Mirany pulled herself back into the room. "Alexos knows the way."

The boy looked unhappy. "I don't. I've never found it again, Mirany."

"Then we'll have to use this."

She went over and brought it out of the bag she had placed in the corner, and held it out, her eyes never leaving Seth's face. She saw what she had expected, that flicker of amazement, of desire. Unmistakable.

"What is that?" he breathed.

"The Sphere of Secrets." She handed it to Alexos; his thin hands clutched it tight. "The merchants brought it as an offering to the god. It needs to be deciphered. Kreon says it's a map of the way to all we desire. The Well of Songs."

Seth reached out, impatient, and snatched it as if he couldn't wait any longer. He held it up, turned it, fascinated. "The text is archaic. Pre-Second Dynasty at least. They used a half-syllabic, half-symbolic alphabet—I've seen it on scrolls in the Room of the Crocodiles."

"Can you read it?" Alexos asked, anxious.

"Odd words. *The road . . . gates of . . . Beware . . .* I'd need to get it back to the City and work on it."

"The City!" Mirany said. "Would it be safe?"

He looked at her. "As safe as on the Island."

He was right, of course. She had had to sleep with the bag that contained it tied to her hand in bed. Chryse had been in her room after the dawn Ritual; when Mirany had come back from breakfast the blond girl had been sliding breathlessly out. "Looking for you," she'd said.

There was no safety in the Upper House.

Seth's eyes were bright with pleasure. "It shouldn't take long. There are word lists there, translations."

"You won't show anyone?"

"Of course not." Preoccupied, he barely listened. The silver Sphere glimmered in his hands.

She glanced at Alexos; the boy smiled at her, and then reached out and gently patted her arm, an old man's reassurance. "Don't worry, Mirany," he whispered. "It will be quite safe with Seth."

"And what about you?" she said. "Going into the desert? Into that terrible desolation?"

He shrugged. For a second, bleakness filled his eyes, ancient and anguished. "I was Rasselon. It was all my fault. How long has it been since the rivers dried up?"

"I don't know," she mumbled.

He nodded, then brightened and grasped her hand. "Let's go and see my new presents," he said.

She thought of that elaborate music box later, the way it had played tune after tune, and how he had danced happily around it with the monkey screeching. She thought of it as she stood in the stifling heat behind the smiling mask of the Bearer-of-the-God, with Chryse fidgeting beside her and the great bronze bowl in her arms. There was a scorpion in it, just one, and it sat motionless in the bottom, its tail rigid and quivering. She had no idea if it was the god. When she asked, no one answered. But there was music here, too, a harsh brazen clamor of cymbals and zithers and horns, and the scorpion crouched, seemingly flattened by the noise. Tense, she waited for it to scuttle, then flipped it expertly back into the bowl. She was calm, licking salty lips. Being Bearer demanded constant concentration.

Around her, on the steps of the Temple, the evening was hot, the light of the setting sun a red furnace that burned them all. Hermia had spread the last of the great scarlet silks down the marble slabs; now she knelt and bowed down to the ground, the openmouthed mask touching the rippling cloth.

"Scorpion Lord, Bright One," she said clearly, her voice ringing. "Your people wait. Your sun burns. Your land scorches. Your day ends. On the feast of your Reconciliation with the Shadow, bless the fevered and the thirsty, those who suffer."

The scorpion's tiny pincers scratched the bronze. It seemed to explore the incised lines of decoration. Mirany felt sweat run down her forehead. Her arms ached.

Hermia sat back on her heels, and behind her, the Nine came forward, forming a semicircle, and beyond them the people crowded, the sick, carried on stretchers, limping, hobbling, children, aged.

Argelin's soldiers kept them back, a firm line of armored men, spears crossed. Behind them, in elaborate litters, the aristocracy watched, the guildsmen and eminences of the City, the scented actors, the polite, curious merchants. Prince Jamil was there; she saw him through the eye slits, sitting in the shade of a great canopy. Then he stood, and she knew the Archon had come.

Risking a glance, she turned her head to the Temple.

Alexos stood on the highest step. For a second, in that garish light, she felt sure that the statue of the god within had stepped down from its pedestal and come out here. But the sun dazzle blinded her; when he stepped down she saw it was only him, a tall thin boy in a white tunic, with the gold mask on his face, the beautiful grave mask of the god, his dark hair almost hidden by its feathers and looped hanging crystals. He raised one hand and beckoned.

Behind the Nine, Argelin nodded. His guards separated, making a gap in the line, an avenue of spears. Slowly, the people began to stumble up.

These were the ones who would have been able to pay. She knew very well that anyone who wanted to get near the Archon would have had to bribe not only the general, but his officers, and probably the scribe of accession, and maybe even something for the Island coffers. Those who couldn't pay were at the back, and stood no chance. From their wails and cries, they knew it.

Argelin was on his white horse, his bodyguard standing around him. She saw how he watched Hermia, covertly, and there was a preoccupied, moody look about him.

The sick stood in a row, and Alexos moved along them. From here she couldn't see, but she knew he was touching them, his frail hands on their suppurating sores, on their ulcers and fractured limbs, their fevered faces. Silent, masked, he was the god and the god was their last hope. Gulls cried over him, high in the warm air. Stillness fell, the sun descending, the distant mountains flushed with its light. For a moment the peaks caught her attention; the highest glimmered white, cleft and unscalable. Was there a Well up there, a place like Kreon had spoken of, untainted, a pure Oracle between the lands of the living and the dead?

The faintest touch nuzzled against her thumb. She glanced down and froze.

The scorpion was balanced on the rim of the bowl.

Beside her, she felt Chryse's utter stillness.

"Don't do this!" she breathed. "If this is you, don't kill me. Not yet. Not here!"

To serve the god means treading the edge of death, Mirany.

"I know. But you need me!"

There is so much suffering here. Look at it, Mirany. Do they expect me to cure all of them, to take away all that brings them to me? If they were not hurting, would they even remember I existed?

She took a careful breath. "They want to live. I want to live."

But the garden of the Rain Queen is so much better. You know. You've seen it.

"Please. My friends are here."

I thought you were different, Mirany. The voice sounded peeved. **But you're just like all the rest of them.**

A gust of wind fluttered her dress. The scorpion fell with a scutter, sliding helplessly down into the depths of the polished metal. Mirany closed her eyes; her whole body ached with tension.

"Thank you," she breathed.

There was no answer.

Except that a great cry came from the line of sick. One of them jerked back, screamed.

Hermia stood quickly; behind her Argelin barked an order and soldiers raced up the steps, but the Archon held up his hand and they slowed, reluctant.

It was a woman, and she was sobbing now. She was holding out her hands to the crowd, and she screamed, "I'm cured! The god has cured me! *I'm cured!*"

The crowd went wild. They surged forward, breaking the cordon, a great wave of people racing up the steps. Argelin yelled, furious.

"Mirany!" Chryse gasped. "Quickly!"

The Nine clustered together on the scarlet silks. Below her she saw all the crowd's thousand faces, all the hope, the excitement, the terror. It came at her like a wave and she almost stumbled, but the soldiers had regrouped; savagely they beat and forced the people back, and the front rows were crushed and screaming until a voice said, "Keep still, all of you."

A clear, petulant voice.

A voice that came from the golden mask of the Archon.

Mirany licked her lips. The crowd fell totally silent. Their astonishment was huge. The Archon never spoke. His voice was never heard until the day he gave up his life. The only voice the god had was the Speaker's, but now Hermia was standing still, and judging by her stiffness, as astounded as any.

"I have something to say to you, and I know it's against the rules. But the rules only go back a little way, and I can remember when there were none, and the Archon spoke freely to his people. When I talked to you, even without a mask."

A stir in the crowd. Argelin had dismounted; he was pushing desperately forward, his men shoving people aside.

Alexos had noticed; his voice quickened. "We've become separated; it's all gone wrong somehow, hasn't it? What use is an Archon who only helps you by dying? So I've decided. I'm going to put things right."

Argelin had almost reached the steps. *Quick!* Mirany thought.

"I proclaim, here and now, in front of all of you, that I intend to make the great pilgrimage of the Archons, to make the journey that each Archon made, centuries ago."

She moved.

As the general leaped up the steps she stepped right in front of him, blocking his way. The bronze bowl clinked against his breastplate; the scorpion scrabbled up the side. For a split second of horror, he stood still.

And Alexos cried, "I will make the journey to the Well of

Songs. I will drink of the water, and bring it back for you, from beyond death and the desert. **I will make the rivers flow and the crops grow for you. I will save you, my people.**"

There was silence. Then a swelling, an indrawing of breath, a great ragged cheering that went on and on, a clatter of shields, a chorus of rattles and zithers and drums.

Mirany gasped. Argelin had grasped the bronze bowl with his gloved hands; he looked at her in fury over it.

"This is all your doing," he whispered, his voice lost in the uproar.

Every Journey Begins with a Toll

"Why you?" Pa said shortly.

"Because the Archon has his closest friends with him."

"And that's you, is it?"

Seth shrugged. "I helped bring him here."

Telia picked husks out of her barley bread. "I don't want you to go," she said, scowling. "There are scorpions and monsters in the desert."

"There are scorpions and monsters everywhere." Seth sat on the wooden stool beside her. Seeing her alarm, he said quietly, "Don't worry. I'll be back in a few weeks."

She tossed the bread down and turned away from him, leaning her elbows on the white windowsill. "You're never here anyway," she said.

Despite himself, it hurt him. His father shook his head and went to the door. "Pity your Archon friend can't help her," he muttered. "I don't suppose you've even remembered to ask him."

Hot, Seth watched Telia's stiff back. She was five now, still too small, a fretful, sickly child. Last year in the terrible drought she had had a fever for weeks. Now he thought there were times when her mind went blank, when for a few seconds she didn't hear or see anything, forgot what people said to her.

"I'm sorry I haven't been here," he said quietly. "It's hard work, being second assistant archivist. There's such a lot to do." On the windowsill were red geraniums. Beyond, roof below roof, the white buildings of the Port tumbled, their labyrinthine alleys and stairs winding down to the noise and scurry of the harbor. It was airier up here, a cooler house than the last. He felt a brief pride that he had been able to afford the rent.

"But you go to see the Archon." Telia turned. "And that girl."

"She's not—"

"And now you're going for miles and miles and miles."

"I have to go!"

She had dark hair, cut straight across her eyes, like his mother's had been. For a moment the memory brought a swell of sadness that startled him. His mother had died bearing Telia, and now none of them talked about her. He usually kept her image out of his head, the endless scrolls and invoices and plans and contracts filling up the empty space. But now he was tired, had been working all night in the deserted scroll vaults of the City by one guttering lantern, painstakingly translating the text on the silver Sphere, and the memories crept in.

Suddenly the house cat jumped onto the sill. Telia reached up and patted it; it arched and rubbed against her hand. "Tammy loves me," she said accusingly.

Seth couldn't stand this. He lifted her on to his lap. "Listen. I'll bring you presents from the Palace. Toys and nice clothes. I'll be back before you've even noticed I've gone."

Her dark eyes were unblinking. "Are you going right now?"

"Yes." It wasn't true; the Archon would leave after nightfall, at moonrise, according to tradition, but Seth knew he wouldn't be back here before then. "Will you kiss me?"

She gave him a small wet kiss under the ear, then scrambled down. "Bye, Seth."

He looked after her at the swaying door curtain, feeling numb and depressed. "Good-bye, Telia," he whispered.

His father came in with a canvas bag. "Spare tunics. Boots. Small sword. Ointments. A cloak, because it's bitter out there at night. And some money."

A small bag of coins. Seth went red. "I don't need money. You keep that."

"Got plenty, have you?"

"Enough. You'll need it for Telia."

Sour, his father nodded. "Her dowry. If she lives long enough."

"Pa—"

"Have you even asked the priestess yet, about getting her onto the Island? Or do all your big concerns put us right out of your mind?"

He took a breath. "Not yet."

His father nodded, that I-knew-it grimness Seth loathed, and then he burst out, "What use is it creeping to the Archon! A boy, without power! You should have got onto Argelin's staff, years ago. I always said so. We'd be a damn sight better off."

White-faced, Seth stared at him. Then he picked up the bag and stalked to the door. He thought he wouldn't be able to get the words out, but at the door he stopped. Without looking around, he said, "I'll see you, then."

A chair scraped the floor. "Let's hope so," his father said acidly.

There was a woman singing on the corner of the leather-workers' street; the high echoes of her voice bounced off the tenements, mingled with the stink of tanned skin, the acid from the vats catching in Seth's throat, stinging his eyes. For a moment the street blurred; he wiped his face hastily with the back of his hand and hurried on, almost running down the steps, ducking between the lines of stiff hides.

What else did they want from him! He worked his fingers to the bone for them, hour after hour, cheated and bribed and schemed for them! Bitter self-pity welled up in him, and a sort of furious, hurt despair that made him want to fling the canvas bag down the steps and kick it all the way to the harbor. Pa! What did he know about the way things worked, the struggle to be promoted, to be noticed, to get out of the teeming throng of slaves and workers and scribes and to be someone more, to be looked up to, to earn enough! Did they think he just had to ask Mirany and Telia would be whisked to the Island?

Coming under the arch at the end of the street, he allowed himself a grim smile. Maybe that was his own fault. Too much boasting . . . *My friend the Archon* . . . *Mirany can't really manage without me* . . . He turned into a small piazza and ducked under the shady portico. All right, he'd ask. Though Mirany was in no position to help.

The fist came from nowhere. It was a crack of agony in his stomach; he was down gasping for breath, doubled up. The second blow over the back of his head was almost a relief, its black dizziness something he could fall into. But they yanked him to his feet and made him stagger, fended him off. His face was gripped, twisted up.

Through the shock and pain a voice said, "Sure it's him?"

"It's him. Cocky little beggar."

He groped for his bag, but they had it. As the red throb in his head receded he could see them, and a new terror tingled down his spine. Argelin's men. A small squad, six men. They lined up around him, said, "Move," and marched, and he had to keep up, shoved roughly in the back whenever he stumbled.

Down the steep streets the patrol hurried, past shops shuttered from the midday heat and a tethered dog that barked, maddened by thirst, through the tunnels below the water tower of Horeb and by the fountains it had once fed, the dolphins and naiads cavorting in a dry basin, their stone torsos cracked and baking. Seth's whole body ached. His throat was parched; he swallowed and tried to think. What did Argelin want with him?

They thought Oblek was dead. The other soldier from the ambush must have recognized him. Instantly he started to plan. What could he offer? "Listen," he croaked. "Do yourselves a favor. You've got the wrong man."

"Shut it." The optio glared back.

"I can pay. Don't take me in. You never found me."

They didn't even slow down. Obviously they could see he wouldn't pay enough. He concentrated instead on getting his breath back, standing upright. He was sure his knee was bleeding.

The fast march took them through deserted streets. Anyone in the way stepped aside quickly. Seth covered his face and head with his mantle. He didn't want anyone from the Office of Plans to see this. Stupid, as he probably would never go back there.

And then in a second of panic he thought of the Sphere. It was well hidden, down in the City, stashed at the back of one of the myriad of pigeonholes where the plans of the Archons' tombs fragmented into dust over centuries. But if he was executed or imprisoned, Mirany would never find it. The Well of Songs would be lost, and Alexos and the Jackal and Oblek would wander in the desert till they died.

Fish-stink. The rattle of ropes, slap of sails. Even in the midday heat the harbor was a place of movement, the breeze shaking and slapping every canopy, the gulls screaming and wheeling over the tip of discarded innards, crabshells, hideous inedible deep-sea creatures.

The general's headquarters was a stark, forbidding building. Once up the steps and past the door guards, there was a wide atrium swarming with people; he had been here before, and he remembered the day he had first met Mirany, and how she had insisted on seeing Oblek. Could she do that for him? Would anyone even know where he was?

The squad dispersed; papers were signed. His bag was roughly searched and the sword taken; then the contents were stuffed back. He was glad he hadn't brought the money, because that would have gone, too. The optio grabbed him, turned him, searched him with careless efficiency, signed another paper, and said, "Follow me. Don't try anything."

They went down some stairs. The place was bigger than he'd thought, made of some dark stone. Corridors led back, lined with doorways, mostly closed, some with grilles in. Cells, he guessed. Sweat broke out on him. Would they torture him?

Down again. The air grew cooler, dimmer. He realized with a shiver of surprise that the building must run back below the houses and streets stacked above it, even into the soft volcanic rock of the cliffs. Masonry began to become patchy; he could see the walls were strangely twisted basalt, glassy and fused at some unguessable heat. A vast round urn full of water stood outside a bronze door, and incense burned before a small statue of the Rain Queen set in a niche in the glittering black wall.

"Wait."

The optio knocked and went in. In seconds he was back. He jerked his head.

Mouth dry, Seth stepped back. "Listen—" he mumbled. Instead the optio shoved him inside.

He had expected a small cell, but the width and splendor of the room he stumbled into made him draw a breath of silent astonishment. It might be underground, but every wall was painted and hung with rich hangings. Tripods of bronze held expensive red-figure vases from the Cascades; a tiger-skin rug was sprawled on the marble floor, its vast jaw gaping. Myriad lamps hung from the roof, bronze and gold and crystal, each bearing a flame that flickered, and an enormous circular mirror reflected them so that the chamber blazed with light.

A round table in the room's center was spread with papers and documents, some held down by lemons taken from a heap in a colorful majolica bowl. Beside the table was a striped day couch, with a woman sitting on it. Leaning on the table, his hands spread on the papers, was Argelin.

"Come closer." He stood upright, watching.

Seth stepped in.

"You didn't expect me." Argelin folded his arms. He was not wearing armor, but a robe of dark red, edged with a gold stripe. His narrow strip of beard and dark hair glistened with oil. "That's good. I've come to think you clever enough to foresee what I'd do."

Seth was baffled, but he tried not to let it show. "Not that clever," he muttered.

The woman was mantled, but she pulled it back. As he'd expected, it was Hermia. The Speaker wore a white pleated dress and her hair was elaborately coiled. She smelled of lavender and some musky perfume, and she stood up, looking at him calmly, a close scrutiny that made him want to squirm, but he held still.

"Clever enough," she said at last, "to plot with a priestess to plant your own candidate in the Archon's Palace."

He said nothing. He had to find out what was going on here.

"Sit down," Argelin said softly.

For a moment Seth thought it was addressed to Hermia, but they were both looking at him. He came around the table and sat on the striped couch. His knee was a scab of blood, he noticed.

Argelin propped himself on the table. He said, "I won't waste time. I'm offering you a quaestorship. A thousand staters a year, but of course you can treble that by your own dealings; as long as the correct taxes come in, I turn a blind eye."

"A quaestorship!" Seth was too stunned even to think properly. That meant one of the elite squad of tax gatherers. The quaestors—there were twelve of them—were the general's agents in the Port, running the whole vast operation of debt collecting, taxation, tolls. They made thousands in bribes. It was an offer that made no sense.

Argelin was amused. "You look a little overwhelmed. Did you think your current promotion was an accident?"

Seth shrugged. "No, but—"

"I obtained it. As a taste for you of what I can offer. You're ambitious. You don't want to spend all your life moldering among the scrolls as a second assistant archivist."

Hermia was watching, her angular face alert. He said slowly, "What do I have to do?"

Argelin smiled, came around the table and picked up a lemon from a pile of papers. He tossed it from hand to hand. "Well. First I want to know who put it into the mind of that boy to announce this unlikely expedition. Was it the priestess Mirany?"

Seth licked his lips. "No. At least . . . no, I don't think so. I don't get to know much of these things. I'm a scribe, that's all. They don't tell me."

"Don't they?" Argelin said smoothly. "The boy must have got it from somewhere."

"The god?"

Hermia glared at him.

"Well, he *is* the Archon."

"Is he?" she hissed. "If I could be sure of that—"

"When did he first speak of it?" Argelin interrupted abruptly. Hermia transferred her glare to him, but before she could say anything, Seth made up his mind. He had to sound assured. If they thought he was lying he'd lose everything. But he couldn't mention the Jackal. The Jackal was as lethal as Argelin, and he was caught between them.

"The day of the announcement. He's got this idea in his head about the Well of Songs. I don't know where he got it, but he's all excited about going there. Something about the water of the Well being pure and filling you with joy. You heard what he said, about bringing it back for the people."

"I heard what he said." Argelin placed the lemon carefully on a parchment. "This is the only reason?"

"As far as I know."

"Nothing else? About discoveries in the mountains? Has

he had secret messages from the pearl merchants?"

Seth was sweating. "Look, I just don't know—"

Hermia stepped in front of him. "Yesterday the Bearer visited the City of the Dead. She asked for you. She brought something away with her. What was it?"

They were both attacking him. He fought for a clear mind. "I don't know. I wasn't there."

"A small wrapped object. Heavy. She took it to the Archon's Palace and you *were* there."

He looked down. He felt tired and bruised. "It was . . . a sphere."

Argelin looked at Hermia. He came close; something changed in his voice. "A sphere?"

"Made of silver. It was old."

"Where did she get it?"

"I don't know." He felt as if a great pressure was forcing down on him. Desperately he wished for water, cool air.

"Was it inscribed?"

"Yes." A whisper.

Argelin nodded. "They would have given it to you to decipher. The boy is illiterate and the girl little better. Have you read it?"

Hopeless, he nodded. A brief memory of Mirany holding up the Sphere came into his mind. He saw, quite suddenly, what he hadn't let himself see then, that she had been watching him. Testing him. And he knew he had given himself away, his leap of greedy interest—she had seen that. She hadn't really wanted to give him the Sphere.

Her mistrust filled him with anger. Defiant, he looked

up. "It's a series of directions for finding water in the desert, and a map to the Well of Songs." He stood, took a ewer from the table and poured, his hands shaking, so that a few drops splashed on the papers. Then he drank, while they watched. When he'd finished, he put the cup down deliberately. "Is that what you want, for me to give it to you, so that they die of thirst out there, Alexos, all of them? Or to alter the instructions, lead them into desolate places? Is that what you want for your quaestorship?"

Argelin smiled. He went and sat on the couch and said mildly, "No. What I want is for them to follow the map. If there are dangers, the Archon can find them first. But you will be my spy. You will give a copy of the map to the officer that takes you back to the City. He will stand over you until you complete it. I, too, wish to know the way to the Well of Songs."

He seemed pleased, glanced at Hermia. But the Speaker's face was cold. She said, "There are too many unanswered questions here. Prince Jamil will be furious. The Oracle has forbidden him the desert, and yet others go there."

"Not at all. No one can go while the Archon makes his pilgrimage."

"And there's the boy. If he really is the Archon—"

"None of that matters," Argelin said quietly, taking her hand.

"*It matters to me!*" She shrugged him off, stalked across the room. All at once Seth sensed they had almost forgotten him; it was each other they were tormenting, and it was an old uneasiness, renewed.

Argelin stood. His face had darkened; he turned to Seth quickly. "Listen to me. Once you have found the Well of Songs, *you will make sure that the Archon does not return.*"

Seth couldn't breathe. A splinter of terror stabbed him. "I'm not a killer."

"Oh, you'll be surprised at how easy it is. A fall from some high rock. Poison. An unfortunate accident. Don't try to betray me, or to double-cross me. Your father and sister remain here, and I assure you I'll have no hesitation in visiting my anger on them. Two more slaves for the market; who knows where they might end up? And when you get back— alone—your office awaits. Work well for me and your career is made. Now go."

Seth glanced at Hermia. Her face was closed but her eyes glittered with anger; she gave him one sharp look.

He turned away and walked to the door.

Outside, as its heaviness slid shut behind him, he closed his eyes and shivered, his whole body wet with sweat. His knees felt weak. He looked at the image of the Rain Queen and then up the corridor and nodded bitterly, crushed with a despair that seared into his soul.

"Well, Pa," he whispered into the darkness. "It seems you've finally got what you wanted."

The Fourth Offering

OF A LOCK OF HAIR

I turned the apples into stars, white as diamond, blue as sapphire, red as ruby. I hid them in the sky and they were lost among billions.

And the rivers dried up.

I was Rasselon, and in his body I wandered my Palace in silence. I saw the fish gasp in the shrinking pools, the flamingos peck at dry stream beds, the crops withering, the flies on the children's faces.

Shame scorches fiercer than the sun.

I have spent lifetimes searching for the Well.

What must I do to find it again?

She Does Not Whisper in His Ear

The sun burned. Its setting scarlet flamed on the Mountains of the Moon, and on the long slender syrinxes of the musicians below on the road.

It burned on the mask of the Archon, and all the sky to the west was a furnace, and the sea a moving gloom of purples and twilight blues.

As Mirany linked hands with the Nine, she saw, from a corner of the eye slit, that a dolphin leaped from the waves, its tail flashing as it submerged, and then another and another, a whole school of them, each a wet gleam of red.

In the center of the sacred circle, Alexos stood. Before him was the dark pit of the Oracle, its faint vapors rising, its jagged sides crystallized with sulfur and basalt.

Alexos knelt. The Archon's mask was almost too big for him, its gold and feathers and hanging lapis, but he used both hands and lifted it off carefully, and she saw his face was hot, his black hair tousled.

He blew the hair from his eyes and laid the mask down.

Silent, their dresses rippling in the wind, the Nine began to intone the chant. It was archaic and crude, a lament not made of words but sounds, the hiss of the cicada, the croon of the owl, the rattle of the scorpion. As the sounds rose the wind gathered them; the Nine stamped their feet, moved in a slow swaying ripple, and the steams from the Oracle drifted and hung, and Mirany felt their acrid power as she breathed them in. Monkeys chattered in the circle, and she could see them, slipping between Chryse and Ixaca, one clutching Ixaca's skirt, and snakes, too, a whole heaving knot of them spilled from the pit and unkinked and tangled on the stone pavement. There were flying things, birds and bats and harpies, human faced, and as she stepped the endless steps she saw how, among the hissing throng, Alexos was calmly cutting a lock of his hair, how he knelt and cast it into the pit.

"An offering from myself to myself," he whispered. "From the light to the dark. From the sound to the silence. From the living to the dead."

Giddy with the fumes, Mirany knew the cut ends of hair were falling, falling down and down into the earth, and out here they were falling on her, too, a drift of dusty rain from the cloudy twilight. It pattered on the stones, a brief drizzle, one of the infrequent downpours since the Archon had come, but not heavy, not enough to fill the irrigation channels in the fields.

Alexos stood. He took his sandals off and tied them around his neck and gripped the wooden staff that the Speaker held out to him. For a moment their eyes met, his dark ones and Hermia's steel-bright gaze; then Mirany saw how the Speaker's mask turned sideways, as if she would whisper something to him. But no words came. Instead, she stepped back into the dance.

Slowly, the sounds died. The Nine stood in silence. The flame in the sky had almost gone; a cool wind gusted in from the sea.

Mirany was strangely breathless; things moved in the corners of her eyes. Small creatures brushed past her legs. Out of the air a tiny cloud of fireflies came and danced.

Alexos said, "I begin my journey here, even as I will end it here. I, Rasselon and Horeb, Antinius and Alexos, Archon once and to come, God-on-earth, Bright Lord, Mouse Lord, Rider of the Sun, begin my journey. I will drink from the Well of Songs. Until I return, pray for me."

A tall boy in a white tunic, he stood simply in the dimness. And one by one the Nine turned away, turned outward, a circle with their backs to him, and as he walked away from them down the broad steps and along the circling path of cobbles, she knew he was passing under the stone door and coming into the road, and that all the people of the Island would be there, a double row, all with their backs turned to the road, for who could see the Archon unmasked?

From here she could see them, and the soldiers lining the bridge, and beyond that, crowding the road to the desert, hundreds of the people of the Port, some carrying torches that guttered and sparked. As Hermia led the Nine down after him and they walked back to the Temple, a sort of sadness seemed to swamp her, a terrible anxiety for the lonely figure on the endless road between the ranks of turned backs.

"Cheer up," Chryse whispered happily. "He'll be back."

Mirany glared at her. "As if you're concerned."

"I do have feelings, Mirany." Chryse's blue eyes glanced from the mask of the Taster.

"Yes, about what's for supper and what dress you'll wear tomorrow."

"That's not fair—"

Mirany turned on her, tugging her own mask off as they crossed the threshold of the Lower House. "Yes it is! I wish you'd stop all this, Chryse. I can't trust you; I'll never trust you! Never again."

Chryse's eyes had tears in them. But she took her mask off and smiled. "Not even if I tell you a secret?"

"I don't want to hear it." She set off walking quickly up to the Temple precinct. She wanted to see Alexos for as long as she could. But Chryse ran after her.

"You will! It's about Hermia and Argelin. They've had an argument."

"They've had arguments before." The Temple rose above them, a dark facade against the stars. She hurried up the worn steps.

"Yes, but not like this!" Chryse stopped, breathless. "Oh wait, Mirany! Listen to me. Just give me a chance!"

Mirany stopped. She didn't turn around, but waited for Chryse to catch up. Then, with an effort, she said, "Well?"

"It was really serious, Mirany, lots of shouting. It was about the Archon. Hermia is starting to believe that Alexos is the real Archon after all. She doesn't tell me much, but I think it might have started when he brought the rain. And because of the Rain Queen choosing him, though I'm not sure Hermia believes that, because she was drugged at the time anyway."

The warm wind fluttered Mirany's dress around her ankles. She said, "And she's told Argelin?"

"No! She's not that stupid. At least I don't think she has. But he knows. And now Alexos has gone away into the desert and I think she's afraid what might happen. Did you see how she went to whisper to him? I wonder what she wanted to say!"

"So do I," Mirany said thoughtfully. Turning, she strained her eyes to see him, but the tiny flames of the torches on the bridge were too bright, the people too far away.

Rhetia was coming up the steps.

"Oh, not her! I'm going," Chryse said quickly. "She hates me." She ran down past the taller girl, but Rhetia didn't even turn her head, as if Chryse had no more importance than the moths that danced in the twilight.

At the top she stood next to Mirany, looking out at the road. "What did that little trollop want?"

Mirany sighed. "She says she's on our side now."

Rhetia spared her a sarcastic glance. "Don't tell me you believe that."

"Not really. But—"

"*Mirany!* You're so soft! She's getting to you, after all she did. Forget her; anything she tells you is just for a purpose. And don't tell her anything yourself."

Mirany was silent. Which of them was more dangerous, she thought—sly Chryse, or Rhetia with her ambition and a ruthlessness that might bring about war? She stole a sidelong glance at the tall girl, her folded arms, her confidence that seemed even more self-possessed than usual.

"What have you done?" she said quietly.

Rhetia grinned. Then she tapped the side of her nose.

Alarmed now, Mirany hissed, "What have you done, Rhetia? Have you spoken to Jamil! I told you not to!"

Rhetia turned back to the distant, dispersing figures on the road. "Let's just say Argelin's going to get a big surprise. Very soon."

Chilled, Mirany hugged her arms around herself, that sudden anxiety surging back, for Alexos, for Seth, for Oblek. *Be careful!* she thought. *Be careful.*

The first sliver of the moon was rising over the sea. Through the ragged clouds it threw a glimmer on the water like the scrawl of a child's crayon.

I will be very careful, Mirany, the moon said in her ear.

Seth got to the bridge late and had to force his way through the crowds. He was bone-weary; it had taken all afternoon to copy the text from the Sphere with Argelin's man checking every letter. Now, with the excitement of the crowd, the festival air, the torches and sausage sellers, the outskirts of the throng seemed like a harvest gathering, or some festival of wild joy.

But as he made his way through to the road, people were more silent. And then he saw a small figure in the distance and knew the Archon was coming. Instantly people turned around, shielding their eyes and faces. Even the soldiers turned, awkward with their great oval shields and the long ceremonial spears, a clatter of bronze that moved relentlessly along the line, each man turning after the other. Tokens were cast on the path before the Archon; flowers and small minia-ture paintings of loved ones, written blessings on folded strips of lead, scented streamers of bright cloth. Alexos' small bare feet padded around them; he walked quickly, looking curi-ously at the objects, at the mantled backs and shoulders of the people.

And for a second Seth had a terrible desire to do as they did. To cover his face and turn away and let Alexos walk past him. To stop this descent into treachery right now, so that he could get to the harbor and ship out, anywhere, away from it.

But Pa and Telia would be here. And Alexos had stopped.

Seth realized everyone around had turned away; their eyes slid to him, sidelong, astonished.

Alexos said, "Seth? Are you coming?"

Seth licked dry lips. "Of course I am," he said gruffly.

A mile from the bridge the Archon stopped again. In the hushed remains of the crowd a tall man stood waiting, only his eyes showing above the mantle that was wound around his face and hair. He was dressed for a journey and had a pack on his back. His arms were folded. He waited patiently. Alexos pointed. "You."

The Jackal stepped out. The rising moon sent his frail shadow down the road. Together, the three of them walked on.

The crowd grew thinner. Once past the last few hovels, in the scrub at the desert edge there were only lepers, huddled at a distance, having nothing to throw.

"Blessings on you, boy," one called, his voice cracked and hoarse.

"Move back," the nearest soldier growled, raising his spear. Alexos stopped. "Let them be." Raising his voice, he called, "I'll bring you back songs, I promise."

They murmured, dissatisfied. Seth pulled Alexos on. "The Archon should never be heard," he muttered.

"I told you, I'm going to change all that." Alexos shook his head earnestly. "When I get back, it will all be different, Seth. It will be like it was long ago. Before Argelin. Like the great age of the Second Dynasty, before the rivers died."

The Jackal nodded, amused. "That will take some doing," he murmured.

There were no more people. Only soldiers, a bronze line of them stretching to the last milepost beyond the City of the Dead, its towering facade a dark horizon to their right, the vast seated Archons black against the stars.

"My statue will be just there," Alexos said thoughtfully. "There on the end where the line stops. It won't look like me. None of them look like me."

Seth was sweating. He stumbled; Alexos waited for him kindly.

"Were you all mad," the Jackal asked politely, "and made Archon by conspirators?"

"Oh no. I was found in many different ways. Once by being lifted up by a bird, snatched from the cradle. Once by being born during an eclipse. I can't remember them all." He sighed. "I wish I could have seen my mother in the crowd.

You did send her the money, Seth?"

"Yes."

The Jackal glanced at him sidelong. "You're quiet. Missing your desk already?"

Seth didn't answer.

The last soldier swung his spear in a salute, and after him the road was empty. As they walked on the silence of the desert gathered, the faint scuttle of tiny invisible creatures suddenly loud, their own footsteps echoing.

On each side the scrubland was gray and formless, a void of shadow. Stunted juniper bushes made small stands of darkness, and the air seemed to vibrate with bats and the heat that rebounded from the cooling rocks.

The Jackal drew his long knife and said, "We should be wary from the start. There are many animals in the desert, and many dangers. You, scribe, keep to the rear. I'll go a little ahead."

Before Seth could answer or protest, he strode off, pulling the covering from his head. At once Alexos whispered, "Did you read the Sphere, Seth?"

"I read it. Mirany was right; it's the map to the Well. I've got it safe, don't worry. But don't tell him."

Alexos glanced at the Jackal's back. "You think he'd take it and go by himself?"

"Who knows what he'd do. As long as he thinks you might know the way, you're safe." *But not from me,* he thought, and almost stumbled again.

Instantly the Jackal stopped.

Seth came up close. "What is it?"

"Someone. In the shadows." His voice was calm. Ahead a solitary olive tree hung over, almost bent to the ground. Something clinked in its tangle.

Then out of the dark a low call came, eerie, the cry of some ground-nesting bird. Seth breathed out, but to his amazement the sound was repeated, this time from the Jackal, a soft sly whistle.

Two shadows came rustling out of the tree. *Ambush*, Seth thought, and grabbed at his sword, but the voice that roared across the rocky track froze him instantly.

"Archon!"

"Oblek!" With a laugh of delight Alexos was running; the big man caught him up and swung him around, giddy against the stars.

"Did you think I wasn't coming with you? To the Well of Songs itself!"

Breathless, Alexos grabbed him and steadied himself. "I told you, Oblek! I told you we'd go one day."

The big man clapped an arm around him and pulled him tight. "So you did, old friend. And now I'm with you there's nothing can harm you. Nothing and no one."

Defiant, he looked at the Jackal, and Seth, and the scornful figure of the Fox, squatting on his heels, his striped robe bristling with weapons. "All of you remember that."

The Jackal smiled his cool smile. "So nice to have us all together again," he said acidly.

The First Stirrings of Unease

Mirany was in the middle of fastening her new pearl necklace when she remembered. It came back to her like a flash of light, like a touch of the god. *The slave woman's son!* How could she have forgotten!

Chryse put her head around the door. "Hermia says hurry up. The litters are all waiting. I'm going on ahead with Ixaca." She had gone before Mirany could speak, still staring horrified at herself in the polished bronze mirror. What if the boy had died? She'd promised medicines and sent nothing!

She flung the necklace down, ran out onto the loggia and down the white stairs at the end. Ignoring the waiting litters, she vaulted the low stone wall and dived into the rooms below, where the girls who served the Nine cooked and washed and scoured. This afternoon was the dedication of a new shrine in the Port, the sacrifice of a goat to be buried in the foundations. The shrine was being paid for by the Guild of Barley Growers, whose crops had failed again, for the second year in a row. All the Nine should be there. But this was so important!

"Genet." She caught the floury arm of a woman. "Where is she?"

"There, holiness, but you shouldn't—"

The girl was turning a spit at the fire; a row of birds were dripping fat. Mirany said, "Genet, listen to me. Leave that, this is urgent. I want you to get blankets, some food—broth, nourishing stuff—and a warm mantle from the storeroom. Small, for a boy."

"Lady—"

"It's *urgent*. Go to Sehen and tell him I said he's to give you a box of ointments—you know what to take. The boy has a cough and sores around the mouth. You're to take them straight away to the City, to a cleaning woman called Khety. She works at the Office of Plans. I promised her." She frowned. "Tell her I'm sorry it's so late."

The girl stood, after a glance at the woman who was baking.

"A cleaning woman?"

"That's right."

She nodded, bemused. "I'll go now, holiness."

All at once Mirany sensed that her request was interfering with all sorts of duty rosters and hierarchies. She backed out hastily. "Thank you. I'm really grateful . . . really." Turning, she bumped into an old woman; she recognized her as Rhetia's servant, the one who had tasted the bread for her. The woman had a jug of wine in her hand, as if she had just come from the cellar. Mirany stared at it. It looked cool and fresh, and vine leaves kept the lip clear of flies.

"Who's that for?"

The old woman looked at her. "My mistress."

"The Nine are going to the Port." But as she said it, like a cold shiver, the truth came to her.

"Not the Lady Rhetia. She feels a little unwell." Even the servant didn't sound convinced.

Barely hearing her, Mirany shoved past, raced up the steps to the courtyard. One litter was left, the slaves sitting in the shade. "Wait," she snapped, then took a breath and walked quickly to the Upper House.

It was silent.

The white loggia with its statues looked cool and remote. From an open window a fine gauze curtain drifted in the sea breeze. Bees buzzed in the roses below.

Voices.

They were coming from Rhetia's room, and one of them was deep. A man's.

It was strictly forbidden for men even to be in the precinct. Mirany slipped her sandals off and padded barefoot on the cool marble. Argelin came here. But this wasn't him.

Reaching Rhetia's door she waited, staring at the word CUPBEARER in gold and the scorpion above it. The door was tightly shut.

Mirany put her cheek against it, feeling the fine grain. It was cedarwood and smelled sweet. Rhetia's voice was so close it startled her. "I assure you, I know this is so. It's been so for several years. There are people who are starting to get tired of tyranny and deceit."

"Including yourself?" The voice was grave and deep.

Mirany closed her eyes. She knew it was Prince Jamil's.

"Including me. You may have heard of what happened two months ago."

"At the Archon's Choosing?" There was a pause, then, "Rumors reached the Empire. That the choice was not Argelin's."

"He was wrongfooted by a group of . . . associates. People who know the true intentions of the god."

"Also including yourself."

"Led by myself."

"The god has spoken to you?"

Rhetia's dress rustled. Then she said quietly. "He has spoken to me from the Oracle."

Mirany jerked her head back and stared at the door. Rhetia's nerve! It appalled her.

At the end of the corridor she was aware of the servant woman, holding the jug, watching her. Waving her away would be no use; she'd tell Rhetia later that Mirany had been listening. Embarrassed, on a hot impulse, she opened the door and walked in.

Rhetia was sitting near the window, the pearl merchant on a zebra-skin stool. Both stood in alarm.

"What are you doing here!" Rhetia snapped.

Mirany decided to be very controlled. "I should be asking that. Aren't you going to introduce me?"

Rhetia took a breath of fury, but she said, "Prince, this is the Lady Mirany. Bearer-of-the-God."

He bowed. "Holiness. I think we have met before."

"One of the *associates* Rhetia mentioned." She watched

his face. It was calm, gave nothing away.

As the door opened and the servant woman brought in the wine, there was an uneasy silence. The woman poured carefully, into two cups, then said, "Shall I bring another cup, holiness?"

"No," Mirany said, knowing the question had been for Rhetia.

As soon as the woman had gone she sat on the couch and said, "Prince Jamil, I'm sorry your expedition was forbidden. But I think you should be very careful about—"

He lowered his body, massive under the encrusted robes. "Lady, if the Oracle is corrupt, this is a matter of vast importance to all the world. The Oracle is the world's center. Every ruler trusts the words of the god. Any breath of scandal, any hint of corruption must be cleansed away. The god, if no one else, would demand it of us."

Mirany felt despair settle on her. She felt very small, very powerless. Things were racing away from her. The Pearl Prince looked on her kindly, as if she was a little girl. "Holiness, I understand your fear. But I must communicate this news to the Emperor."

"Don't," she said sharply.

He stopped, frowning. "Lady—"

"Don't." Ignoring Rhetia's scowl, she stood up. "Your army is vast, your chariots and elephants and infantry. Here in the Two Lands we have very little. The country is destitute from years of drought, and only trade in salt and the pilgrims to the Oracle keep us alive. If you spread this . . . rumor, you won't need a war to destroy us." She came up to him, and though he was sitting, his face was level with hers, a dark, grave face. "Don't tell anyone. Defy Argelin if you want. Go into the desert. Go to the mountains and start your silver trade. Leave the cleansing of the Oracle to us."

"Mirany." Rhetia was icy with anger. "You're meddling in things you don't understand here."

Prince Jamil held up his hand. Then he stood. "I will consider what you have told me," he said, and he was saying it to Mirany. He glanced at Rhetia. "And your concerns, holiness, I will consider and send you word."

At the door he turned to them. "It may not be possible to act without many deaths. Are you prepared for that?"

"Yes," Rhetia said calmly. "If the god wills it."

When he was gone, they both sat in silence. Mirany expected an outburst, but Rhetia just stood up after a moment and went to the window, looking out. "I suppose it's a little late to go to the shrine now," she said thoughtfully.

Astounded, Mirany stared at her back. "I asked you not to tell him! What have you started!"

Rhetia turned. Her anger was cold and remote. "One of my slaves died this morning. After merely tasting one segment of an orange here in my room. It seemed fresh, but when I looked I found a tiny hole where a sharp needle had pierced it. It was poisoned, Mirany."

Chilled, Mirany clasped both hands together. "Hermia?"

"Who else?" She turned, her back straight, her head held proud. "War has begun, Mirany. And I didn't start it."

*   *   *

They reached the Oasis of Katra about an hour after midnight. Alexos was tired out and had been riding on Oblek's back for the last few miles. Seth felt footsore already, his calves aching and the sand gritty in his boots. He scowled to himself. He wasn't used to so much walking, and it would get worse. He was a scribe. Scribes sat at desks.

The oasis was a darkness ahead, lit with the dull red glimmers of campfires. There were always people here; it was the last watering place before the arid country, and it marked the crossroads where the road turned northwest, to the salt plains. Caravans of nomads worked this route all year, long strings of camels that brought salt and opals and some forms of crystal down to the Port. Seth had often seen them; browned, dried-up men, all in black, their wives rarely unveiled. They spoke a strange dialect and had strange ideas. He had even heard they had their own gods.

The Jackal stopped. "Now," he said, "be wary. Tell no one who we are or where we go."

Oblek scowled. "We're not stupid."

"That's a matter of opinion." The tomb thief turned to Seth, the moon slanting obliquely on his face. "There will be men here who might know something of the mountains."

"We don't need them. We know the way."

The Jackal's long eyes watched him. "I'm pleased to hear it."

"Let me down," Alexos said sleepily. He slid to the ground and pushed his dark hair back.

They walked on, a tight group. There were trees at the oasis, Seth realized. He could see the fringes of their branches against the stars, tall pines and cypresses. Coming closer, he smiled with surprise, because the smell of the place rolled toward him over the desolation, a sweet smell of mingled flower scents and crushed grass and the dung of animals. A dog barked, sharp and anxious. Figures moved before the fires.

"Stand still, strangers."

From the shadow of the trees on the left a man emerged, another behind him. The first man held a chain and on it were three great dogs, of a kind Seth had never seen, black faced and heavily muscled. The beasts broke out into a low ferocious growling that terrified him, pulling their handler after them. If he let go, Seth thought—

"Where are you from?"

The Jackal stood, alert. "The Port. Traveling west. Is there room here for another group?"

"If you don't have pox, or vermin." The man in front spoke, and as he came out into the moonlight Seth heard Alexos gasp in horror, and his own stomach gave a squeamish lurch.

One side of the man's face was a pitted mass of scars and seared skin; his left eye was blank, his whole cheek as if it had once melted and reset.

If the Jackal was shocked, it did not show by one flicker. "We have no pox, friend. Show us where we can make our camp, and we'll be no bother to you."

The scarred man walked forward. "There are over a hundred of us, lord, so I doubt you could be."

Lord, Seth thought. The Jackal had altered his voice, but

not enough. It might be a bad mistake. As they followed the man past the guard dogs and into the dimness under the trees, Seth rubbed his face wearily with one palm. He was desperate to sleep.

There were tents pitched under the trees, many of them, wide leather structures. Camels were tethered beside them in long rows, and their curious aloof faces watched him as he stumbled by. Some men still sat around campfires. As the strangers passed they stared impassively, their eyes red glimmers, the smoke of their pipes fragrant.

"You have tents?"

Oblek shrugged. "No. Ours is a pilgrimage. We walk light."

"Then you may use a spare one of ours, if you wish. It contains only grain sacks."

"Thank you," the Jackal said graciously.

The burned man nodded, a grim nod. "Not at all, lord." He showed them the leather structure, and the Fox dived in first, tossed a few things around, then thrust his ugly head out of the door flap.

"Safe, chief."

The Jackal turned. "We will only be here one night."

"If the god wills. But the desert has her own moods."

"The weather?"

"There may be a dust storm. It should be brief."

Oblek had a hand on Alexos' shoulder; he thrust him down and into the dark opening. "What do we call you?" he growled.

The nomad turned his scarred face away. From the other

side, he looked normal, a handsome man. "My name is Hared. Once leader of this tribe."

He took three steps away, then turned back. "May the god give you a good sleep," he said quietly. "And may you give us your blessing, Lord Archon."

Alexos was crouched in the tent door. He reached out and gripped Oblek's knife as it whipped out of the sheath. For a moment he and the nomad looked at each other in the scented darkness, and when he spoke his voice was old, and cool as the stars.

You have it, my son.

A Private Matter

It had to be a girl.

Lying awake in the morning he realized that, because a girl would have the best chance of getting right up to Mirany and giving her the note. It lay warm in his hand under the blanket, carefully written in thin graphite strokes. PA AND TELIA IN DANGER. GET THEM TO THE ISLAND. PLEASE. She could read, maybe not that well, but well enough. But he had to get the note to her, and only the nomads were going the right way.

Hared had been right about the dust storm. Seth could hear it now, a peculiar dry rustle against the leathery sides of the tent, even over the grunt and whistle of Oblek's snores. Carefully, he raised his head.

The Jackal's blanket was empty, neatly folded. The Fox too was missing, but Alexos lay curled up, only the top of his hair visible, and the big man was sprawled next to him, flat on his back. Seth crept out from his blanket, pulled on his boots and pushed the note carefully down inside, next to the knife he kept there. Then he put his head out of the tent.

The oasis was a maelstrom of red. There was no air but a swirling mass of dust, gritty in his eyes and tasting oddly salty on his lips. He pulled the mantle tight around his face and crawled out.

There were trees, many of them, and under them a glint of water; he made toward it eagerly, head down. A small pool, its surface scummed with redness. Camels leaned and drank from it, one wary eye on him.

"Boy!" The voice was indistinct, muffled. He turned and saw an old man beckoning him toward a larger structure than most, with smoke coming from its top.

Seth stumbled over.

The man grabbed him and pulled him inside. "Drink in here," he growled. "More comfortable than lying on your face in the dirt."

Breathless, Seth uncovered his face. "Thanks," he muttered.

It was some sort of communal gathering place, and there were plenty of people inside. In one corner a fire burned and a kid had been spitted over it; the meat was still raw but the stink of fat clouded the high roof. A circle of women sat near it; he thought they were sewing, or weaving, but their hands moved so expertly among the dark wools and intricate frames of hanging weights that he wasn't really sure how the bright cloth was being made. They glanced at him, and he went red, and they laughed, light, scornful giggles. He could see why the nomads kept them veiled in the Port, because they were beautiful, dark haired, dark eyed, and garlanded with ropes of crystals.

"They're all married," the old man said.

Seth turned in alarm. "No disrespect."

"Then keep your eyes to yourself. The food is this way."

There was plenty. Jugs of water and watered wine, and olives, figs, cheese, a hard, seeded bread. Seth ate hungrily. "Where is everyone? All the men?"

"Saddling up. Taking the tents down. We leave for the Port as soon as the weather settles."

Seth chewed a fig thoughtfully. "What do you do, when you get there?"

The old man spat and laughed. He had few teeth left; he moistened his bread in a dish of water and then slurped at it. "Pay the general's taxes! He takes half, at least. Then we have the business of unloading onto the ship, if our contact is in port. Haggling. Bartering."

"Do you go," Seth asked quietly, "anywhere near the Island?"

"Sometimes Hared's wife goes, or the other women. They give an offering to the Temple. He wants a son but his wife ... well ..." He shook his head sourly. "If you ask me, he should get another."

"Which is she?" It was a risk, but he kept his voice faintly bored.

"The one with the long earrings."

She was young, Seth thought. Not much older than Mirany. Glancing at her, he saw her raise her head and look back at him; for a few seconds their eyes met. She didn't giggle, and her smile faded. After a moment she looked away.

Seth gazed around the tent. A few men smoked and played some sort of dice game on the other side of the fire, but they were absorbed and barely looked up. Of the Jackal there was no sign. Nervous, he said, "Where are my friends?"

"The tall lord, he's with Hared. Buying supplies." The old man looked at him curiously, eyes bright. "You didn't bring a lot with you."

"The Archon has to travel without anything. To live on what the god brings us."

The old man nodded. "But you must take water. West, toward the mountains, there's very little."

Seth thought of the silver globe in his bag. For a moment he was afraid it might already have been stolen, but then Oblek was sleeping right over it. It would take an earthquake to move him. "Have you been that way? What is out there, in the desert?"

The old man settled more comfortably on the worn rug. With a sudden sinking feeling Seth recognized that smug look. Now he'd get an hour of traveler's tales, about crawling for days without water and giant scorpions and birds with wings of metal. He should never have asked.

The old man said, "I've heard things. Passed down, from father to son. The tribe holds the memory of the desert. West of here, the road turns, but there is a track that leads the way you want to go. Very faint, often sand blown. It's marked with a rock, with an image of the Rain Queen carved in it, so old that her face is smooth now."

Seth nodded. That was on the map.

"After that, for a day southwest, there is scrub. Look out

for small desert rats; they make good eating. The ground rises slowly. You will come to a place of dead trees, if you keep the star of the Archon directly ahead of you. Beyond the dead trees, a way beyond, is the first Animal."

Seth glanced back at the women; one of them had made a joke and they were all laughing, a merry uproar that made one of the dice players look over and mutter something.

"What are the Animals?" he asked absently. "Who made them?"

The old man shrugged. "I have seen the first, but only from a distance, from a hillside. Their true shape can only be seen from above, so that makes it clear that it was the god who drew them on the desert. There is a tale that says when the god was young he wanted a place to play, so he made a great ocean of sand and built hills and palaces and populated them with monsters."

"Monsters."

"You will see. The Animals he drew with his finger in the sand. Don't halt near them at night, or when the moon is waxing." He mused, remembering. "When I saw the first one, the great cat, it shone in the moonlight."

He ate the last of the bread, then drank the water in the dish. Licking it dry, he put it into a pocket in his robe and said, "But the Archon . . . he knows."

"He's only a boy."

"He is the god. He has walked this path a hundred times. One day he will find it again, the Well of Songs. They say it lies high in a sacred cave. There he will make amends for his theft." Suddenly he stood, said, "Eat. I'll be back. An old man's bladder is weak."

Alone, Seth took an olive stone from his mouth and tossed it down. Then, deliberately, he turned to the circle of women and kept his voice low. "May I speak with you?"

He said it to the young one, but there was no chance of getting her on her own. It would have to be all of them, a huge risk. Startled, the girl looked at him, then flashed a glance beyond to the dice players. They were counting coins and arguing.

"It isn't permitted," she said quietly.

"Please. I . . . the Archon needs your help." He took out the letter quickly, before the men saw. "The Archon needs this parchment to be taken secretly to the Island, and to be given into the hands of the Bearer-of-the-God. *No one else.*" He held it out to her, but she made no move to take it. One of the other women said, "What does it say?"

"That is hidden."

"He is the god. He can speak through the Oracle."

None of them were weaving now, though they kept the looms clacking, the sound covering their words. He saw how they looked at the letter, intrigued. None of them would be able to read it.

"To the Speaker, yes. But this is to the Bearer. A private matter. Please, I need you to take it."

Ignoring the others, he looked at her. "Only a woman can do this. Your husband need not know. No one need know."

Her fingers came up from the wool; they were long and slim and the nails had been painted darkest red. She took the letter from him and looked down at it, at the seal stamped with the signet of his office, the snake and scorpion of the City of the Dead. Then she looked up at him. Her voice was almost a whisper. "I need something in return."

Seth glanced at the other women. Each one watched him, all merriment gone.

"I need a son." Her hands came over the letter and touched his; he almost jerked back at their warmth. "My husband . . . you've seen him. The scarred man."

Seth nodded. He was old enough to be her father, he thought.

She licked her lips. "He is kind. He was burned in a great fire, in one of the black tar pits. His honor is destroyed, and he is not able to be the father of the tribe now, because a leader must be without disfigurement, and beautiful. Like the Archon." She looked down. "Hared was beautiful once, they say."

The dice players threw again. The sound made her uneasy; her eyes darted that way. "To restore his honor he and I must have a son, or he will put me aside. Ask the Archon to send me a son. Then I will take your letter."

The door curtain lifted. Seth crushed the parchment into her fingers, murmured, "I will," and turned and snatched up the water jug, pouring with a shaky hand. He didn't look up but could hear men coming in; they came and sat around him, and when he drank, he saw the Fox leering at him and the Jackal sitting with Hared, red dust drifting from them at every move.

"Where's the musician?" The Fox took the jug from him.

"Asleep."

The Jackal glanced over. "Get back there, Fox. Bring them here."

"Think they'll run off?" Seth was agitated; he was listening to the murmur of the women behind him, the clacking the looms made. Hared was murmuring to his wife; then the scarred man came over and sat. Seth made room for him.

The Jackal watched Seth with his strange gaze. Then he said, "We have purchased some grain, water, and fruit. The storm is subsiding and in a short time, according to our friends here, it will be safe to leave."

Seth nodded, preoccupied.

"Is anything wrong?"

"No." He tried to sound normal; the Jackal missed very little. "Well, maybe I'm concerned. Alexos . . . he's only ten. This will be a terrible ordeal for the strongest of us."

The tomb thief drank, his fair hair long on his shoulders. "Worry about yourself. A scribe doesn't get a lot of exercise."

"My brains do." Seth was annoyed. "And you'll need them."

"As I remember," the Jackal said icily, "your cleverness consists mostly of treachery."

"And yours of dishonesty."

Hared was watching them, a faint astonishment on his marred face. "Are you not friends?" he said quietly. "It is folly to go into the desert together unless you trust each other. In the desert men have only one another. It's a place that strips away everything and lays a man's soul bare."

Seth looked away. The Jackal said calmly, "Let's hope, then, that it doesn't prove too much for us."

The old man was coming back, and behind him, sleepy and tousled, was Alexos, and Oblek, looking grumpy. The women stopped their looms and watched the Archon. Something new came into their faces as they saw him, a tenderness, a consciousness. The girl who was Hared's wife seemed to have tears in her eyes.

Alexos sat down and took some figs. "These are my favorites," he said happily.

Oblek poured wine, downed the whole cup and poured again. His hands were shaking, the skin on his face and bald skull pitted and scabbed. His small eyes were puffy, his clothes soiled.

The Jackal watched him. "There'll be no wine in the desert."

"Except what I can carry."

"We carry water, fat man. Water and only water."

"Yes, Oblek." Alexos turned to him sternly. "You mustn't take any wine. It's not good for you, and it spoils your playing."

The big man looked at him, then blearily reached over and ruffled his hair. "I'd better drink as much as I can now then. As for my playing, old friend, it's finished. The songs are drowned."

"We'll find them." Alexos looked at Hared thoughtfully. "Thank you for your kindness. My blessing is on you and on your people, and on your children."

The man turned his good eye to him. "I have no children," he said bleakly.

Alexos shrugged. "This is a crossroads," he said. "There

are all sorts of ways from here."

Into the puzzled silence the Fox put his red head around the door flap. "Storm's over, chief," he said. "We can go."

They each had a heavy burden of food and water, except the Archon, who had nothing except the staff that the Speaker had given him. He played with it now, teasing the chained dogs who barked joyfully and even rolled over for him. Seth envied him, pulling on the pack and adjusting the straps. Its weight crippled him. The thought of slogging under a burning sun with it filled him with dread, but there was no point in complaining. The Fox, he knew, was waiting for him to do just that, so he kept an obstinate silence.

Hared said, "Good luck and the Rain Queen go with you, and the favor of the Shadow."

"Shadows," the Jackal remarked dryly, "are just what we need."

He set off, walking quickly, and Oblek and the Fox tramped after him, and Alexos waved and said, "Good-bye!" and ran barefoot ahead, using the staff to vault stones.

Seth took a few steps and looked back. The women had come out of the tent and were watching; he saw the young one, her face half veiled, and their eyes met. He would speak to Alexos, but what could Alexos do? The letter was a secret. For a moment he thought about telling the others about it. Why not? Why not tell them Argelin was blackmailing him, threatening his family? He turned, and trudged away from the despair in the girl's eyes. He knew why not. The reason was that he could barely admit it even to himself. The reason was that if nothing else happened, he would have to do what the general wanted.

And if the Jackal or Oblek found out, they would slit his throat.

After a while he looked back again, but the camp was deserted. In front of him the land was dust red, a sere, parched, shimmering silence.

He hitched up the pack that was already an ache in his shoulders, and trudged on, dispirited. Into the desert.

The Fifth Offering

OF THE SPILLED WINE

There is a world all around these people that they know nothing of.

In this world the land contorts into the shapes of great beasts, and trees are women, and the stars fall like ripe fruit. The only ones who see this are the poets and the singers, and when they forget, they grow unhappy, and search for the Well.

For whoever drinks of the Well becomes like a god, knowing the truth of dreams.

I am worried, though, about such knowledge. Such knowledge is dangerous.

And the Well, therefore, must be guarded.

She Sees the Cosmos Crumble

Mirany.

The voice was a whisper. *Come outside and look, Mirany! Come and see.*

She opened her eyes and looked around the silent room. It was bright with a silvery moonlight and there was no sound in it at all but the far off wash of the sea.

Alert, she sat up slowly, her eyes going to every corner, her hand to the knife she always kept under the pillow.

"Is that you?"

Who else? I have something I want you to see. Go out on the terrace. It will be safe. I promise.

She felt strange, a weak light-headed hunger. For days she had been eating nothing but fruit and eggs, things that would be difficult to tamper with, she had thought, but since the death of Rhetia's slave she had been almost too scared to touch anything. She and Rhetia had their food prepared separately now by trusted servants, who then had to taste it first themselves, but even so, Mirany knew that death was close. Maybe Seth would get back to find a new Bearer, a new hierarchy altogether.

No one will see. Look back, Mirany.

Halfway into her tunic she glanced behind and almost screamed. A great terror surged through her; she had to clutch her own mouth. In the bed, lying curled and fast asleep, another Mirany lay, as if she herself was a ghost, a wraith that had risen up from her own body.

Don't be scared. That's not you. You are you.

"Am I dead?"

He seemed to laugh, a happy sound. **I was going to do that, but you were so scared before. So I've brought you into the world of the gods, just for a while. Now come outside.**

She felt dizzy, but her hands and feet were cold, her body as solid and real as before, she was sure. The dry skin on her heel where her sandal chafed still itched. So she couldn't be dead. Crossing to the door, she opened it a slit and peered out.

The loggia was silent, striped with moonlight. The statues of the Speakers gazed out to sea, their faces throwing elongated slants of blackness. The nearest one turned to her and the face was marble, cool and curious. Sure now this was a dream, Mirany stepped out.

The floor was cold under her bare feet, and it was wet, running with water. The water was running down the facade of the Upper House like a waterfall, a glinting, splashing stream, rainbow-tinted with spray.

Below, the rest of the precinct was in darkness, except

that in the shadowy courtyard, bats were flitting, and a few of the Temple cats slept in small furry heaps.

"Is it real water?" She cupped some, put it to her lips.

As real as anything is real. It runs here always but when you are awake you don't see it. Look up. To the right of the moon.

The sky was black, the stars brilliant. Small dark flickers across them showed where the bats darted and swooped after invisible insects. Mirany waited. "I don't see anything."

This is the way it starts, Mirany. The way wars and wonders are prefigured. With the falling of stars and portents in the sky. Look.

A flash. It shot across the blackness and she gasped, as if it had seared her sight. And instantly the night was full of falling stars, a vast shower of tiny bursting meteors that made a silver rain high over the Temple roof, completely silent, an extravaganza of brilliance.

"The stars are falling!" She gasped. "All of them?"

Not all. The three I stole must plummet to earth. One is already here. Now the others are coming . . .

Two scorches of light, out of the east. They flashed in front of her, and after them came sound, a terrible tearing, a rumble that made the very walls and terrace of the house shake, so that one of the statues toppled and smashed, an explosion of smithereens.

Doors opened. Someone shouted. A guard dog howled.

Two stars fell. Low over the roof they swished, out into the desert, far to the west. In their wake the meteor shower fell like rain, and it *was* rain, she thought, a silver wetness that fell into the sea and coated the surface, gleaming on the flying fish as they leaped, on the vast leviathans and monsters that rose up from the depths, hideous whiskered mermen, beautiful naiads who stared at the sky.

Rhetia's door was flung open; the tall girl ran out. She took no notice of Mirany, her upturned face lit with radiance. She looked amazed, then exultant, a fierce delight that chilled Mirany.

"Can she see me?"

No one sees you. But it is time to go back.

"They fell in the desert. Does that mean—"

Seth has one. They must find the others, or my theft can never be remedied. There have been so many thefts, Mirany. From the living and the dead. Go back now.

She opened her eyes. Rhetia was shaking her hard. "Come and see! The stars are falling! It's a sign, Mirany, a great sign!"

Mirany sat up, dizzy. Her face was stinging, as if from some great radiance. And the soles of her feet were wet.

Two miles past the rock that marked the trail, the Jackal made his move.

Oblek was at the back; he stopped, scratched, turned his back, fumbled with the pack. Before he could get the flask to his lips, an agile arm slid around his neck and jerked; the point of a knife was thrust into his back. Oblek swore, furious, swung like a bear. "Seth! Treachery!"

Seth didn't move.

The Fox ducked, gripped his left arm expertly and twisted it up. The musician howled with rage and agony.

"Well." The Jackal turned and strolled back. "Just as I thought."

He took the flask and sniffed the lip. Then, very slowly, he tipped it and let the wine pour in a slow heartbreaking trickle onto the stony track. It lay in the dust for a moment in glistening globules.

Oblek gave a great jerk; the Fox gripped him tighter. "You scum!" the musician raged. "Poxed, backstabbing, bastard scum!"

The Jackal didn't flinch. He tossed the empty flask down. "It's for your own good. Tell him, Archon."

"He's right, Oblek," Alexos said sadly. "I told you not to bring it."

"Is there any more?" the tomb thief demanded.

"*No!*"

"Fox."

With one movement the Fox kicked Oblek's pack over, the Jackal picked it up and rummaged through it thoroughly, ignoring the stream of curses Oblek hurled at him. But when he pulled the second flask out, the musician fell silent. The Jackal looked at him straight.

"No!" Oblek said hoarsely. He turned to Alexos. "Old friend, listen to me. One flask! That's all. In all this desert! We might be dying of thirst soon, we might be desperate for it. Don't let him." He licked his lips, watching the Jackal. "Don't let him!"

Seth had never seen such a change. Oblek was terrified,

the bluff, reckless man brought down to abject despair. Alexos shuffled. But when he looked up, his eyes were innocent and without mercy. "He's got to, Oblek."

"Indeed," the Jackal said, breaking the seal. "We have no choice. The nomad was right when he said the desert strips a man bare. We have to trust one another out here. Our lives will depend on that."

Oblek didn't answer. His body slumped; the Fox let him go and he almost fell forward, his small eyes fixed on the stream of wine that emptied with a wet gurgle onto the sand. It sank in and was gone.

For a moment no one said anything. Seth was tense, waiting for an outburst, a fight. But Oblek seemed too stunned. He stepped forward, picked up his pack, and swung it on. Then he walked past them all, staring straight ahead, saying nothing even to Alexos. He seemed smaller, as if something had been knocked out of him.

The Fox sheathed his knife and came over. "It's only the start, chief."

"I know." The Jackal stared after the big man. "Watch him. He's your responsibility."

The Fox gave a grimace, his toothless mouth downturned. "Nursemaid, me."

"He'll need one."

The one-eyed thief nodded, settling the knife back into his belt of weapons. "And if he gets to be too much trouble?"

The Jackal gave a glance toward Seth and Alexos. "We leave him somewhere, Fox. We leave him for the vultures."

"It's a good thing you don't mean that," Alexos said,

walking on, "or I might get cross."

"Oh, I mean it"—the tall thief bowed gracefully—
"*holiness.*"

Seth was sure he did. Alexos was safe while they thought
he knew the way, but he and Oblek were expendable, and
should watch each other's backs, though the big man was too
absorbed in his despair to be relied on. Coming last along the
track, Seth trudged into the hot afternoon, head down, footsore. Already the skin of his face was being burned by the
sun; he had taken to winding cloth over his lips and cheeks,
but his eyes were almost blinded by the glare from the pale
desert sands, the shimmering tricks the heat played. As the
old man had warned, for the last day the ground had risen
slowly in a smooth, seemingly endless slope, a gritty track
with some sort of rock under it, and rocks on each side.
Yesterday they had passed the dead trees, a parched and
dessicated forest of trunks bleached to pale gray, so tinder dry
and frail that barely any strength was needed to snap them
off, but at least last night they had made a great fire; then first
the Jackal had kept watch while the others slept, and then the
Fox. Seth had meant to keep an eye on them both, but he'd
been so weary he'd sunk into a deep sleep and Alexos had
woken him before dawn by sitting on his chest. The plan was
to start early and sleep out the hottest part of the day in any
shade they could find, though shade was a rare thing out
here, and would get rarer.

Trudging at the back, Seth looked around. The desert
was not bare. Small scrubby plants still grew, their leaves
fleshy and thick. There were holes too, scrapes and burrows,

though he'd seen none of the rats the old man mentioned. Maybe they only came out at night.

Insects plagued him, buzzing around his face. He brushed them off, watching the others as they walked ahead.

Oblek was far in front, stumbling with a dogged ferocity. Alexos chatted to the Jackal, the tall thief walking easily. Then the Fox kept alert watch, of the sky, the distant hills, sometimes turning back to glance at Seth.

He couldn't help thinking about it.

How he would do it, if he had to. If there was no choice left. Alexos was eager to explore; he poked holes, grubbed under cacti. Everything fascinated him. It would be so easy, too easy, to push him, let slippery rocks or quicksand do the evil deed. But even as he thought it he was revolted, furious at himself. He liked Alexos. The boy was strange and friendly and totally without guile. And it wouldn't stop there, because there was Oblek, and even the Jackal, though Seth couldn't work out how the Jackal would react, not if they'd already found the Well. Even if they hadn't, it was he, Seth, who had the Sphere.

He realized he was weary, worn out with the worry of it. Surely he could outwit Argelin! He tried to make himself confident, lifted his head, thought of the way they'd got Alexos to be Archon, despite everything! He was Seth! The plotter, the one who knew all the dodges! And yes, once Mirany got the letter, Pa and Telia would be safe.

On the Island.

He frowned. For a moment he had the distinct idea that the Island was as dangerous as the desert. Maybe worse.

They were an unheroic group, to set out on such a quest. Thieves and madmen and conspirators. None of them trusted the others. Stumbling, he wished Mirany was here. Though maybe she didn't trust him that much either.

At the height of the sun they stopped, though the only shelter in the desolation was a thicket of spiny cacti. Alexos crawled in and went to sleep straight away. The Fox checked the ground scrupulously for scorpions, then drank and curled up, three of his knives stuck upright in the sand, ready.

The Jackal gave Oblek a dry smile. "Feeling better?"

The musician was red-eyed. His hands shook. "Drop dead."

The tall man nodded. "Take care with the water. Ration yourself."

Oblek looked at him murderously over the water flask. "Don't worry. When mine runs out, there's yours."

The Jackal glanced at Seth, then leaned back on one elbow. "Go to sleep, fat man," he said calmly.

Everyone slept, or so Seth thought. But hours later, when a stone in his back made him groan and turn over, he opened his eyes and saw that the Jackal was on his feet, standing out in the heat with his back to them, looking at the mountains. There was a rigidity in his stance that was disturbing, the way his face was raised to the distant peaks, the faint breeze moving his hair. He turned, as if he'd sensed someone watching. Seth closed his eyes instantly. When he opened them again, the Jackal was sitting, his back against the heaped packs. His strange gaze scanned the wasted land.

Late in the afternoon they packed up and walked on,

into the abrupt night, a darkness that rose up out of the land before them, though the high peaks still shone with light for a while, as if up there lay the country of the gods. As darkness deepened, the desert cooled, the insects giving place to moths and clouds of mosquitoes that hung and clustered and danced over certain spots. A breeze sprang up, and then dropped just before midnight, leaving a tense stillness that made the Jackal pause and look up at the sky.

"Chief?"

"Wait, Fox. Listen."

They stood in a tight group, Oblek with an arm around the boy. The night seemed so silent Seth thought he could hear the faint slithers of sand in the burrow mouths.

"I'll set a few traps, if you're stopping," the Fox said hopefully.

The Jackal gazed east. His voice was a whisper of awe. "Archon?" he said. "What are you doing to the sky?"

Alexos stopped yawning. Eyes wide, he stared. The sky was a sudden explosion of falling lights, a cascade of brilliance. Under its splendor, Seth felt cold terror creep into his heart.

"I'm not doing it," Alexos gasped. "At least I don't think I am. Look at it, Seth!"

The shooting stars scorched and crackled, sudden streaks almost too fast to see, outlining the watchers' faces with silver; Oblek's great head shiny with sweat and starlight.

And last of all, in a great rush, two stars came loose and fell, with a rumble and crack of thunder so low that the desert shook, and Seth dived to the sand, feeling the others crash beside him. Molten flame burned; they felt heat scorch over them.

Amazed, they watched the stars flare into the dark mountains.

A distant concussion shook the world.

Then there was silence.

After a while, pushing himself up on his elbows, the Jackal brushed sand from his face. "More falling stars. This is a good portent, I hope." He picked himself up, an elegant shadow, his long hair glinting. He had made a good effort at keeping his voice calm; but Seth knew he was more shaken than he wanted to show.

Sore, Seth scrambled halfway to his knees. And then his fingers clutched in the cold sand. The brilliance of the meteor shower lit the desert for miles ahead. In its radiance he saw eerie lines, ghostly and faint, whirls and tangles of phosphorescence scrawled on the desert, a great spread of them, intertwining and linking as if some huge secret symbol had been marked out by a giant finger, and as he turned he saw it was all around them, that they had walked blindly into the heart of it.

"*What is that?*" he breathed.

It was Oblek who answered, his voice thick with disuse. "Don't they teach you anything in your precious scrolls, ink boy? This is the first of the great Animals." He put his arm around Alexos' shoulders uneasily.

"This is the Lion."

He Couldn't Care Less

"It has to be done." Alexos was earnest. "As Archon, I have to walk the ritual path of the Lion, and that means even if it takes all day. So now we've had something to eat I'll start. All right?"

Seth shook his head. "Why bother? Why not just go past it?"

"It wouldn't be right, Seth. This is why I've come. Otherwise the Lion will come padding after us, and there'll be trouble. I have to talk to it."

It was useless, Seth knew. Once Alexos had an idea, he stuck to it. He glanced at the Jackal, who was picking meat from the last tiny bones of the desert rat. "Start when you want," the tall man said. "Just don't expect us to wait around."

Alexos put both hands on his hips and drew himself up. "I wouldn't advise you to cross me, thief king," he said, his voice echoing in the emptiness. "Remember who I am."

"Oh, I remember." The Jackal wiped his fingers on a square of cloth. "The mad child who says he knows the way to the Well of Songs."

"Which makes me the god."

"If you say so." He stood and began to put things into the pack. Then he said to the Fox, "The moon will rise soon and there are about five more hours of darkness. I think we should use them. We can stop and sleep when the sun gets too hot."

"You're not listening to me!" Alexos stamped his foot in fury. "Stop talking as if I wasn't here! Tell him, Oblek."

Oblek scowled. "Leave the boy alone," he muttered without conviction. He sat where he had slumped when the fire had been lit, silent and morose. He had eaten nothing. His head hung, as if it was heavy. Now he took another mouthful of water from the emptying flask; Seth noticed how his hands trembled helplessly.

The Jackal noticed, too. Alexos gave him one glare, then turned and walked to the nearest of the strange lines. Seth went after him. The lines seemed to be formed of some lighter material. He scuffed at one with his foot, and it glinted even in the starlight, like powdered crystal, crushed glass.

Alexos stepped onto the line and began to follow it, as if it was a path. With a careful, upright walk he paced the twisting line, his bare feet on the cool gritty stuff. The line snaked on itself, spiraled like a maze. To follow it around the vast outline of the Lion would take hours, Seth thought. He went back and picked up his pack.

The Jackal strode straight across the desert, ignoring the

lines, and the Fox came behind with Oblek. The big man trudged without looking to right or left.

"Come on," the tall thief called.

Alexos took no notice. He tiptoed steadily, arms out, along the pale lines of the god's outline.

The Jackal said, "Get him."

"Get him yourself," Seth muttered.

The thief's long eyes looked at him. Then he went over, grabbed Alexos and swung him off his feet. The boy gave a yelp. "No! Leave me—I've got to do this."

He kicked, but the Jackal had him firmly around the waist. "Your being mad was quite amusing in the Port," he said mildly, "but this is no place to start playing games."

"But I'm the god!"

"Indeed. Well, strike me dead with a thunderbolt and go back to your fun."

"*Oblek!*" Alexos was distraught, but the musician had plodded far ahead; if he heard, he didn't turn around.

"I'm afraid Oblek is suffering a little frustration of his own just now." The Jackal looked after him, over the boy's back.

"Put me down!" The Archon was struggling so much, Seth thought he would choke himself.

"Let him be," he said quietly.

"If I do," the Jackal said sternly, "he walks with me. No running off." He let the boy down but kept a firm grip of his arm. "I don't want to tie you up, but I will." He strode off; with a jerk Alexos was yanked after him, after one wild look back.

"This is a mistake," he said, his voice full of fury, his eyes wet. "And you'll regret it. The Lion is following us now."

"What a pity," the Jackal said, acidly. "The god will just have to deal with it, won't he?"

They walked for hours, into a darkness that paled behind them. The ground grew softer, the bushes sparse. Finally Alexos was so tired the Jackal had to carry him, asleep on his back, and Seth and the others took turns with two packs, an unbearable weight.

The desert was strange at night. The sky was immense, and there were stars in it that Seth had never seen before, brilliant reds and blues, millions of stars. He knew the names of some of the constellations, of the Scorpion and the Running Man, and the Rain Queen's Necklace, but even the familiar shapes seemed lost in the welter of glittering points of light. He stared at them until his neck ached, and at the mountains ahead, black pinnacles that seemed no nearer than they did from the walls of the City. How could four men and a boy ever reach them? No one had come back from the mountains since the rivers had dried. He must be mad, even being out here.

His feet ached. The muscles of his calves felt stretched, the constant slither of the fine sand tugging at them. His back and shoulders were an agony of stooped bruising. Sand was in his eyes and rubbing them made it worse; it was in his hair and nostrils and even caked the folds of the scarf over his mouth. And he was so thirsty. A mouthful at a time, every precious swallow, the water in the leather flask was going down. There would be a time, he thought wryly, when he would be praying to have its weight crushing him again.

The Fox stopped and waited for him. "I'll take the pack, pretty boy."

"I can manage."

"Sure. But we take turns."

Teeth gritted with effort, Seth heaved the thing off. The relief was huge; his own pack felt like nothing. He grabbed the straps and helped the Fox on with it; the one-eyed man was wiry and swung it onto one shoulder as if it was nothing.

Then the Fox turned on his heel. "What was that?"

"Where?"

"A sound. Listen."

They waited, unmoving in the dark. Behind them the desert stretched into mists and glimmers, a faint wispiness that seemed to emanate from the ground. It hung, a layer of gray, closing in.

"I didn't hear anything," Seth said at last. "What did it sound like?"

The Fox's one eye stared into the mist. "A stone rattling." After a second he said, "Maybe I was wrong."

"Trouble?" Far ahead, the Jackal was waiting.

"Nothing, chief." But under his breath he said to Seth, "Keep your eyes open. This is bandit country."

They walked faster. Seth was uneasy, not wanting to be at the back anymore. The predawn chilliness grew, the mist creeping after them, prowling around the spiny bushes, slinking low. He began to hear sounds, a clink, a shuffle. Sand slithered; a whisper of moving crystals. Something touched his ankle.

Seth stopped. He turned and saw the mist was almost up to him, sand-gray and silent. There was movement in it, a shape that loomed and padded. He took a leap back and opened his mouth but before he could yell the fog stuffed itself in, choking him, rolled over him and was all around; instantly he lost direction, blind.

"*Oblek!*" he gasped.

Someone answered, muffled. He crouched, hands in the grit. It was out there. He could hear it, its paws soft on the stony unstable ground, its great body lithe. Cold with sweat, he scrambled around. It was behind, in front, everywhere. He groped for his knife and drew it; it was wet with condensation. The mist was breathing on the blade, becoming a maned beast putting its face into his, licking him with a soft tongue of cloud, slashing a paw out and rolling him over so that he yelled and screamed and scrabbled backward, into spines and cacti.

"*Oblek! Jackal!*"

The mist split. Tawny rays like whiskers seamed it, an eye of gold opened in it. Dazzled, he put a hand up to protect his sight, saw a sudden fan of brilliant yellow rays pierce the fog, turning it amber, dissolving it, thinning it. His body grew a long spindly shadow, and so did a rock nearby, and the stump of a dead tree, and far, far ahead, frighteningly far, the sun was rising over an empty horizon.

A touch on his shoulder made him jump; the Jackal was there, armed, and the others, watching.

"What did you see?" the tall man asked quietly.

Seth ran a hand over his face. His voice sounded scared

and hoarse. "A lion. In the mist."

"A lion."

"I saw it."

"I told you." Alexos looked bone weary but he folded his thin arms. "You should have let me talk to it."

The Jackal nodded slowly. "So now we are pursued by demons." The sunlight lit his face; he turned away from it. "For some of us, that's not new."

"What does it want?" the Fox said. He caught the Jackal's eye. "I mean . . . not that—"

"To stop us." Alexos glared at him. "To consume us."

"No problem." The Jackal walked on grimly. "We can always tether the fat man to the sand. He should make quite a meal, even for a lion made of fog and fear."

"It was *there*," Seth growled, still shaken.

"Of course it was. In your head. What do you say, musician?"

Oblek looked up. His eyes were vacant; he had to force his cracked lips to speak. "I couldn't care less," he croaked.

"Exactly." The Jackal turned. "Nor could I. Now we walk. Fast. The foothills are still far away, and we must find water in the next two days, or we die out here. That's our real danger, not mirages and dreams." He grabbed his pack from the Fox and hauled it on, his elongated shadow stretching toward the hills. "Come on."

Alexos came and walked by Seth. "I believe you, Seth," he said. "It's back there, snuffling." He glanced behind, at the empty land. "And look at our footsteps. So easy to follow." His voice lowered. "What does the Sphere say?"

"That the first beast *must be appeased for its nature is anger, and it prowls in the mind and its jealousies are claws.* There was something else about *flowers* but I couldn't translate a few phrases, they were too worn." Seth raised his head, struck by a sudden doubt. "There's something wrong here. If the Jackal thinks you know the way to the Well he must believe you are the god. And yet he obviously doesn't." He looked up. "You don't think he could know about the Sphere?"

"How?"

Seth's mind was working rapidly. "He has a spy in—" For a moment, a heartstopping moment, he almost said, "*Argelin's headquarters,*" and bit his tongue. "All sorts of places. Maybe he knew Mirany brought it to you." It sounded lame. But if the Jackal knew about the Sphere, why not just take it and go? *And if he knew about the Sphere, did he know about Seth's orders?*

"Then we'd better be careful," the boy said gravely.

"You're right," Seth muttered. Suddenly he swung the pack down, rummaged in the secret compartment he had made in the bottom, and took out the parchment with the translation of the Sphere's script on it. He read it quickly.

"What are you going to do?"

"Destroy it. The Sphere will tell them nothing. They'll need me alive."

Alexos nodded. "Good idea. If you can remember it."

"I'll remember." He memorized it quickly—not difficult, as he'd been working on it for so many hours. Then he tore the parchment into tiny shreds and scattered them on the desert, watching the Jackal's tall back.

There was silence for a few paces. Then Seth licked sore lips. "Archon—"

"What?"

"The nomad woman. She asked me to ask you for a son for her."

"That would be nice," Alexos said dreamily.

"And . . . I mean, I know you're the god. I saw you change the stones . . . and bring rain. So, if you are, you must be able to help her. And you must know . . . things . . ."

It was useless. Alexos was using his staff to vault stones. He seemed quite unconcerned at anything Seth was saying. "I know things."

"About me?"

Alexos laughed. "I know you're clever, Seth."

He closed his eyes. "Clever."

"And you're my friend." He ran on, toward Oblek.

Seth looked at his thin body in the dirty white tunic, the bare feet, the dark tousled hair. "Beware of your friends then," he whispered.

By noon they were all worn out. The sun had crawled overhead, a molten inferno. Its glare was a weight; they bowed under it. But there was no shelter, though the Fox scouted a little way ahead, his keen eye the only visible feature of his wrapped face. They had entered a dry valley of slithering stones, as if a watercourse might once have run there, centuries ago. But now nothing grew in the merciless heat, and the whole landscape shimmered and blurred without even a breeze to relieve the scorching furnace.

Seth drank a few mouthfuls of warm water and crouched. "We've got to stop."

"Not here." The Jackal's lips were crusted with sand. "No shade."

"Then we'll have to do without. Alexos is worn out."

The tomb thief looked at the boy, already asleep. "Cover him or he'll burn."

Oblek took a cloak from his pack and spread it over Alexos, then pulled out the flask and drank thirstily. Water dripped down his chin, his great throat working.

"Take it easy," Seth whispered.

Oblek's small eyes were lit with smothered fury. His face was scabbed, and the scarf he wore around his head made him seem like an outcast, a leper. "Leave it to me," he growled. "We'll have water enough, the Archon and me. Soon."

Finally, they had to sleep in the burning sun. Curled under his spread cloak, Seth sweated. Tiny sand flies hopped on his nose and cheeks, on his tightly closed eyelids. He was stifling in an oven, but he slept, too weary to care.

A murmur woke him.

A stifled gasp, almost of fear.

He opened his eyes, lifted the edge of the cloak and peered out. Light dazzled him, the sand surface red hot as his fingers sank in it.

He saw the Jackal, sleeping a little way off. The man was well wrapped, and lay on his side, but wasn't still. His body twitched, as if he was crawled over by ants, and as Seth stared, the thief gave a low sharp cry of pain, his eyes opened, and he sat up with a convulsive gasp, glancing around.

For a second he looked haggard and lost, totally unlike himself. Then he rubbed his face and drew up his long knees and sat, breathing hard, recovering. The Fox came and crouched, and gave him the water flask. They talked, so quietly Seth couldn't catch any of it. The Jackal drank, and then laughed, a shaky, mocking sound. He stood up, brushing sand off, and the Fox lay down in his place.

Seth lowered the edge of his cloak and lay in the dark, thoughtful. A nightmare. Not the sort of thing he would have expected the Jackal to suffer from. For a moment there, a brief second, the tomb thief had been afraid.

Seth turned over. Drowsily he thought of Pa and Telia. Had the message got to Mirany? Could she do anything? As he drifted back into sleep, the desert stirred under him. He realized with strange clarity that he was lying curled against its great warm flank, that its body itched with lice, its hills and valleys were muscles and bone under a fur of shifting sand. He told himself he should get up and shout a warning.

But it purred in his ear, and he slept.

Yelling.

A furious roar.

Instantly he had the knife out, was up, flinging off the cloak.

He had slept too long. The sun had sunk, the sky to the west a dull copper red, ominous. All the dry valley had blossomed. It had become a sea of rustling yellow flowers, stiff crisp growths that had sprouted and shot up and burst into seed in some bizarrely rapid lifetime, triggered by who knows what—a breeze, a drop in temperature, the levels of light? All before him, high as his chest, acres of crisp flowers made tiny jerky movements. Seed pods cracked, petals dried even as he looked at them, detached, dropped.

And in the heart of the brilliant crop, the Jackal and Oblek were fighting. A roaring, crashing, vicious struggle, with Alexos yelling anxiously and the Fox holding him well back. Seeds and fluff made a cloud; through it Seth ran to see Oblek's great arms around the thinner man, how he hefted him off the ground, flung him down, crushed him. But the Jackal was lithe; he twisted in the bruising grip, jerked, elbowed Oblek in the stomach. As the big man lurched, he was out, behind him, one stringy arm around his neck, choking.

Oblek roared and floundered. Alexos screeched. "Don't hurt him! He doesn't know what he's doing!"

Waist-deep in the dessicating sunflowers, destruction raged. Oblek was too strong; he broke out, his face red with fury, his broad hands clawing the Jackal's arms, punching him hard, once, again, with a clumsy blind retribution.

Seth gasped, "What happened?"

"Fool tried to steal our water. Stay clear." But the Fox pushed the Archon at Seth and moved in, alert, a knife in each hand.

"They'll kill him." Alexos was white, his eyes wide with terror. "Don't let them kill him, Seth."

Hesitant, Seth gripped dry flower heads with both hands.

He was a scribe. Scribes had no idea how to fight. But he could feel it overwhelm him, that vicious heady anger, and as the Jackal reeled and the Fox went in hard against Oblek he dived in, too, not even sure who he was fighting for, wanting only to hurt, to attack. Grabbing the big man's arm, he twisted; Oblek yelled and flung him off so easily he crashed into the stiff flower stalks with all the breath knocked out of him. Scrambling up, he saw the Fox's knife slash down, embed in the sand an inch from Oblek's eye; then the musician was pinned, the Jackal bruised and worn, coming from behind and stamping hard on his arm, kneeling on him. The tomb thief glanced up, his yellow eyes cat bright.

"Do it!" he snarled.

"No!"

It was as if the desert screamed. A roar from everywhere, a huge voice, a rumble.

The earth shook, boulders dislodged and rolled.

Alexos spread his hands wide. **"I will not permit this."**

They stared at him. He was white with fury.

"I told you to let me speak with the Lion. The Lion is here, we walk on his back. The Lion is inside you! His anger is yours. And mine!"

Around him, in great circles radiating from his feet, the flowers were dying, their brief lives over; they crisped slowly, curled, bowed, fell to fragments. And as they crumbled Seth saw the desert floor was crawling with life, beetles and rats and scorpions and ants, tiny flitting lizards, scuttling spiders of enormous size, feeding on the seeds and one another, ferociously killing.

Alexos twisted east, the way they had come. He hissed, **"Let them see you."**

And as the millions of flowers crumpled, Seth saw the Lion. It was enormous, its great paws the outcrops of hills, its body the valley sides. A vast slab of projecting rock turned and was its head, the muzzle wired with thick whiskers, the eyes amber, their black pupils growing crevices that widened as they stared at him.

In the silence the only sounds were tiny scrabbles, the dried-out flowers falling, Oblek's breath, a hissed curse from the Fox.

The Lion watched. Its tail flicked. When it spoke, its voice was the slither of gravel. "They dishonored my form and your journey. I should devour them."

"They are sorry," Alexos said quietly. And then, "I'll make sure they look more carefully now. That they honor the signs." He walked forward, a boy in a dirty tunic, until he was below the beast, its nearest paw higher than his head, its claws gleaming. "I promise you that, because I am the Archon, and they are only men. They don't know anything. They didn't know about you."

The Lion opened its mouth and roared. Or maybe it was just a landslip, the last rays of light making the hills glow.

Because at that instant the sun sank behind the Mountains of the Moon, and there was no lion.

She Is Hindered in Her Quest

The elephants had walked down in a long line, each holding the tail of the beast in front. Now they waded into the sea, foam curling around their great thighs. Gulls cried over them, amazed. The animals sprayed one another with salt water; their keepers scrubbed them with long brushes. Urchins from the Port whooped and splashed in the shallows, keeping a safe distance, and the wash of the disturbed water sent moored boats lurching and their ropes dipping and dripping, taut.

Chryse moved a little farther into the shade and said, "I wonder if they drink through those trunks. I mean those are their noses, aren't they?"

Mirany leaned on the white balustrade and looked down. "I suppose." She wasn't looking at the elephants. Beyond them, some of the merchant ships had sailed out to sea. Others were unmoving, gathered like a fleet. Surely they must have heard from the Emperor by now. Something was happening; she saw running sailors, sails being hastily dropped. Could they be going home?

"They are, you know." Chryse touched her own snub nose. "It must be horrible."

"Chryse, for the god's sake!" Mirany glared around at her. "Haven't you got anything to do?"

The blond girl shrugged. "I've swum and had lunch and had my toes painted. What else is there?" Then an alertness came over her face, and she edged closer. "Why? What's going to happen? Have you heard from the Archon?"

"No." She said it quickly.

"Not even through the Oracle?"

Chryse's voice was oddly smug. Mirany gave her an irritated glare. "Not even through the Oracle."

"That's a pity. Because I have."

Mirany turned. "What?" For a shattering second she thought Chryse meant the god had spoken to her. She felt a pain like indrawn breath, a shocking jealousy. Then she thought, why shouldn't he speak to her? Even her?

"It was yesterday." Chryse sat on the white marble bench and smoothed her dress. "After the dawn Ritual. You and snobby Rhetia had gone off on your own, as you always do now, and I was last out. There were pilgrims there, you know, like there usually are. Wealthy ones, with offerings. I was going past them when a woman stepped out and said, 'Holiness?'"

She glanced up under her lashes, saw Mirany's stare, and smiled. "I said, 'Yes?' and she looked all around, as if she wanted to see if anyone was listening. One of those really pretty desert women, Mirany, and her hair was so glossy and her lips so red. What do they use for that, do you think?"

"I haven't the faintest idea." Mirany came and stood over her.

"Well, you can't get it in the market. Anyway, there were other women with her, so she must have been important. She said, 'You are the Bearer-of-the-God, aren't you?' I don't know why she thought that. Someone else must have pointed me out, and got it wrong. I mean, with the masks on . . . So I said yes."

"Chryse." Mirany was tight with fury. "*What have you done?*"

Unperturbed, the blue eyes met hers. "In fact, I did you a favor, Mirany. Because if I hadn't taken it Hermia might have got her hands on it."

"It?"

"The letter."

It was no use screaming at her. Mirany made herself take a deep breath. Ominously quiet, she said, "What letter?"

Chryse smiled. "Well, I'm telling you. I had to hide it, you see. This woman, she put her hand out of her robe—she had lots of those fabulous silver bangles—and she held it out. 'He said I had to give it only to you,' she said. She sounded really scared. So I took it. It had a seal on. I said 'Thank you,' and she said, 'Tell him, tell the Archon, that he has done something wonderful for me. Hared and I are so happy.' There were tears in her eyes, Mirany. I don't know who Hared is."

"And the letter?"

"I told you it's hidden. I've got a secret place." She was

so smug Mirany wanted to grab her arm and twist it behind her back.

Instead she sat hopelessly on the bench and said, "What do you want for it, Chryse?"

Chryse smiled happily. "That's what I like about you, Mirany, you know how things work. But all I want is to show you that I'm on your side. For you to trust me. I could have given the letter to Hermia, after all."

"You might already have done that. Did you open it?"

Chryse pouted. "Yes."

"What's it about?"

"I don't know! I couldn't read it."

Mirany nodded. Chryse couldn't read at all, she was sure. "Did you show it to anyone?"

"Oh of course not, Mirany! So is it a deal?"

What choice did she have? "Yes."

"And you'll have your breakfast with me from now on, just to prove it?"

She might be arranging her own death. But she had to see the letter. "Yes! Now give it to me."

They ran to the Lower House, and Chryse made her stay out in the courtyard, well away from the building. Scarlet flowers made a bower there, and the bees hummed in them as she waited impatiently. A servant hurried by, carrying plates of sweetmeats. Mirany caught her arm.

"What's happening?"

"The Pearl Prince is due to visit the Speaker, holiness."

Surprised, Mirany nodded; just then Chryse came out, looking slightly flustered. "I've got it."

She held out the parchment. It was very small, and grubby. The seal was broken but Mirany recognized the emblems of the City, and when she opened it, she saw the letters were Seth's, carefully drawn, as if he'd been afraid she couldn't read them.

PA AND TELIA IN DANGER. GET THEM TO THE ISLAND. PLEASE.

"You've had this since yesterday! Why didn't you give it to me before!"

Chryse looked surprised. "Is it that important?"

Mirany swore, a word she had heard Oblek use, then tore the note rapidly into tiny pieces and dropped them into the incense burner, poking them down until she was sure they were burned to ashes.

"Well?" Chryse said expectantly.

"Something Seth wants done."

"Oh Mirany, you *promised*—"

"I'll tell you! As soon as I've done it."

There was no time to waste. It was urgent; she knew that by the small word at the end. *Please*. It sounded scared. Not a bit like Seth. Leaving Chryse to follow or not, she ran hastily down and found six litter bearers; when the litter was ready, Chryse was first in.

"Where are we going?"

"The Port. Don't talk. I want to think."

She told the men to hurry, but the road was hot and crowded with fruit carriers and donkeys and pilgrims. All the way she fretted. Why was his father suddenly in danger? From Argelin? And to get them on to the Island was too risky, even for the little girl. Hermia would know at once. She frowned and shook her head; he had no idea, *no idea at all*, how things were for her. The only place where they would be safe was with Kreon. She would have to get them to the City and down into the tombs. There was nowhere else.

She hadn't been to his new house and was surprised to find how high up it was. Impatient, she gripped the seat as the bearers lurched around corners, asked the way, avoided strewn rubbish, climbed the hot steep streets. Finally the litter wouldn't fit under an arch in the narrow alley so she jumped out and ran, yelling at Chryse to come, racing up steps and through the winding lanes, filthy with refuse, higher and higher into the stifling tangle of white cramped buildings, hurtling around the last corner till she stopped so suddenly Chryse almost thudded into her.

This was the house. One of Argelin's guards leaned outside the door.

After a moment she whispered, "Wait here," and walked forward. The soldier glanced at her.

"The family that lives here," she said, breathless. "The man, the little girl. Can I speak with them?"

"They've gone," the guard said laconically. He obviously had no idea who she was.

"Gone where?"

He gave her a leer and sucked his teeth. "Argelin's dungeons, darling. They've been arrested."

"She showed it to Hermia."

Eight of the Nine sat in a circle with Chryse in the middle. She was already crying, and Rhetia had barely started.

The tall girl stood over her, threatening. "She must have. She had the note for a day. Enough time for a message to Argelin and for the soldiers to go in. You just can't trust her, Mirany! You should know that by now."

"I didn't!" Chryse sobbed. "I didn't, I didn't, I didn't!"

"She's no airhead, though she wants you to think so." Rhetia looked at the blond huddle coldly. "I used to think that. She's dangerous." She turned to the others. "What do we do with her?"

Mirany stood by the window, uneasy. She felt hot and worried and angry. Seth had begged her to help and she'd let him down. But still she said, "She gave me the letter. If she was in Hermia's pay, why do that? Why not just lose it? I'd never have known it existed."

"Yes!" Chryse's kohl-streaked face shot up in hope. "That's right!"

"It's all part of her game. Use the message to arrest these people, then use it to insinuate herself into your trust." Rhetia shrugged, already bored. "It's obvious, Mirany." She turned. "I think we should punish her. The punishment of exclusion."

Chryse wailed with misery.

Mirany turned to the window. No one could lay a finger on the Nine in theory, though she knew Rhetia might have incited some of the others, Ixaca, maybe, to agree to have Chryse poisoned. So exclusion was probably better, but Chryse might not think so. No one would speak with her, eat with her, touch her. All her possessions would be broken, her necklaces unstrung, her perfumes spilled on the floor, her dresses torn. Catty comments would be constantly made in her hearing, and when she finally lost her temper and screamed out, they would hold her down and Rhetia or one of the others would slap her, or punch her where the bruises wouldn't show. And it would go on and on. Mirany knew; she had had a week of it once, when she first came. She had cried herself to sleep every night, desperate for home. For someone like Chryse, who only wanted to be liked, to be part of everything, it would be unbearable.

Mirany turned. "No. You need all our votes for that and I won't be part of it. It's petty and spiteful and it will only drive her back to Hermia. Besides, Rhetia, you want her excluded for yourself, not for us. You want it in case she finds out about your war."

There was an appalled stillness. A gull gave a long mournful cry out over the waves. Mirany had no idea how much the others knew, but their faces were wary, fascinated.

Chryse, tears forgotten, whispered, "What war?"

Mirany looked at Rhetia. The tall girl was watching her intently. She would not lower herself to plead, even threaten. But under her loosely coiled hair, her eyes were cold.

Mirany looked down. Then she said, "Rhetia has told Prince Jamil that the Oracle is corrupt. She has asked him for armed forces to use against Argelin and Hermia."

A split second of utter disbelief. Then Chryse jumped up. "And she calls *me* a traitor!"

"Is it true?" Ixaca, the Anointer, was on her feet.

"Yes." Rhetia was calm. "It's true. We all know the Oracle is being betrayed, and I'm doing something about it. I intend to be Speaker. All of you, if you still want to keep your places, will back me."

But all the time her eyes were on Mirany.

Mirany licked dry lips. She was so tense she thought she would scream, but she said, "I'm going to Hermia."

Chryse stared. "Why?"

"To try and stop this. If she stepped down. If she accepted Rhetia as Speaker—"

Rhetia took a step forward. "She won't. And if you do that, Mirany, if you dare do that, then you've lost us. All of us. You'll be on your own, caught between sides."

It was a moment of pure fear. Because it was true. Seth was gone, and Alexos and Oblek, and now the Nine were against her, and Hermia would still hate her. There was no one in all the world to help her.

Except me.

Mirany jumped. His voice was so quiet, so sad. But it gave her something, an uprising of courage. She nodded. "I know that," she said, and was answering both of them. And then she turned and walked out.

There was a slave dressing Hermia's hair, but Mirany said, "Leave us, please." The girl looked at the Speaker; Hermia nodded and the girl went. Slowly, Hermia stood, as if she could tell by Mirany's rigidity, by the way her hands were clenched, what was coming.

But all she said was, "You should be dressing for Prince Jamil's visit."

"I doubt he'll be here." Mirany looked up. "Hermia, I

know you hate me. For everything that's happened, for getting Alexos to be Archon, for the things I've said to you. But now I've come to warn you—"

"Warn me?"

"To beg you, then, to stand down. To let us have a new Speaker. You're almost the age to leave. If you don't—"

Hermia laughed, a harsh, uneasy sound. "Are you threatening me?" She came forward, suddenly vengeful. "You, who think you can hear the god? Who think you know what the god wants?" She smiled, cold, the careful curls dark on her white skin. "I thought that once, Mirany. When I was young and naive, I thought I knew what the god wanted, but then I realized it was my own voice, my own desires. When I became Speaker, I thought it would change. That the Oracle would pulsate with sound, roar with a great voice."

Her fingers picked up an ivory comb, turning it over. "That first day I was so terrified I could hardly breathe. Some city in the east had sent to know if they should invade their enemy's territory. I put the question, and then I waited."

She turned. "Can you imagine how that feels? That silence? The pit with its fumes, an open mouth out of which nothing comes? Nothing. The slow horror of realizing that these men with their foreheads on the pavement are waiting for an answer, now, immediately? That a thousand Speakers before you heard his voice, or said they did? That no one will ever know how many of them were lying? *Or will know if you should lie?*"

Shocked, Mirany stood silent. She had never seen Hermia so agitated. The Speaker's eyes darted to her.

"You would have failed. Many would. I didn't. Because the next thought, almost as breathtaking, almost as exultant, was that the fate of cities, of the lives of men and women was in my hands. That whole empires could rise and fall by what I said, that kings could be deposed and that a woman would look for her lost ring in the right place, that farmers would grow the crops I told them, merchants voyage to the ends of the world if I gave them permission. Me!"

She took a breath, her eyes bright, laying the comb down with a click. "That power is intoxicating, Mirany. I will not leave the Oracle, not for you, not even for Argelin. And not for anything Rhetia thinks she can do."

"You know?"

"I know there's some conspiracy with the Pearl Prince. The general knows."

Mirany stepped forward. "You can stop it. The Oracle—"

"So you want me to say the god requires my retirement?" She laughed, cold. "You, so keen to cleanse the Oracle, want it to speak what you want. What a hypocrite you are, Mirany."

"And the Archon?"

She asked it quietly. It fell into a clamor of disturbed gulls, of distant voices.

Hermia raised her head and gave Mirany an uneasy look. Finally she said, "I'm sorry about the Archon."

"Sorry?" Mirany went cold.

"I had started to think that perhaps you were right about the boy. There is something . . . was something . . ."

The bleakness of her voice made Mirany come forward

and catch her arm, a grip so hard she frightened herself. "*What do you mean, 'was'?* What's happened to Alexos?"

Hermia pulled away. "It is the fate of the Archon," she whispered, "to be sacrificed for his people. Especially if he is the god."

The door crashed open. Six bodyguards marched in, fully armed. Behind them Argelin stalked, hot with haste, his armor dusty, his cloak red as blood.

Hermia turned. "What's happening? How dare you! . . ."

"I dare, lady, because the root of treachery turns out to be here."

"Here!" Wrathful, she faced him. "Are you accusing me?"

His smooth face was calm. "You rule the Nine."

"You know I'm not responsible for anything Rhetia does." For a moment they faced each other, in stony mistrust. Then, as if something was reassured in her, Hermia stepped close to him and her voice softened. "What is it? What's happened?"

His tension broke; he waved a gloved hand at the window.

Mirany looked, and gasped.

The sea was blue, but not empty. Rank on rank of galleys rose and fell on the smooth waves, caravels and slave ships, quinqueremes of banked oars, a great flagship with the Emperor's blazon of a ruby horse galloping across it. Alarmed clouds of gulls screamed over them, and beyond, in the Port, was chaos, the uproar of hasty defenses, fleeing people, spilled fish, the dragging out of great defensive catapults along the stone quays.

"Jamil's ships slipped out to join them, without the wretched elephants," Argelin said bleakly. "The Port is blockaded and I've closed every gate in the wall. The City is barricaded, but the Island is defenseless. You must come back with me, where you'll be safe."

"No." She flickered a glance at Mirany. "My duty is here. I will not abandon the Oracle."

"Hermia, I haven't got enough troops—"

"The god will protect his own."

He put a hand out and touched her arm, and then, as she stiffened, quickly withdrew it. "So be it," he said coldly. "But the rest of the Nine will be under house arrest. Anyone who tries to leave will be killed. The time for caution is finished." He glanced at Mirany. "I suppose you're happy now. Blood will flow in the streets because of you."

She swallowed, dry with fear.

He leaned forward, his face dark with fury. "Am I so terrible, lady, am I so relentless, for my downfall to be worth so much?"

The Sixth Offering

OF A SCATTERING OF FEATHERS

There are many things they think I want.

Thousands of gifts come to me. Birds, creatures, emeralds, silver. What can you give a god, who already has everything?

My shadow wants nothing, the darkness. The Rain Queen dispenses her life=giving arts for no reward.

But I have thought about it, and there are things I want. Your heart and mind. The three stars.

Not to be left alone.

Their Needs Torment Them

There had been the Monkey, and now the Spider. Tiny in the distance, Alexos walked the winding paths, a patient, plodding figure.

"What does he think about?" the Fox rasped, "out there?"

Seth shook his head. It was too painful to speak. They were down to one gulp of water each every three hours, and his tongue was swollen, his throat choked with dust, swallowing a terrible effort, and yet he kept wanting to do it, having to stop himself.

According to the Sphere, the next water hole was two hours west. He had to get them to it. Or Alexos did.

The Archon turned, pacing back. Once he fell and Seth stood, alarmed, but Alexos picked himself up and completed the track, his small feet stumbling with weariness. Then he came and sat by Oblek.

Silent, the Jackal handed him the water. He drank carefully, one tiny swallow.

Oblek's red eyes watched, bloodshot and sore. For two days he had hardly spoken, dragging himself along. When he slept, he sweated and cried out; even now he was darting scared glances at the dimming landscape, his eyes dull, terrified. Things were out there, he had whispered to Seth. Following him. Demons and dogs with great eyes. Dead men, crawling, unraveling.

Seth knew it was the heat and the mirages, and above all the drink, or lack of it. Oblek was drying out; his body craved wine and the lack of it tormented him, the heat and thirst deranging his mind. They'd be better off without him, Seth thought sourly, and it might come to that, because he could barely stumble now.

Without a word, the Jackal stood and looked around. Wearily, they followed him.

The Animals were appeased, at least. Alexos had insisted on walking their outlines, talking to them, burying a small lock of hair at the threshold of each. Seth rubbed the sandpaper skin on his face and remembered the Lion, the anger it had infected them with. They had seen nothing alive since then, not even a beetle. Now the mountains loomed large; he could make out individual valleys and peaks, though at dawn and dusk the topmost heights were lost in mist. Sometimes a white glimmer tantalized him. Was that snow up there? He had never seen snow, only read of it in old travelers' tales. Solid water. It hardly seemed possible.

They walked.

Over hours, the journey became an agony. Each step burned. There was no end to it. Under their stumbling feet the ground was hard and cracked, a vast salt plain brilliant with encrusted crystals. Only their eyes were uncovered, and even those they had to protect with their hands, blinded.

Mirages moved with them, of distant misty trees, of a shimmer of light on water; three times the Fox had to drag Oblek back from them. The musician rambled, talking nonsense. The water was gone.

The world was a shimmering furnace and Seth trudged across it, with not enough moisture in him even to sweat anymore. Stories and snatches of baby rhymes floated through his dissolving memory. He forgot where he was, who he was.

He forgot everything except staggering, one foot before the other.

And the unbearable, choking thirst.

And then, this place.

It stank. A bitter, raw stench that caught in the throat and made him cough. The desert had sunk into a great depression, and as they stumbled down, the floor of it became sticky, oozing a dark stuff that clotted and couldn't be wiped off. In places it had gathered into pools of thick black murk, too viscous and slow to be called liquid, though it flowed, if you watched it long enough. Bubbles rose to the surface, taking long minutes.

In front of him, Oblek stopped. He tore the wrappings off his face. "There!" he screeched. His great hand grabbed at Seth, hot and shaking. "See it! Look at it!"

Whatever the musician saw was terrifying him. Seth swayed with weariness. From the pools, fumes rose, acrid.

Peculiar blue fire flickered over the surfaces, and every few seconds the whole quagmire gave a great belch and fat bubbles splatted, as if something down there had turned over. Could anything live in that? If so, Seth didn't want to see it.

"Demons!" Walking backward, Oblek seemed to notice the pools for the first time. He stumbled, fell on his knees in the oily mess, then saw the stuff on him and tried to rub it off, terrified. "Archon! Save me! I can smell them, Archon, the birds with metal wings, the fat coiled snakes! Look, they're creeping toward me. Archon!"

The Jackal pulled the covering from his face; his eyes were gritty with sand. "He's finished," he said, his voice a rasp.

"No." Alexos looked bone weary. He barely had the strength to talk. "There's nothing there, Oblek, and we have to get out of here. There's water ahead. Very close."

Oblek didn't seem to hear. "Leave me," he moaned. "Let me stay here. The birds are out there. I can smell them."

"That's this black oil—"

"Or I'll go back. Shall I?" Oblek looked up, his face lit by a manic cunning. "Back to the Port? It won't take me long. An hour. I'll go back and get us water. Wine."

The Jackal and the Fox exchanged glances. Then the tomb thief pulled Alexos away. "Come on," he said.

"I'm not leaving him." With a jerk Alexos stood his ground. "I'm not."

"He can't go on. Even you can see that. His mind's gone, and he's dangerous."

"He won't hurt me."

The Jackal frowned. "Boy, he'd cut your throat for a glass of wine."

"I won't leave him. Tell them, Seth."

Seth sucked dry lips. Getting the words out was agony, and gazing down at Oblek's pitiful huddle made him feel despair. To his own surprise he said, "The water's close. We can get him that far, between us."

The Jackal made no move. Then he smiled his cold smile. "Well. The desert does bring out hidden things, scribe."

"And hidden names, Lord Osarkon."

That surprised him. He couldn't hide the flicker in his eyes; Seth felt glad.

"So you've done some research. Is there a file on me, in the City of the Dead?"

"On your family. Their tombs. One of them was Archon, long ago."

"The worst Archon. Rasselon."

"Even he would not have left a man to die in the desert."

The Jackal eyed him coldly. "What do you owe the fat man?"

"He caught me once. When I was falling."

Oblek, behind, gave a grunt of memory. For a moment he looked at Seth and something of the old fierce light was in his eyes.

The Jackal shrugged, came forward and put his arm under Oblek's, a firm grip. Seth closed in to help. Together they hauled the big man to his feet, dragged his arms over their shoulders.

"Lead on, boy," the Jackal said sourly. "You've got an

hour, no more, to find water. Or we lie down and die."

But the oily landscape clogged them, slowed them down. Mists and fumes dimmed even the sun, and breathing them left everyone sick and dizzy. Staggering along, Seth prayed Alexos could remember the directions he'd whispered to him a few hours ago, to keep the cleft in the mountains ahead, to watch for the rising ground, the scatter of cacti.

But after another hour of blazing heat they had barely escaped the oil field, and there were no cacti, and Alexos collapsed on hands and knees and sobbed.

Seth stared at the desert. If the spring had dried . . .

"What's that?" The Fox pointed.

Birds.

They were high, soaring on thermals.

The Jackal was clutching his side, looking up. "Is that the place?"

Alexos glanced at Seth; Seth gave a nod, tiny. But the Jackal saw it. Instantly he let Oblek drop and drew a sword, a bright, lethal blade.

"Chief?" The Fox had two knives out instantly.

The tall man came and leveled his blade at Seth's neck, lifting his chin with it. The sharp edge was warm; he felt the sting of a cut.

"Tell me," the Jackal croaked, "what is going on here."

"Nothing."

He gasped. With a swift slash the strap of his bag was cut; it fell and the Jackal kicked it over.

"Search that."

In seconds the Fox had the Sphere out; he threw it and

the Jackal caught it one-handed. He stared. "First a star. Now the moon itself! What else are you lunatics hiding from me?"

"Filthy thief," Oblek growled. "If I could get on my feet—"

The Jackal ignored him. He sheathed the knife and examined the Sphere rapidly, his fingers touching the incised letters. "Very old. A map?"

Grudging, Seth nodded, rubbing his neck. It was sore, nicked open.

"To the Well, no doubt. You've read it. Where's the translation?"

Seth was silent. The tomb thief raised an eyebrow. "Would you believe this, Fox? He's holding out on us again. Just like last time." He came up close. "I suppose you've memorized this, too?"

"It's no good to you without me."

"No? What if I can read it, too?"

A flicker of panic must have crossed his face; the Jackal laughed painfully.

"I was educated, *scribe*, by better masters than ever taught you. I may not be so practiced, but I think I can decipher this. Here, look, is where we are." He touched the signs for the oil field, the cramped wedge-shaped letters, the device of the trapped vulture that it had taken Seth ages to work out.

"And this hieroglyph at the edge is the spring."

He looked up. "The landscape has dried. There have been centuries of drought since this was made. But it may still be here."

* * *

Half an hour later, with Oblek in a shuddering stupor and Alexos curled up beside him, Seth straightened the agony of his weary back. "I've found it!"

The Fox leaped into the pit, grabbed the wooden spade and worked frantically. Limp with relief, Seth climbed out and knelt on the burning sand, his hands raw. All the time he had been digging, the Jackal had sat and watched him, and even now the man's long eyes did not turn away, his fingers tight on the Sphere.

"Water, chief."

The hollow was barely knee deep, but the bottom was sludgy. Already the sandy mess was dark; as Seth watched, a slow pool accumulated. The Fox scooped some up carefully, tasted it, then spat. "Fresh. But it will take time to settle."

"Widen the hole. We'll need to fill every container."

That took another hour. Maddened, burning with thirst, they waited for the sand to settle out of the water hole. The sun had set; far to the west the birds they had seen earlier circled against the foothills. Alexos was watching them.

"Those aren't birds," he said suddenly.

The Jackal chewed a dried olive. "Indeed?"

"They are people with wings."

The Fox snorted.

"Don't you believe me?" Alexos looked at him, surprised. "I'm the Archon. I know things."

"You don't even know where your brains are, goat boy."

Alexos scowled. "He believes me."

He pointed to the Jackal, who tried to swallow the last of the olive and failed. "Indeed, Fox, he's right. I do begin to believe. The last Archon was a crazy old fool. He may well be reborn in this boy."

The Fox grinned, but Alexos knelt up in the sand. **"That's not what I meant,"** he said quietly. **"And you know it."**

Night had come. Quite suddenly its relief was all around them. The Jackal and Alexos faced each other; when he spoke again, the thief's voice was dry. "For a moment that time, when the rain came, I will admit that perhaps I thought . . . I *wondered* if you might not be the Archon in truth. But the god does not use thieves and fat musicians and lying scribes to work out his purpose. I do not think I am such an instrument of destiny."

"Everyone," Alexos said gravely, "is used by the gods, Lord Osarkon."

"Even the lowest of the low? Even those who rob the dead?"

Alexos watched him, his flawless face calm. "Do you hate yourself so much? Is it the dead that you dream of? Do they torment you, at night, in the dark?"

The Fox went rigid. Even Oblek watched, his bleary eyes fascinated.

After a moment the Jackal brought his face close to the boy's, his long eyes dangerous. "What do you know about that?"

"I know what it is to suffer remorse. I stole the golden apples."

"Remorse?" The Jackal managed a smile. "For what? Do the dead miss their treasures? Do they resent the water and food that can be bought with their jewels?"

"You know they do."

The thief's eyes almost flinched. Seth thought he would lash out, strike the boy, but instead he whispered, "I have thought it. Sometimes."

"Their footsteps haunt your dreams."

"The god must know."

"I do, my son."

"Then take them away, holiness. I beg you, take their weight off my soul, and I'll gladly believe you are the god. Show me your powers. Cleanse me of guilt. I want to believe." There was a look in his eyes Seth had never seen there before, a hollow pain. Then he straightened, it slid away, and he said languidly, "And while you're about it, why not make the desert into an orchard full of balbal trees."

The Fox wheezed a grin. Partly of relief, Seth thought.

"You're making fun of me," Alexos said sulkily.

"If you're the god you know exactly what I'm doing, and will do." He stashed the silver globe carefully in his bag. "So I need have no fears for your safety, need I?"

A slurp interrupted him. Lying full-length on the sand, Oblek was lapping at the water like a dog.

Hours later, deep in exhausted sleep that lulled and held him like a warm cocoon, Seth saw the water hole flood. All night as he slept the water had risen, and now it gushed over the sides, the sandy edges crumbling, plopping in, and it spread on the surface of the desert, a great lake shining under the moon.

And on the lake there were ships, a whole flotilla of warships of all sizes, and they were sailing toward him, their sails full though the wind had dropped. Heavy keels ground on to the shore.

Mirany was next to him, and she said, "I came in a ship like that from Mylos."

He nodded.

Soldiers were leaping from the boats, men in the intricate armor of the Emperor. Elephants trumpeted, and all around the waters were thick with leaping dolphins, flying fish, and nereids.

"What will you do?" he whispered anxiously.

She shook her head. "I don't know, Seth. I don't know whose side I'm on anymore. There's only me left, all alone."

And the fleet was gone and she was on a rock, a tiny rock in the empty sea, and he was drifting away from her, the current taking him, and he couldn't swim, and he was drowning.

"Oblek!" he gasped, but there was no answer.

Far below, deep beneath his feet, Oblek's bloated, drowned face stared up at him.

He woke.

Someone had hold of his arm, was shaking him urgently.

Wiping sweat from his face, he rolled over.

"Seth," Alexos said. "Listen. What did he mean, earlier, when he said a star?"

"What?"

"The Jackal. What did he mean? He said, 'first a star and now the moon.' What star?"

Seth let his forehead sink back onto the softness of his

cloak. He felt utterly worn out, his hands still raw from the digging. "Will you go to sleep!" he growled.

"It's important!" Alexos sounded almost distraught. "Please!"

"A star. I bought it. He took it." The words were mumbled into the darkness, the warm delicious oblivion that was closing over him.

"A real star?"

"Ask him—the Jackal."

And he was asleep again. Until the tiny distant voice said, "I can't. He's gone."

For a full second Seth lay without moving. Then he opened his eyes.

"Who's gone?"

"Both of them."

With a jerk he rolled, sat up, stared. Then he swore, and leaped to his feet.

Oblek was snoring by the water hole. Two full packs lay beside him.

All around, in all the silent, predawn wilderness, nothing moved. A faint pink light showed in the east. To the west the mountains shone, their pinnacles bright. And the desert was empty, to every horizon.

Freedom Is Bought and Sold

The terms were clear.

The Port was to surrender, disarm, and hand over Argelin. Once the Emperor had installed a satrap, the Oracle was to be ritually purged. A new Speaker would be appointed. "By Jamil," Chryse said breathlessly, "because you can bet he'll be this satrap thingy."

Mirany nodded, impatient. "They don't seem to realize Argelin won't let anyone hand him over. What else?"

"Tribute. Five million staters, paid to the Emperor. What if they put some foreign woman in as Speaker, Mirany!" Appalled, she gripped the seat as the litter lurched.

Despite their house arrest, Argelin had sent a sudden order for the Nine to be brought to the theater. Mirany wondered what he and Hermia were planning.

"Argelin will fight," she said.

Chryse nodded. "The guards outside the Lower House were changed at noon. The ones coming up from the Port were full of it. A man in a boat brought the letter with the terms in. Argelin set fire to it in front of everyone. He had the messenger stripped of all his jewels and clothes, had his ears cut off and sent him back in rags, and said that was all the tribute Prince Jamil would get from the Two Lands. Then he ordered the bombardment."

She could hear that for herself. The great catapults on the quay had been working all morning, the clatter of their winding gear clear even from the Island, the whizz and hiss and loop of the released rope, the splash as the stone balls plunged into the sea, the sizzle and stink of burning pitch.

"But it's useless," Chryse said, looking wide-eyed through the window, "because the fleet is keeping well out of range."

"Then he should save his ammunition." Mirany fidgeted with the mask on her knee. She knew a siege, however short, would be a disaster. The Emperor's ships were blockading the Port. Nothing else could get in or out, and this was a land that lived only on its imports. Little grew here, and the land was arid. At their backs was only the endless desert. In a few days the shortages would begin. Hunger, fighting. Without the traders, the people of the Port would starve and the thousands of clerks and workers in the City would have no pay. She dared not think about the riots that would bring.

As the litter lurched hurriedly through the marketplace she saw panic had already begun. Peering between the curtains, she glimpsed empty stalls, anxious queues, soldiers everywhere. Prices had shot up; sacks of grain were selling for three times their worth, and a woman was screaming curses at one stall owner, who had three huge slaves at his back. But people would pay it. Food would be hoarded like jewels now, the scraps thrown away last week dug up from midden heaps.

"What about us?" Chryse whispered. "Will the offerings still come?"

"I don't know. For a while. But the Island is better off." After all, it was the only green place for miles, she thought. Olives grew there and lemons, and oranges. The granaries under the Temple were always full. But how long before starvation drove these people there?

Then she grabbed the balsa frame of the litter and screamed, "Stop! *Stop! Now!*"

The six slaves jerked to a standstill; the central one turned awkwardly. "Holiness?"

She jumped out, thrusting the Bearer's mask into Chryse's hands. "Hold that."

"Where are you going? Oh Mirany, the soldiers! . . ."

She pulled the mantle over her head. "Quick. Give me your jewelry, Chryse."

"*What!*"

"Now!" She snatched the rings as Chryse tugged them off reluctantly, then whipped the earrings from her ears. Chryse screeched. "Not those!"

"Wait here." She grabbed the slave's arm. "Keep the curtains closed." Then she was racing across the littered square, between dogs fighting over scraps and donkey dung and the snaking food queues. She stopped, glancing around. She had seen him. Where were they!

Then a flicker of bronze caught her eye.

•

Two soldiers were marching him down to the slave market. Pa had a rope around his wrists, the other end looped around the soldier's shoulder, but at least he wasn't chained. Mirany sped after them.

They turned a corner, and by the time she had caught up they had entered a small white stairway that led down to the next terrace. An arch spanned the alley, with a few red flowers growing in a tiny barred window above it.

"Wait! Wait! The god commands it!"

The guards turned. One lifted his spear, but when he saw she was alone, he lowered it, reluctant, then dropped his eyes. The other, more insolent, stared straight at her.

"Do you know who I am?" she said rapidly.

"One of the Nine."

"The Bearer. The Bearer-of-the-God." She stepped right up to him; he was young and hard eyed and she had no idea how to handle him. *Help me*, she thought. *I need you to help me now.*

The guard made a jerk with his head. It might have been a nod.

"This man. There's been a change of plan. You're to hand him over to me."

Pa was standing very still, carefully not looking at her.

The guards exchanged a glance. "We were told—"

"It doesn't matter what you were told." She drew herself up, lifted her chin. "*I'm* telling you now. He comes with me."

The guard holding the spear licked his lips. She was sure of him, but the other one only stared, and it wasn't a stare she liked. He said, "That's more than we know. Argelin wants him sold. We're ordered to bring back the money as proof."

She nodded. His eyes did not leave hers. "So you see how it is."

"Then I'll buy him."

It was too quick; she was betraying her haste, her fear. Seth could have done it, the pretend reluctance, the holding out for a price. But there wasn't time; if soldiers came looking for her—

She held out the jewelry, her own, and Chryse's.

Despite his care, the guard's eyes went wide.

"We're not—"

"From you. I'll buy him from you. All this, for you. Sell some of it, give Argelin the coins. Keep the rest. It's the price of ten slaves. But it must be now, and it must be secret."

Pa's hand tightened on the rope. For a moment there was a silence filled only with gull cries. Then the soldier moved. He grabbed the jewels, slapped the end of the rope into her hand.

Instantly Pa turned and ran, Mirany close behind. Rounding back into the square, he yelled, "Where's Telia? Have you got Telia?"

"The litter. Over there."

Chryse was standing; the slaves had put the litter down. As Mirany ran up they gaped, but she shoved Pa inside and screamed at Chryse, "Get in! Quickly!"

Hastily the slaves bent and heaved. The extra weight slowed them, so Chryse put her head out and snapped, "Hurry up. We're late."

Breathless, Mirany lay back on the soft bench. Opposite, Pa crumpled.

"Where is Telia?"

"I don't know! He asked me to look after you. When I got to your house you were gone."

"Argelin had us arrested." Pa was watching her. He looked drawn, his face haggard. "I don't know why." Then he said, "They must be using us to get at him. They took Telia away this morning. Where is she? What are they doing to her!" His voice was an agony.

Mirany pulled the mask over her face. Her voice came out muffled, echoing. "I promise you. We'll find her."

The tracks were clear. They led west, and Seth trudged in them. Beside him Oblek plodded, the pack on his back. Alexos wandered wearily out to the right.

The wind that had risen hissed sand at them, a searing heat. It had taken hours to fill all the leather bottles with the sandy water, and all the time Oblek had cursed the Jackal, his house, his parents, his parents' parents. Despite the empty sands, none of them could really believe he and Fox had gone. Seth found himself gazing out, shading his eyes, watching for them.

Finally, when they realized it was true, the arguments had started. Seth had suggested that they turn back, and Alexos had insisted on going on.

"We'll never get him to the Well!"

"But it's Oblek we're going for, Seth. It's Oblek who needs the songs!"

It had only ended when the big man had put a hand down on the sand, heaved himself up, and swung the pack on his back. Then he had looked down at Seth.

Something had changed. His eyes were steady—sore and red from grit, but steady—they no longer searched out demons, and his hands were less shaky. He pulled himself upright and wrapped the scarf around his face and head, shoving it into the neck of his filthy tunic. Then he took the short sword the Fox had left thrust into the sand and felt the edge of it with his thumb. His voice was raw and rough with disuse. "I owe you, ink boy."

"I owed you. Twice."

The musician nodded. "He would have left me. As it is, there's water, food. He's given us the chance to go back. If you want to, go. You might get through."

"Not long ago you were desperate to—"

"Not long ago I was out of my head. Now I feel like death, can't stop shaking, my legs are jelly and small red maggots feel like they're crawling inside my skin. But I'm Oblek again. And I'm not going back or taking mercy from any tomb rat." He tried to fold his arms. "Once I was a musician. The best, the rarest. I've tasted life without that and it stinks. I won't be dried up, scribe, I won't be without the songs. Whatever's out here, I'll get through it if I have to crawl every inch of the way." He glanced down at Alexos. "So take me to your magic Well, old friend."

Now, hours later, Seth watched him. He had to admit the big man was tough. The raging heat was enough to kill anyone, but Oblek had the shakes and was barely out of delirium, a descent into some personal hell Seth could only guess at. The Jackal had been wrong to write him off. He scowled. The tomb thief had the Sphere and didn't need them. But they had their own journey to finish.

Oblek glanced over. His voice was raw. "Need to drink."

Seth nodded.

They crouched. There was no shelter, no rocks, no growth. The Jackal's tracks were lost on the desiccated ground.

The leather bottle moved from hand to hand, their eyes fixed on it as each sipped. Oblek licked a drop carefully from his burned lips. "Tell me the route. If something happened to you—"

Seth shrugged. Then he whispered, "We've passed the region of the Animals. There are others: a vast Beetle and a thing that looks like a crocodile, but they're far to the north and our path doesn't cross them." Just as well. The Sphere had said of the Beetle, *"This is the beast of decay and the redemption of corruption. Its power resides in the inmost places, in the films and mildews of entombment, in the contagions of pestilence."*

Its revenge, if unappeased, might have been horrific.

"Then?" Oblek rasped his chin. His hands were shaking; he clenched them.

"Difficult. The text was worn. Something about the migration of birds overhead—roosting places." He scratched peeling skin from his knee. There had been another word, too, but he wanted to keep it to himself.

"Tell us," Alexos said quietly.

Seth looked up, alarmed. He swallowed. "A hieroglyph. It took hours of searching old scrolls to decipher it. There's a syllabary written in Sretheb's time."

"What the hell did it mean?" Oblek growled.

Seth frowned. Then he said, "Devouring. Eating alive."

They were silent. "Might it mean a place where there's food?" Oblek muttered.

He shrugged. None of them really believed that.

Alexos said, "Could the Jackal have read that sign?"

Seth was savagely scornful. "No chance. He's full of himself, but even I had to search for hours."

"*Even* you." Oblek nodded. Looking out at the shimmering land, he brooded. "He shouldn't have left us. I'll tell that to his princely face before I smash it in pieces."

"Now that's the old Oblek."

The Archon was looking up, at a faint circling spot far in the west. "Birds?" Seth asked.

"Not birds." The boy looked at him, one of his closed secret looks. Then he said, "I think they've escaped. From his dreams."

The theater was packed. Every seat, the curving stone benches crammed with men, women, scribes, sailors, traders, whores, ranks of slaves standing at the top. The roar of the noise and the clatter of Argelin's guards as they kept order astonished Mirany; it rang down onto the stage as if the steep hillside penned it in, a babel of fear. Inside her mask all the voices reverberated; drops of sweat tickled her forehead. When the soldiers all crossed their spears in a clashing tight phalanx around the stage, it sounded like cymbals, announcing the performance.

The Nine sat on perfectly arranged stools, silver gilt. A brazier burned in the center, and behind it an image of the god looked into a mirror; twin opposing faces of purest white marble.

Alexos. What had Hermia meant about Alexos?

She was standing now, tall and regal, and the crowd fell silent as Argelin climbed the steps to stand opposite her.

The rest of the Nine stood, with a rustle of white, the feathers and looped lapis of their headdresses clinking, their calm smiling masks facing the crowd. High overhead in the empty blue sky, three birds circled.

Argelin bowed courteously to the Speaker, then turned to the crowd. "Citizens. We are under attack. Our land is threatened with invasion from a great empire, stronger than we are, with more ships and more weapons. Our trade is cut off, and the Port beseiged, all because the Princes of Pearl desire to control the greatest treasure of our lands. The mouthpiece of the god himself."

The acoustics were perfect; he barely had to lift his voice. Silence answered him, the faintest murmur of his own words journeying around the topmost tier.

The breeze raised frail edges of mantles and robes.

"They want surrender. They want to rule and tax and sell you all into their slavery. They want the power to tell the world what the god says. I say, they will never have that power. The Oracle will teach us the way to win this battle. The god will save his people!"

A cheer. Ragged and uncertain, but then the soldiers roared and the theater rang with voices. Argelin watched, his smooth face calm, his narrow beard perfectly trimmed. *An actor*, Mirany thought. A great actor who knew his audience feared him. He held out his hand; the noise subsided.

"They want you to hand me over to them. If you want that, I'll go. You have only to say the word."

Utter silence, except for a tiny squirm of scorn from Rhetia. Nobody moved; it was as if the crowd was frozen in terror, as if the slightest movement might condemn them. Argelin's eyes scanned the rows; the soldiers watched, impassive.

They're all too scared to breathe, Mirany thought.

You have a mask to hide behind, remember.

She almost gasped with surprise. Chryse's eyes in the mask slot shot to her.

You! You don't want me to speak, do you? Not here, in front of all these?

You could. "Give yourself up!" you could cry. People might join in, stamp, clap. The bolder ones. You could call his bluff, Mirany.

The silence was terrible. She felt it smother her. The god's voice was grave and cold. **No. So don't feel such scorn for them, Mirany, because they're all just like you.**

Argelin bowed. Then he looked up again. "Your trust, friends, honors me." There was the faintest scorn there, but she heard it, and Rhetia heard it, too. The Cupbearer took a small step forward.

The rest of the Nine froze.

Hermia turned quickly, raised her hands, tossed a cloud of incense on the burner; it cracked and spat, fragrant smoke rose.

She breathed it in, arms wide. Argelin stepped back. "Tell us, Speaker-to-the-God. What does the Oracle advise? For the Oracle is here, wherever you are. The god is here, and only you can hear him."

Mirany turned. Rhetia was very still, a stillness that might move.

Don't let her!

I cannot stop her. But I think she will not take a risk. She thinks Argelin will lose this war.

Will he?

Quiet, Mirany. I can't hear myself speak.

Hermia was swaying, the openmouthed mask making tiny gasping sounds. Chryse and Ixaca hovered behind, in case she fell. Argelin said, "Bright One, Lord of the Sun, Mouse Lord, Scorpion King. Advise us."

Words came from the mouth. The whole theater heard them, echoing. They said, *"A sacrifice. Give me the most precious thing you have."*

"They killed something?"

In the dimness Seth was kneeling, examining the hollows in the sand. "Maybe. This is blood. And look, feathers."

"With what?" Oblek growled. "Fox had no bow." The big man had his arms wrapped tight around himself. He was sweating uncontrollably.

"Maybe it flew down. On some carrion."

Alexos had the feathers. He was looking at them close, his dark eyes fascinated by the barbs, how they linked and unlinked, his long fingers smoothing them so no gap appeared. "But these aren't from one sort of bird, Seth. There are all different sorts."

Seth stood. His shadow stood with him, stretching out up the dunes of soft sand that had been clogging their way since noon. Now it was night, as suddenly as ever, the moon low over the mountains.

He reached out and touched them. Small yellow feathers. One long white-and-black one, broken. A handful of gray fluff. Pink plumes from some flamingo.

"And here, look." Alexos was tugging something out of the sand. "These are from gulls."

"No gulls in the filthy desert."

"No, Oblek, I know that. And look at this."

It was the corner of a piece of cloth. The boy tugged, and it came out of the sand so suddenly he fell back, and it was dark red and striped, a gaudy rag. Silent, they stared at it, the great tears slashed through it, the bloodstains. It was Oblek who said, "Fox was wearing that. Around his head."

Seth put a hand down and turned it over. There was a lot of blood.

"What sort of bird can do this?" he whispered.

Alexos looked up suddenly. Far to the west, almost hidden against the range of the mountains, something dark flapped.

"Whatever it is," he breathed, "it's coming back."

They had dressed her in a white robe with feathers to trim it.

Through the eye slits Mirany saw her brought up the steps, through a cloud of released doves that burst like a fluttering white pain from the baskets the soldiers opened.

Telia.

Someone in the crowd gave a howl like a dog. If it was Pa, she prayed they would hold him back.

The little girl stood quietly and turned to confront the crowd. Her face was calm, with that intense concentration Mirany had noticed sometimes, and she looked out at the sea of people without fear.

Argelin came and put his hand on her shoulder; she looked up at him gravely. He led her to the stone altar, and lifted her onto it; her bare feet hung over the side.

Then he turned to Hermia. "Bright One. The Archon is not here. He cannot give his life for the people. So we bring you another in his place."

Small Things Crammed Together

The bird was enormous.

Its wingspan seemed almost too great to keep it in the sky; it hung motionless on the currents of air, idly turning over the searing heat that came off the land. Then it soared down.

Slowly it zigzagged, its eyes never leaving the disturbed surface, the scattered feathers, the bloodstained cloth. All around the place the sand was humped and heaped, as if some great fight had happened, and hollows that were footprints led there and stopped.

The bird's fierce scrutiny was unwavering. Its talons waited, tight below its body. In all the night land nothing moved, not a mouse, not a beetle. There was nothing, anywhere, for miles.

What can we do? Mirany asked.

We?

We have to do something! He asked me to look after

her—don't you see, this is all my fault! She wanted to cry out, to leap up and scream. The thought of Seth was an agony.

That's silly, Mirany. Lots of people act together. Chryse didn't give you the letter; Argelin arrested them. People always think their own actions are so important. He sounded almost sulky. Appalled, she thought, "You're not going to accept her?"

There was silence. Then, **That's another thing. People always think they know what's best.**

Smoke, and incense. The rising heat of thousands watching, the heat of the day stored in the stone benches, the flagged stage. She clenched her fingers.

"I won't let them do this."

Telia was watching her, dark eyes under a ragged fringe. Argelin turned and nodded; a slave came forward and helped the girl lie down, quite calmly. She had probably been drugged. All at once it struck Mirany like a wave of heat that Hermia had helped to plan this, that he and Hermia had things all worked out.

The Speaker came forward with unsteady, dragging steps. A scent of dark spices hung around her, her headdress seemed too heavy, her graceful neck bowed. She placed both hands on the altar and looked up, the glint of her eyes watching the crowd like a hawk. . . .

"I accept your offering, my people. And, believe me, I will save you."

Cheering roared down. Real, this time, a raw, hoarse savagery of relief. Behind it, unmistakable, the rattle and whip of the artillery down on the quays.

They think it's you speaking. Mirany was trembling with anger. *Why don't you show them—*

Why don't you? he whispered.

The bird circled. Its beak was long, a hooked horror.

It rose high, swooped, circled again.

Every instinct told it its prey was there, but the desert was huge and something had shuffled far to the east, a scuttle and scrape, a tiny vibration of paws.

It turned, flapped. Was gone.

In silence the wilderness was unchanging under the moon. Then it erupted.

An arm flailed from the sand, another, a spitting face. Seth gasped huge mouthfuls of air, spat out the hollow straw, heaved armfuls of sandy weight off his belly and legs. "Oblek!" he yelled, but the mound beside him had already opened; like one of the dead the musician rose from it coughing, streaming with sand, his face and body forming out of shapeless terrifying masses. Seth knelt up, blinded. He scraped hair from his face, groped, felt for Alexos.

"Archon! It's gone! It's safe!"

A meaty hand shoved him aside. Oblek forced fingers into the heap, grasped for the boy's body, paused, dug again, hard. "Alexos?"

He glanced at Seth, a flash of disbelief. Then they were both digging, flinging sand aside, hands wide, churning the desert till Seth leaped up and stared around, at the emptiness.

Oblek's roar was an agony of terror. "Archon! *Where are you!*"

* * *

The bronze bowl was empty; it lay at Mirany's feet, and though she had stood at the Oracle for long minutes this morning, nothing had crawled into it. But Hermia must have thought of that. Because as she stood over Telia her hands were not empty; she held a sharp curved knife, its haft beaded with emeralds and pearls, its bronze blade serrated.

Mirany stood in a terror of cold sweat. If she objected she had no doubt she might get half a dozen words out; then the soldiers would close in and it would be announced the lady had fainted. She glanced at Rhetia; the tall girl stood rigid. Would she let this happen? Probably. Rhetia was ruthless; if Hermia made a sacrifice and the war was still lost then what easier way to prove she did not have the god's favor, to turn the people against her? Rhetia didn't care about one small girl.

But I do. And you'll help, won't you? I know you will.

He was silent. So she lifted her chin, squared her shoulders, and stepped forward.

"Wait!"

It was a small word, but it rang. Shocked by the noise it made, she jerked in fear, her own command returning at her from every side, sharp, angry, fierce.

The Speaker's mask turned instantly; Argelin's face was edged with red light.

Before they could snap orders, she said it again. "Wait!" And then like a sudden peace flooding her, the moon came out and shone on them all, a gold light and she knew he was behind her, at the back of the stage on the high arch where the god appeared at the end of all the plays. She knew it from their faces, the soldiers' rigidity, the way the front rows were standing stricken, then kneeling, a ripple of awe that seemed to go right around the theater, up and up into the highest seats like a wind through a cornfield.

She turned. "The god is here," she said, her voice high and clear. "The god."

He did not move at first. Instead he looked out at the people, a tall figure, his tunic white, his face masked and as beautiful as the statue in the Temple, as pure, with that hurt look in his eyes she saw there every morning. The only light on him was the moon, and it caught his hair as he walked swiftly down the steps past her, past Hermia's frozen awe to the altar, as he caught Telia's hand, forcing her to stand, and then he lifted her onto his shoulder, and she sat there, sleepy, rubbing her eyes.

The silence was full of sound. Not the bombardment, not anymore, but birds, rows of crowded birds singing at night when they should never sing. Full of the cries of disturbed gulls, the gathering of millions of insects, whining and crackling as they crawled out of stones and crevices, of the skitter of mice. And the cats had come, the million mongrel scrawny cats of the Port, running in under doors, over lintels, sneaking under the feet of soldiers, their eyes green as emeralds. All the god's life was scurrying and hurrying toward him. And most of all, the scorpions.

Argelin hissed a curse; Chryse breathed a stifled, petrified sob.

For the stage around them was moving, crawling, alive. The moonlight caught carapace and claw, a jointed, stilted scramble. Out of holes they came and chinks in the stonework, from under benches and flags and marble columns. They fell from chiseled acanthus architraves, from the roof, from the pediment where the Rain Queen sat, her stone face calm. Red and gold and black, tiny, huge as lobsters, the scorpions attended their lord.

No one on the stage dared move a muscle.

And the god said, **There will be death, if you want death. There will be peace, if you want peace. All I can do is put back the apples I once stole, and show you the way to the Well, so you may drink. And yes, if you wish it, to make the rivers flow again.**

He put Telia down gently, next to Ixaca, who grabbed her hand. Then, ignoring the slithering scorpions, his bare feet walked to Hermia.

Mask to mask, they looked at each other, only their eyes visible in the gleaming metal.

"Who are you?" she whispered.

Hear me, Speaker. Don't shut me out.

Stricken, she stared at him. "Can it be you?"

No sacrifice. Not until I return, and then, if there's need, it will be me. As for who I am, you know that. He turned away, walked to the back of the stage and paused at the exit, perfectly lit, perfectly timed, like an actor. **Don't be scared, Hermia. You've known it for a long time now.**

"Seth. Tell me about the star."

Seth jumped, turning like a cat. Alexos was sitting by the

water pack, legs crossed.

"*Where did you come from?*"

"I dug myself out." The boy looked at them both strangely. "Did you think I was suffocated?"

Gray with sand, Oblek stared at him. Then he swallowed, and rasped a hand over his face.

"Why did the Jackal say he had a star?"

Seth glanced at the musician. They both knew the boy had not been there an instant ago. Oblek reached unsteadily for the water, saying nothing. After a glance at the sky, Seth let himself sit slowly down.

"I bought the star as a gift for you," he said huskily. "The Jackal took it. He has it with him."

"It fell? Like the others?"

"Into the sea."

"Then that's the three." His dark eyes lit up. "Don't you see, the three apples I turned into stars? I thought I'd fixed them securely, but they came loose and now they're here, and we have to take them with us." He nodded, happily.

Oblek muttered, "Old friend. Where in the god's name have you been?"

Alexos looked at him, puzzled. "I've been here, Oblek, haven't I?"

The musician licked burned lips. "Not here. We looked for you. We were worried for you."

He was watching the boy with a fear Seth had never seen before. Oblek's eyes slid to him; he said, "When the bird was gone, you weren't in the place we buried you."

Lightly, Alexos shrugged. He stood up. "I was talking to

Mirany. She's looking after Telia, Seth."

Horrified, Seth felt the blood drain from his face. "Is she?" he breathed.

"Yes. Like you asked." Alexos smiled his grave smile. "Let's hurry, shall we? I want to catch up with the Jackal. I want my star."

Neither of them said anything else. Three shadows, they walked in silence under the moon, alert for the sweeping hunter in the sky. Wrapped in a long thin mantle, Seth thought quickly. If he knew about the letter, what else did he know? About Argelin's orders? What was going on behind them? Were Argelin's men following? There had been no sign of them. And what sort of bird was it that was as huge as that? Had it killed the Jackal? Would they stumble on bones soon, half eaten by sand crabs, picked clean?

"Seth."

It was Oblek's rumble, and the big man had stopped, ahead.

For an instant of cold fear, Seth knew that was exactly what he'd found, and was surprised at his own dread. What good had the Jackal ever done him?

But the musician just pointed. "What's that?"

The land had been rising for miles. Now, black against the starry sky, a building rose. Walls, turrets, a broken battlement. At first he thought it was perched on a crag, a towering outcrop of the Mountains of the Moon, and then as his eyes adjusted, he saw that the whole rock was fortified, what had seemed stone was crumbling battlements, the whole mass of towers and minarets so broken it was hard to tell what was rock and what masonry. It looked black, but the sinking moon glinted on slabs, making them glimmer.

As they stared, the sky paled. Behind them, leagues away, lifetimes away, over the Island and the Port and the sea, over the City of the Dead, the sun was rising.

Seth gasped. "It's covered with people."

"Not people. Small things. Crammed together." Under his hand, Oblek's small eyes were screwed up against the dusty wind. "Millions of them."

Alexos nodded. "Birds," he said simply.

Lights were lit, torches, all around the arena. They drove the scorpions back into the dark and the insects away and the cats back to the houses. The people were a different matter; they clustered around the lights, talking, weeping, going over and over the events of the vision, the message, as if, Mirany thought, it had all been some bizarre performance. Maybe it had. Argelin had withdrawn, his bodyguard closing around him, and though he had given Hermia one concerned look, she had not returned it. In fact she had swept out without a word to anyone, had rushed into her litter and closed the door in Chryse's face when the girl had tried to join her.

Disturbed, the rest of the Nine looked at one another.

Mirany took her mask off and blew hair from her eyes. She went and took Telia's hand. "Do you recognize me?"

"You're that girl. Seth's friend."

"Mirany."

"He likes you." Telia watched Pa hurtle down the steep stone steps. He grabbed her and held her tight. When he looked up, his face was years older. But all he said was, "Where can we go?"

Mirany thought quickly. "The City. Use Seth's pass. Find a cleaning woman called Khety and tell her I sent you. She's to take you to Kreon. Stay with him."

"The albino?"

"He's . . . more than that. He'll know you're coming."

Pa looked beyond, at the impatient soldiers. "What about you?"

"I'm more use where I am. Go quickly!"

He nodded and hustled the child away. At the bottom of the steps he turned back. "I can never thank you enough. He came because of you."

She was almost too tired to answer him. Then, from the Port, as he ran, came a great crash, a roar of voices, a sound she had never heard before, clashing bronze, a raw-throated, terrible rumble. The optio grabbed her instantly. "Lady! Hurry!"

Half flung into the litter, she felt it swing up and the men begin to run. "What is it? What's happened?"

Her face alight, Rhetia had the curtains open. Flames flickered red on her skin, and her face was joyous.

"Jamil's attacking," she whispered.

The Seventh Offering

OF A BLUE EGG

Don't think the gods are strong. We are frailer than you.

How easily we are forgotten! Faith in us is fragile; we depend on you for it, and how fickle you are.

You have made gods of trees and birds and strange demons; you've worshipped stones and spun a million mythologies about us. You have laughed at us in your strength and prayed desperately to us in your weak=ness.

I hold the world like a blue sphere in both my hands, but one cry from you pierces me, and I cannot destroy it.

Gods are children before you.

A Nest of Horrors

Finches, he decided, stepping cautiously under the arch.

Millions and millions of finches, lovebirds, parrots, macaws, sparrows, species he didn't know, species blown miles off course, species with plumes and long tails that looked as if they belonged in stories with djinns and white-skinned princesses.

They covered the ruined city, a feathered layer always stirring, the uproar of their chirruping and fighting and re-arranging ringing in the ancient tumbled stones, the blown hills of sand. The ground was white with droppings; as Seth walked his boots sank into a gummy mess, accumulated over centuries. The air stank, too. Oblek had his face well wrapped; only Alexos seemed not to mind, trying to entice finches onto his arm with a fragment of hard bread.

The birds watched them, beady eyed. The tiny bodies were crushed into long lines on sills and roofs, some this way, some that, hanging on, falling off, fluttering, pecking, a never-ending motion.

The city seemed empty but for them.

At a hanging gate Oblek paused. He glanced around it carefully, then waved Seth on. The farther they went the more ominous the city became; they had been climbing its smashed streets and plazas for at least an hour, the sun already making the brown brick walls too hot to touch.

"Keep up!" Seth glanced back at Alexos.

"So many birds, Seth! What do they all eat?"

It was a good question. Nothing grew here; there was no sign of water. Above them the ruined buildings rose to the heights of the crag. Empty, dust-deep rooms, their roofs gone, columns that rose alone, statues of broken torsos, giant-sized, dessicated by the desert wind. As they crawled under the remains of one, Seth looked up at it. A leg and body in a short tunic, and at its back a great shattered stump of rock. The smashed pieces all around it were a barricade they had to climb over; as one slid under his feet Seth staggered, and putting his hand down, he turned the stone. It was carved with feathers. Close together, huge. A wing. Beyond that there was no doubt. A double line of vast winged beings squatted on both sides of the paved road. None had faces; it was as if some revenging army had stormed through centuries ago, tearing everything down, smashing the faces of bizarre deities.

"Are they gods?" he whispered.

Oblek shrugged; they looked at Alexos. Tiny below a black basalt figure, his face looked pale and weary. "If they are, Seth, let's hope they have no worshippers."

All the way up to the citadel the dark headless masses crouched, their wings furled. Up here the wind gusted hot from the desert. High up, one dot circled.

"Would the Jackal come here?" Oblek muttered.

"The Sphere says the way leads through. There's a well marked. They'd look for it."

"If they're still alive."

The inner gateway was massed with birds. Thousands of eyes watched them approach, a restlessness that grew noisier, more frantic.

"Keep to one side," Seth whispered. "Don't disturb them."

Oblek's small eyes moved from side to side. "You first," he breathed.

Seth glared at him, then took a step toward the darkness of the arch. As he walked the stench grew worse, the road coated with white. He had to pick his way, small careful steps, utterly silent, and above him as the gateway loomed, the birds seemed a weight smothering his mind, an intent, breathless scrutiny. He was closer now, and there was a path, a way through the rubble. Stones had been lifted aside, cleared. Then, on the dusty track over a heap of shattered debris, he saw them.

Silent, he glanced back at Oblek and pointed.

Footprints. Boots, maybe two men, maybe more, and around them, others. Bare feet. Strangely shaped. The toes long, almost hooked, an odd spur jutting from the heel.

He heard Oblek's indrawn breath.

It was nothing, barely a sound, but it was enough. A bird squawked, fluttered. Another took off, startled, and in an instant they were all rising, a mass of panicking, screaming beaks, of wings that clashed and beat in urgent, mindless terror.

"Get down!" Oblek grabbed the Archon and flung him onto the path, one hand protecting the boy's head, the other beating off the wings and beaks. Seth dived under the arch, the air already a swirl of frantic bodies, crashing themselves to death against stonework, diving at his hair and face, tearing his hands as he curled into a terrified knot. The noise was unbearable; he knew that all down the streets they had climbed, all down the city in a ripple of screaming frenzy the birds were rising, a vast multicolored alarm for whoever lived here. Because someone did. Or something.

"In here!" Seth screeched.

Oblek tried to get up, but the birds slashed at him. Doubled over, arms around Alexos, he cursed and swore and staggered toward the arch, and Seth leaned out and grabbed him; they all tumbled in together, bruised, stinging with cuts. Birds were flying everywhere, uncontrolled, slamming themselves into the confusing curves of the arch, desperate to get out. Jerking back from a savage slash at his eyes, Seth felt something hard give behind him; he turned instantly.

A door.

He shoved at it; rubble blocked it but it shifted. Then Oblek was there, and with a heave he had the door open and they scrambled through. Steps led up, into darkness, and without stopping they ran up them, only slowing gradually as the racket fell away below and the clamor of their own breath and shuffles became the only sounds.

Then Oblek stopped and slid down the walls,

breathless. "God," he managed.

Seth bent over the pain in his side. Then he sat, too.

Alexos was crying, a silent awed fear. He had a scratch on his face, but that was all. The backs of Oblek's hands were raw, torn by the birds' terror and menace. Seth felt he was one mass of bruises, dry as dust, his throat caked with sand. Taking a flask of water out, he downed some gratefully. Then he passed it over. Silent, Oblek's shaky hands took it without spilling a drop. When the big man had drunk, he shook his head, dust scattering from sweat-coated skin. "What nest of horrors have we walked into?"

After a while, Seth looked up.

The stairs led into dimness. Far up, a slant of sunlight angled down from some window, a brilliant rod of light. A bird fluttered into it, then out. It was cooler here, as if the walls were thick enough to keep out the scorching heat.

"There's no point going back down. If we keep up this way, we should come out at some upper level. We need to keep climbing now, to find another gate."

Oblek heaved himself up. "No point tiptoeing, either. Are you all right, Archon?"

"I don't like it here, Oblek."

"Nor do I, old friend."

"There are creatures here. Like the birds. Full of frenzy."

Oblek put a huge arm around him. The boy looked up, his grave face dirty. "I love you, Oblek," he said suddenly.

"And I love you, old friend. When we get back I'll make such songs for you as you'll never have heard in all your thousand lifetimes. Now, let's move on. This is no place to linger."

The stairs were wide. On the first landing broken doors led to rooms, most of them empty—the ones with no roof aswirl with birds. They explored a long corridor where the rags of curtains that might once have been red drifted in drafts. The whole place was empty, and silent, except for the screeches of macaws and parrots, distant now.

Then Alexos stopped. His hand tightened in Oblek's. "I can hear voices," he whispered.

The litter rocked. Mirany held on desperately. "They'll drop us!" she gasped.

They were at the gate of the City; the guards yelled a warning and the litter went down with a thump. Rhetia was out in seconds.

"Open this gate!"

"Lady, are you mad?"

"*Open it!* The Nine must return to the Island."

The gate commander looked around helplessly. "The Port is under attack!"

"All the more reason for us not to be here." Rhetia advanced on him fiercely. "Or do you want to be the one responsible for our deaths!" When he hesitated, she drew herself up. Mirany saw her triumphant smile. "Open it," the man said sullenly.

Behind him, the guards ran to the great wooden bars. Without waiting for the litter, Rhetia slid through as soon as the gates were ajar, and Mirany ran after her. The desert was hot and silent. Behind them, from the area of the harbor, came the clash of swords. Mirany wondered where the invaders had landed, and if the wall was breached. Racing after Rhetia, she saw the black palisade of the City of the Dead over the desolate ground, the statues of the great Archons tawny in the afternoon light. A jackal ran, head down, then stopped and looked back at her.

She ran after Rhetia, thinking, *Where are you, Seth?* And as they passed the gardens of the Archon's villa she thought of all the animals in there, the jungle of monkeys and gifts. *And where are you, Bright Lord?*

This time, there was no answer.

Then Rhetia stopped and looked back. Behind them the gate was opening again. A few figures flitted through, in flimsy dresses. They walked, upright and with dignity, along the sandy road. Mirany caught at a stitch in her side. "Hermia."

Rhetia scowled. "I thought she might be too scared."

"Not her. Don't underestimate her."

The Speaker strode up to them. She was pale, her nose long and straight under her eyes, the manicured perfection of her eyebrows. Despite the heat her hair stayed in its elaborate coils. But there was something different. Hermia was shaken, Mirany realized. Like the Port, her defenses had been broken.

But she faced up to Rhetia. "Cupbearer. You and the Bearer will walk behind me."

Rhetia was cold. "I didn't think you would come. After what he said to you."

The Speaker came close. Eye to eye, the two were matched in height, in cold anger. For a moment Mirany thought Hermia would strike. Instead her voice came, precise and chiseled with wrath. "I am the Speaker. Not you. The

Port is unimportant. What Jamil wants is the Oracle and only we can deny him that. Not by violence. But by silence." She nodded calmly. "We won't let the whole land burn for your ambitions, Rhetia. We, the Nine, will stand together. We will keep the angry silence of the god. Before Argelin, before Jamil. Until there is an end to this." She glanced at Ixaca and Gaia, who closed in. Behind them Chryse watched, wide-eyed and flushed with excitement. "We all have to stand together. Are you with us?"

Rhetia stepped back. She glanced at Mirany, at all of them. Then she looked down at the crowding ships, the pall of smoke rising over the Port.

"For now," she muttered.

The words were louder. Strange harsh words. Seth crawled under the last of the red curtains and found Oblek blocking him; the musician inched aside, then pointed with a stubby finger.

Seth bit his lip. Beside him, he could feel Alexos' astonishment.

They were high on a narrow balcony. Below was a vast hall, its wall pierced with windows so that sunlight slanted across it, barring everything with stripes of heat.

In the center on a stone platform was a bizarre construction, rickety and intricate. It seemed to be made of wood, pieces of brittle twig woven together, hundreds of them. Where had they come from, because the nearest trees were miles across the desert?

"It's a nest," Alexos breathed.

Seth stared. A nest. But for no bird. Because a staircase had been built up to it, a winding, patchwork contraption, leading through the teetering layers of wood, the pieces of jaojao bough nailed together to a top-heavy mass of broken chairs and tables, splintered screens, bed legs and slabs of mahogany and teak from precious carved objects. And high on the top, reclining among pillows and cushions and down and billions upon billions of feathers, was a figure that turned his heart chill.

Gigantic, bloated, she sprawled on the incongruous bed. Her robe was feathered, and her mask a hideous black and red, beaked with an eagle's cruel beak. Her fingers seemed swollen; even from here he could see each one was tied with elaborately knotted strings, red and blue and yellow, and the same strings were woven in her dank, greasy hair. She held a fan, made of some dark skin, and she fanned herself with it idly as she spoke in a throaty, cold voice.

It was the Jackal she was speaking to.

Seth's eyes widened. The tomb thief looked terrible. His pale hair had come loose, and there was a cut right down his face. The Fox was worse, crouching on the floor in obvious pain as if he couldn't even drag himself upright. They were in some sort of cage, made of pieces of white ivory, or perhaps bone. Bone. Seth swallowed. They looked like human bones.

Around, there were men. They wore the hideous bird masks, and clothes stitched with feathers, but they were men, and they were armed with spears tipped with what looked like stone or some vitreous sharpened mineral.

Oblek scratched. Then he breathed, "Now who's in trouble, thief lord?"

The Jackal gripped the bars of the cage. "I had no knowledge," he was saying tensely, "of your religion, or your rituals. We had no idea that birds were sacred here. We were simply trying to obtain food."

"You are thieves."

Even from here they could see the Jackal raise an eyebrow. "Not at all," he snapped.

Oblek allowed himself a grin. "Lying scum."

"You attempted to kill the High One. Then you came here and we know why. You seek the star. You will not find it."

Alexos wriggled up beside Seth. "The star! One of those that fell."

"And now"—the woman held up her hand—"we have yours."

It gleamed in her hand, a white shaft of pure light. Seth scowled, thinking of the hundred and fifty staters he still owed for it, and the Archon gave a small breath of recognition. "So long," he whispered. "So long since I've seen it."

The Jackal spread his fine hands. "I assure you, madam, one star is enough for anyone."

It was the wrong thing to say. The bird-men closed in angrily. The woman held up her hand. Her voice was very strange, an oily sound, as if something had been done to her throat.

"The High One has devoured the star."

"Birds," Seth muttered. "She means that vast bird."

"Condor?"

"Something similar."

"Eats more than carrion, then, I'll bet." Oblek was looking around the hall, noting a doorway in the corner, another opening high in the east wall.

"It can't have!" Alexos looked devastated.

The Jackal said, "We mean no disrespect. Keep the star. All we ask is to go free." His voice was taut, but Seth had to admire his composure. He must know perfectly well there was no chance.

A sound, glutinous and sinister. The woman was laughing. She nodded her head to the bird-men. Then she said, "Your souls will be free. On the wind, high in the sky, as will your rags of flesh. Wherever the High One takes them . . ."

Jerkily, with a lurch that made the Jackal stagger, the cage began to rise. The Fox gave a howl of fear, stifled at the Jackal's wrathful glare. The tall man pulled himself upright. "On your feet, Fox," he muttered. "After all our years of pillaging him, death is finally getting his own back."

Seth squirmed. "We can't leave them," he argued against the silence.

Oblek wriggled back. "We could."

"No!" Alexos breathed, and the big man tugged his hair. "Only joking, old friend." He grinned. "If anyone finishes that scum off it'll be me. That's the only reason we're bothering, understand."

Alexos nodded, grave. "Of course it is, Oblek."

The woman stood. It was a great effort, as if she hardly ever rose from the bed, and there was a great depression where she had lain, in the feathers. Something pale glimmered among the down. Seth stared. "What is that?"

Alexos' dark eyes went wide. Then he said, "It's an egg."

He Spoke to Me Face=to=Face

The egg was enormous, as long as Seth's arm. It was palest blue with odd splotches, and it nestled in the warm down and the woman covered it carefully, piling cushions and coverings on top. Then, awkward and clumsy, she began to descend the stairs.

"She *incubates* it?" Oblek looked amazed, then disgusted. "They think birds are gods and they hatch their eggs?"

"One bird. That huge one." Seth looked around quickly. "We have to cut the cage down. The bird will come through that opening in the wall." He turned quickly. "Archon, can you help? Can you do something?"

"Of course I can," Alexos said eagerly. "Anything you want."

"I mean . . ." Seth glanced at Oblek. "Something . . . magical."

The boy frowned. When he looked up, his eyes were dark and his voice echoed slightly in the closed spaces.

"Is it fair for one god to work against another?"

"In the stories it happens all the time," Seth said, unwavering.

"I don't write the stories, Seth." He looked up, worried. "But I think the bird is coming."

The cage was high now, swinging below the vaulted roof. The two men waited, watching the window, glancing down at the floor. Seth knew the Jackal was calculating the jump, planning. Below, the bird-men and their queen moved back, and for the first time he saw that the floor down there was ankle deep with the same gooey whiteness that clotted all the fortress, splashed and dribbled under the great beam that crossed the roof.

From outside, a harsh eerie squawk turned him cold.

"Oblek. Find a way down and deal with the spearmen."

"All of them?"

"Unless you want to climb across and cut the rope."

Oblek leaned out and looked at the thin ledge along the wall. Then he clapped Seth on the shoulder. "All yours, ink boy," he said, and was gone, squirming back with Alexos ahead of him. Seth licked dry lips.

He put one leg over the balcony, and then the other, hands gripping tight on the corroding metal. Then he lowered himself onto the ledge, his foot stretched, feeling for it. The stonework seemed safe, but as it took his weight he felt its edges crumble, and he clung desperately to the bars of the balcony, silent, summoning up courage.

Then he let go, grabbed at stone.

Below him, in dimness, the hall was darkening. Torches

were being extinguished, and a faint smoke began to rise around him, the familiar smell of incense. A hasty breath of it made him want to cough; he choked it down. Then, sliding his feet, splayed against the smoke-stained wall, he edged toward the cage.

The Fox was praying, gabbling words, over and over. The Jackal was on his knees, too, but when Seth could spare another glance, he saw the thief was working intently at the complex knotting that held the cage door, his long fingers swiftly unweaving the ropes.

Something blocked the bars of light, a great flapping.

Seth clung on, staring, horrified.

The bird flew past outside, so close he saw its cruel hooked beak. It was no vulture. There was a creature in old legends called the roc. Maybe this was it.

A yell made him grip tight, turn his head.

They had seen him. One of the bird-warriors pointed; the woman snapped something and the man grabbed his spear, drawing his arm back deliberately, taking careful aim. The Jackal stared; Seth glimpsed his utter surprise.

The spear whooshed. It smacked into the stonework just to his left and clattered down; sparks fell into his hair. Instantly he stretched his arm out, gripped, and hauled himself a few feet farther, his back and shoulders tense against the impact of the next flung point that would skewer him to the wall.

His hand slid, wet with sweat. He knew if he moved he'd fall; then the Jackal yelled, "Come on, Seth! Come on!" and he heaved himself up, the dark stone crumbling and soft against his cheek, arms trembling with effort.

Out of the corner of his eye he saw the spearmen aim again, knew he was dead, and instantly, with a roar that jerked their eyes away in shock, Oblek was down there, his sword sweeping, crashing into them, sharp pieces of stone being flung from behind him. One caught a spearman in the face; he went down. Oblek's weight sent another crashing.

"Seth!" The Jackal was close, gripping the bone framework. For a second their eyes met, an exchange of astonishment and hope, then his hands slithered, he screeched, grabbed, and with a wrenching of all his muscles had the rope in its brackets in the wall.

"Cut it!" The Fox was up now, hands bunched in fists. "Quick, boy! *The bird!*"

It was squeezing in, rustling its vast body through the window. A fierce-eyed head, the hooked beak, great talons of dark yellow that made horrible scrabblings on the stones of the sill. Below, the bird-people fought to hold Oblek, their vast queen standing back. And her arms were wide and she was singing, a wordless song of clicks and trills, an alien music rising to a racket of harsh screeches. Mesmerized, the bird listened, one golden eye fixed on her.

Seth had the knife from his boot. Desperately he worked it across the hemp fibers; the rope was thick, twisted tight.

The woman ended her song. She and the bird watched each other. Then, with a swiftness that made the Fox screech and the Jackal swear, the bird dragged the rest of its huge body through and flapped with a draft and crack of vast wings to the beam.

One strand snapped. The cage jolted, the men toppled.

Oblek yelled below, a cacophony of blows and fury. The bird leaned forward. One claw grabbed the cage. Then its beak opened; it pecked viciously at the Jackal.

He flung himself back, flattened against the rear wall. Expertly, instantly, the bird twisted it, pecked again; the men hurling themselves away, stumbling. "God! Boy!" the Fox howled. Sweat in his eyes, his arms an agony of aching, Seth hacked at the rope. The fibers dwindled, frayed, untwisted. Then, with a terrible crack that flung him back with a cry of terror, they snapped.

The cage fell. It hit the ground and smashed open; Seth grabbed the wall, missed, fell after it into a blackness that rose up and smacked into him, a winded, gasping, softness under him, that growled, "Get off me! Quickly!"

The Jackal was already up, lithe and sudden. He grabbed a spear, and as the bird spread its wings and screamed down he stabbed upward, a rain of dust falling around him like snow. "Get Fox!" he yelled, but Seth was already struggling up, shoved aside by Oblek.

Startled by the stabbing spear, the bird screeched again. In the wreckage of the cage the Fox was crawling; Oblek had one great arm around him. Seth snatched up another spear, swinging to face the woman.

She took off her mask. Her face was too small, hidden in rolls of fat, her hair razored short. She blazed with fury and defiance; he was frozen by her malevolence, unable to move.

The Jackal had no such problem. He swiveled and ran to her, grabbing the hand that clutched the star, twisting it viciously; she struck him hard in the face, a stunning blow. For a second it knocked him back. Then he brought the spear up into her chest.

"Give it to me!" His voice was cold as ice.

"Leave it!" Oblek yelled.

The Jackal's long eyes did not flicker.

She knew her danger. With a glare at her men picking themselves up, she slowly held out the star, a brilliant glitter on her palm.

"May it be cursed, and you with it."

"Too late, lady." The Jackal took it quickly. "I'm afraid I already am."

"*Seth!*" Oblek's roar.

Seth turned, saw the bird just too late. Its talon grabbed at him; he leaped with a gasp of terror, felt the slash of iron claws down his side, collapsed. The bird-men were on him instantly, one tugging the spear from his sore hands. They were kicking him, Oblek was yelling, wading in, but they were outnumbered, and he knew it was over.

Until a high clear voice rang out over the chaos.

"Stand still! All of you!"

Seth shoved a man off, stared up.

Alexos was standing above them, carefully balanced, on top of the rickety nest. In both hands he held the blue egg.

"Stand still," he said quietly. "Or I smash it."

The Nine crossed the bridge in a body.

Hermia turned to the guards. "Leave this place. You will be needed in the Port now."

"Lady—"

"Do as I say. We'll guard the Oracle ourselves."

Torn between reluctance and the terrifying sounds of battle from the Port, the men eyed one another. Without another word they raced down the desert road. Hermia turned and strode on. The Nine walked silently, each struggling with her fears. Mirany bit her dry lips and wished desperately that Seth was here, and Alexos. The boy was unpredictable and strange, but he was the Archon and the power of the god was in him. She even missed Oblek, his blunt, obtuse violence. Looking at Hermia's straight back, she felt useless, because there were too many plots here, a network of intrigue, a silent maneuvering for power. It was trickier than any battle. She had no idea whom to trust anymore.

At the precinct everything was in chaos. The slaves were building frail barricades of furniture; some of the women were just sitting and weeping. Hermia stood on the loggia and spoke to them all in a crisp voice.

"There is no need to panic. This is the Island, and you are safer here than anywhere. Everything will go on precisely as normal. I will have no interruption in the rites, no insult offered to the god. Those ridiculous defenses will be dismantled and the furniture replaced immediately. Koret"—she turned imperiously to the steward—"have a sentinel placed on the Temple roof. I want constant reports about what is happening in the Port."

Does she love Argelin? Mirany thought. *Is she terrified for him?*

"Preparations will resume for the evening meal. I will

address all the Nine at sunset." She turned, the light breeze rippling the fine pleats of her red robe. "Now I wish to speak to the Bearer, privately. Bring rosewater and sherbet to my room."

She swept away down the marble corridor. In Mirany's ear Rhetia breathed, "Be careful. She's planning something."

The Speaker's room was bright and cool, muslin curtains drifting in the warm breeze. Hermia sat in a gilded chair while a slave reverently placed the openmouthed mask on its stand, arranging the feathers, the strands of gold discs. Koret came in and placed a brass inlaid tray with two red cups and a flask. There was a gilt plate of tiny fresh figs. Mirany suddenly realized she was so hungry she wanted to eat them all. It would probably be safe. Hermia wouldn't poison her here.

Without moving, Hermia looked at her. Her eyes were dark, her face edged with tension, the perfect curls of her hair dusty from the road. Then she reached out and poured from the long-necked jug and handed a cup to Mirany.

They both drank. The liquid was sweet and thick, fragrant with oranges.

Hermia held the cup and stared down into it. "Mirany, I don't know what is happening."

Astounded, Mirany was silent.

"Today, at the theater, I saw him. We all saw him. He spoke to me face-to-face and I heard him as I've never heard him before." She looked up. "It terrified me."

It was an admission Mirany could hardly believe she was hearing. She muttered, "We were all—"

"You weren't. I looked at you, and you were amazed, but

not afraid. Because you know him, Mirany, and I don't." She put the cup back on the tray with a click and linked her fingers. Her gaze was direct and cold. "I have made an unforgivable mistake. I've come to see that you were right about Alexos, and I was wrong. He is the God-in-the-World. His safety is vital. His quest for the Well must succeed. Do you have any way of communicating with him?"

Breathless, Mirany's hands clutched the cup. "Sometimes. That is . . . I talk to the god. He isn't always here . . . at least, he doesn't always answer." She stopped, aware of Hermia's scrutiny, of the glimmer of bewilderment, almost of pain. "I can never be sure," she said gently. "But the god is in Alexos."

"Yes. I think he is." Hermia stood up, drawing herself to her full height. "And so I must ask you to warn him."

Mirany's heart thudded. "*Warn him!* Of what?"

"There is a plot to kill the Archon. Argelin desires that he never return."

In the silence only a gull cried outside the window. Mirany tried to shape the words. It was an effort, but only a whisper came out. "Who is to kill him?"

She couldn't think it. She wouldn't. But the fear in the note he had sent rang in her mind, the word *please* like something undigested, impossible to swallow.

"The scribe. I believe Argelin has his family." Hermia watched her carefully.

Mirany shook her head, numb. "Even . . . He wouldn't . . ."

"There were other inducements. A quaestorship."

Mirany glanced up, her eyes wide.

Hermia nodded. "Now you *are* afraid," she said.

The woman's mouth opened in horror.

No one moved; even the great bird had flapped back to its perch and now preened irritably under one enormous wing.

Slowly, Alexos held the egg up. Its weight made his arms tremble; the bird-queen bit her lip.

"Boy!" she hissed. "Take care!"

The Jackal said, "Back to the doorway. Come on, Alexos. Bring it!"

Step by step, Alexos came down the stairs. The bird-men hovered, terrified behind their masks, but none of them dared make any move.

"Go free." The woman opened her arms quickly. "Leave! No one will hinder you. But lay down the unborn."

"Not yet." The Jackal's voice was urgent. "Bring it here. Take your time."

Alexos nodded, his face set in concentration. Sweat dripped into his eyes, he wiped at them with an arm.

"Old friend," Oblek moaned, "be careful."

He was halfway down. The nest creaked and rustled; parts of it jerked. Above him the great bird stared, its attention caught. It spread its wings; before Seth could yell a warning, it had launched itself, sailing down.

Alexos glanced up, twisted, ducked. His foot slipped; he grabbed at the rail with a yell.

The egg fell out of his hands.

Appalled, frozen, they all watched it fall, a slow, terrible arc down and down through the dusty sunslashed darkness of the vast hall, and as it hit the floor the fracture was in their own bones and skulls, setting Seth's teeth on edge, dislocating his mind—the woman's high scream and the crack of the thick shell, as it shattered on the stones.

They Swear to Keep the Silence

No one moved. Then Alexos gave a great cry of pain, an anguish that cut Seth like a knife. Instantly he ran, climbing up to the boy, leaping the mess on the floor.

Alexos was white with shock. "I killed it," he breathed.

Seth snatched him up. "It's all right. It wasn't your fault."

The eggshell lay in pieces, ridged and jagged. From inside it a colorless fluid oozed; a wet gangly wing projected. Seth carried Alexos away from it and turned his head in disgust. Then something caught his eye.

"Look!"

But Alexos was sobbing.

Seth jumped, bent over the ruined shell. Ignoring the spear that jabbed his neck, he gently reached in and picked up the glimmering object that lay among the pieces and held it up, brilliant in his fingers. It was a star, blue as sapphire—

"The second star!" The Jackal had been grabbed and

was flat against the wall, but his astonishment was clear. "It was in the egg?"

"Kill them." The woman's voice was hoarse with grief. "Kill them now."

"*No!* Wait."

Alexos turned, tears streaming down his face. He took a breath, then said, "This is my fault, not theirs. If anyone has to die, it should be me."

Seth's heart gave a great leap. For a second he thought, *If they do it, I won't have to,* and then he hated himself with a hatred that burned like fire. He turned fiercely on the boy. "That's rubbish! Do something about it. You're the god, aren't you? You make things happen, make things live and die. Show them who you are."

"He's right." Oblek looked at the woman. "Show her what a proper god really is."

Alexos looked at them, hope lighting his face. "Should I?"

He glanced down at the broken egg, then up at the bird. It sat motionless, unblinking eyes on him, as if he was a small morsel of prey far below. "I'm sorry," he said earnestly. "This should never have happened. I'll do what I can, but there are things that can never be put together again, moments that can never be repeated."

The bird screeched, a harsh sound.

Alexos knelt among the wreckage of the egg. He looked up at the woman. "If I succeed, will you let us go?"

"Who are you?" she whispered, her voice choked.

He did not answer. Instead he put his frail hand into the mess and stroked the twisted limb of the unborn chick, the gentlest of touches. From the corner of one eye, Seth saw the Jackal's tension. Oblek waited, patient, faintly smiling.

"Be alive. Be reborn, who was never born. Because gods are always born in strangeness, in impossible ways."

A feather moved. Or was it the breeze?

Seth stepped closer.

"I call you. From the Rain Queen's garden, where the trees are always in leaf. Where streams drip into cool pools and dragonflies flit. From where you sit in the topmost branches."

It moved. The woman put a hand over her mouth. A shiver, a jerking of limbs.

"They need you. They need us. Because without us they are empty and hollow and they turn on each other. They need us to blame and to curse. To love. To destroy."

It was staggering up. Ugly wings splayed, the bald head lifted on its scrawny neck. The chick opened its beak. A faint squawk rang through the hall.

Alexos scrambled back. He looked at the woman and his face was weary, with dark hollows under his eyes.

"I give you your divinity back."

Then he looked at Seth, a long look. **"Divinity,"** he said, **"is fragile."**

Seth went cold; at the same time the Jackal shoved back his guards, took the second star from Seth, and strode to where his pack lay across the room. He hauled it on, threw another to Oblek, and dragged up the injured Fox. "Now we leave," the Jackal said briskly. "Before they get any more ideas."

Oblek crossed to Alexos. "Come, old friend. Come with us."

The boy turned to him. "I feel so tired, Oblek." He sighed.

"Then I'll carry you. Oblek will carry you all the way to the Well." Picking him up easily, the big man followed the others out of the hall. Seth hurried after them.

"Wait."

He turned at the door. The woman was standing over the chick, watching its ungainly movements. Above her the great bird eyed its offspring critically.

"We have something else of yours."

"Something else?"

"A silver egg. With markings on its surface. We took it from the tall man."

The Sphere. He stared at her.

"Do you wish for it back? You are a dangerous people, we can see that, when even your children perform miracles. Maybe you are gods yourselves. We no longer wish to be enemies with you." The woman beckoned a bird-man. "Fetch it."

He started toward the nest, but Seth said, "No." He licked his lips. "Keep it. As our gift to you." He turned and was almost out the doorway before he turned back.

"It will never hatch into anything, though."

The woman put her mask on, and its black-and-red beak turned sidelong to him. "Who knows what the gods can do?" its voice murmured.

Running after the others, he grinned to himself. Without

the Sphere the Jackal could never leave them behind again. From now on, only he knew the way.

No one obstructed them. All the gates were open, the doors wide, the streets of ruined statues silent and still. By the time they climbed to the top of the destroyed network of towers and toppled pylons, the sun had long since set behind the mountains, and the myriad birds that flocked overhead in dark clouds, swooping and rising and falling, had settled into deafening chirruping rest on the headless images. At a stroke, as one, they fell silent.

Night had come.

The road was silent, the stars overhead brilliant. Mirany had run as far and fast as she could; now she hobbled along, a stone in her sandal, a pain in her side. No time to stop for either of them. She felt like crying, but she wouldn't, because she wouldn't believe it. Seth was ambitious but he would never hurt Alexos. Surely! But as she clutched her side and smelled the artemisia and lavender that lined the road, the knowledge deep inside was that she couldn't be sure, not of him, not of Chryse, not of Rhetia. She only trusted the god, and the god was not answering her, and his silence filled her with terror.

Besides, gods were unpredictable. You never knew what they would do.

The stone door leaned in the warm twilight; she ducked under it and followed the spiral path through a drift of moths. Cicadas chorused all around her, the voice of heat, and far off the waves hissed on the beach. Smoke and noise rolled from the Port. She had no idea what was happening down there.

When she came to the stone steps, she climbed them and stood at the top, on the flat platform. From here the sea stretched to the horizon, black and gently heaving. She turned, saw the outline of the Mountains of the Moon, their ghostly pinnacles against the stars. How high was Seth, and the others? Had they found the Well, or the Jackal his gold? Or were they already dead of thirst in the wilderness, still shapes crawled over by ants?

She shook the thought away and crossed to the Oracle.

In the shadow of its guardian stone, the pit opened.

"Listen to me," she said. "Listen!" She leaned down, lay on her stomach, her hair in her eyes. Then she put her face into the misty darkness and screamed. "Kreon! Listen to me!"

She had no idea if he could hear her. Seth had said the chamber was far down, that voices came muffled and broken, but surely no one had shouted like this, hung so far into the smoke, been so terrified. It was making her dizzy; her eyes blurred and she closed them. "Warn Alexos! Seth has been ordered to kill him. *Can you hear me?* Show me you can hear me!" Why didn't he answer her? Where was the voice in her head when she needed it?

Behind, from the precinct, came the soft shimmer of a gong, the signal for the meeting of the Nine. It was to be held here, so she had time. "Kreon," she moaned. "Please!"

Something scrabbled.

She jerked back instantly, knowing it would be a scorpion. Its pincers came out, and then all of it, a large red creature, claws held high, and it ran at her as if she had called it. And if the god was in his creatures then she had, she supposed. It gleamed in the starlight.

Mirany took a breath. Edging closer, holding her skirt above her knees in a tight handful, she wondered if the fumes of the pit had not gone to her head, twisted her brain and eyesight. Because the scorpion had something tied around it.

She went and found the bronze bowl and held it out, brim to the floor. As they always did, the scorpion came close, attracted by the reflections perhaps, the shimmering of its own jerky movements. As soon as it was in, she stood, letting it slide helplessly down to the bottom, looking at it closely.

A bracelet. Thin and cheap and obviously well worn. Very small, a little girl's ornament. Mirany felt a flood of relief. It was Telia's; she always wore it. Telia and Pa were safe below, in the Kingdom of the Shadow. Then her gaze froze in horror. She had told them about Seth—had they heard? What were they thinking?

She clutched the bowl tightly, hearing feet race up the steps behind her.

Rhetia had a dark mantle around her shoulders. She was breathless. "I knew you were here! What's going on? What are you up to?"

Mirany sighed. "Do we all have to be plotting against one another?" Suddenly furious, all the pent-up anger churning inside her, she walked up to the tall girl and let it rage out. "You and Jamil, Hermia and Argelin, what's the difference between you? Lies from the Oracle and tyranny over the people. You used to be so proud, Rhetia, and yet you stoop to treachery now! You said your only loyalty was to the Oracle, but it isn't, it's to yourself! Is ambition worth so much?" Her voice was shaking; she turned away and yelled it at the Mountains of the Moon. "Is it worth killing for?"

There was silence. Then Rhetia said quietly, "You and I were never friends, were we? But I heard the Oracle once, and it said your name."

Mirany swung back. "Don't you *dare* say you're doing all this for me!" she snarled.

Rhetia raised her eyebrows. "Then I won't. But don't you see—you say you can hear the god. I don't know if I can—I've only spoken once to the Oracle, and the answer was that I woke up hours later and found that the Rain Queen had taken my place. I want to hear him, Mirany. I want that power, that knowledge. So when I become Speaker, you can stay as Bearer and we'll work together. But only if Jamil wins. If that doesn't happen, if Argelin wins, then neither of us will be left alive."

Wary, Mirany stared at her. "You really mean that, don't you?"

Rhetia looked sour. "I may have made some compromises, but I don't lie." She turned. "The others are coming."

They were already here, Ixaca and Callia, Gaia looking worried, Persis, the tall new girl, Tethys. Last of all came Chryse, slightly breathless, wearing a pink robe, and behind her, Hermia. None of them were masked.

They stood in an open-ended circle around the pit. The girls who had barely seen it before flicked awed glances at its ominous darkness.

Hermia looked around. "The news from the Port is uncertain. The attack was repulsed by the general's men and the attackers seem to have been driven back to their ships. Several streets are still burning. I don't know how many died."

The warm wind moved between them, billowing skirts, soft with the smells of roses and thyme.

"I have decided on a plan to ensure there will be no more violence." Hermia fixed each of them with her firm gaze. "We withhold the Oracle. Each of us will swear that the Silence of the god's anger will descend until there is a truce. Whatever the threat to ourselves, we stand together, unbroken. Do you agree?"

"Yes," Rhetia said firmly. If Hermia was surprised she didn't let it show. She looked at Mirany, who placed the bronze bowl carefully in the center of the circle.

Rhetia put her hand boldly on the rim. The scorpion froze, its sting raised and quivering.

"I swear to keep the Silence," she said, her voice firm.

Each of the girls did the same, hesitant, eyes fixed on the scorpion and its strange collar, ready to jerk away if it should move. Mirany swore with them. Last of all came Chryse.

The blond girl was wide eyed with horror. "I can't!" she breathed.

"Move slowly," Mirany whispered.

Chryse's fingers reached out; she gasped, "I swear to keep the Silence," and snatched them back with a shriek as the scorpion burst into life and raced toward her.

Only Mirany noticed that not even the tips of her

manicured nails had touched the bronze rim.

Hermia nodded. "Thank you, all of you. This loyalty to the god comforts me. Jamil claims this war to be over the truth of the Oracle. Argelin says it's about trade and silver." She raised her head suddenly. "Now we'll see."

Lights. A glow of red torches, the crackle of resin. Between the olive trees the flames approached, the harsh clatter of metal behind them.

"Soldiers, here!" Rhetia turned instantly on the Speaker. "Is this some treachery?"

"Not on my part." Hermia watched, intent, her mouth hard.

The soldiers made a double line up the steps and crossed their spears. Some made furtive signs with their fingers, warding the god's wrath; others cast quick nervous glances at the black pit. Hermia stepped forward, her voice cold with fury. "Who sent for you? How dare you come to this place!"

"I brought them." Argelin climbed the steps, looking weary. His bronze helmet covered most of his face; only his eyes gleamed, his beard untrimmed. He stopped and faced the Nine.

"It's convenient to have you all here."

"Do you need a bodyguard with *us* now?" Hermia's voice was icy.

"With some of you, lady, I've needed one for a long time."

He was looking at Mirany. Then he turned. "As you may have heard, the attack is over. This time we held them off. The Desert Gate was overrun, but my men stormed it and recovered it. The enemy has returned to his ships. Next time we may not be so fortunate. I need money, Hermia. I need to buy mercenaries, melt down stores of metals, force the merchants and aristocrats to pay for repairs. Many of them would secretly be pleased if I lost this war. The fools think the Emperor would tax them less."

Hermia watched him closely. "I don't see what we can do."

"You have storerooms of grain and food and treasure, of offerings to the god. I need them now, or we're lost."

She nodded, impatient. "Take them. But the food must be distributed free to the people."

He stepped closer. "That's not all. The Oracle must speak. You must tell everyone the god confirms I'm the only one who can save the Port. He must order them to obey me in every instance." He reached out and took her hands, the moonlight slanting on the bronze of his armor. "In fact the Oracle must declare I am to be crowned king."

The Nine stood in appalled silence. Only Hermia seemed calm, without surprise, and as she watched the Speaker, Mirany knew that the pair of them had discussed this before, that they had planned this moment together.

Rhetia must have thought so, too. She was cold with fury; she opened her mouth but Hermia had already answered. "King? Not Archon?"

He almost smiled. "We already have an Archon."

She nodded. "Yes. And to be Archon might require the giving of your life."

"I would be willing to give it." His smile had faded.

"This land has never had any king but the god."

Hermia's eyes never left Argelin's face.

He dropped her hands. "These are desperate times." A slight impatience had crept into his voice.

"Indeed they are, Lord General." She nodded, manicured nails tapping her ornate necklace of lapis and jade.

"So you . . . the god will speak?" He was alarmed now, Mirany thought. He sensed danger. As if suddenly tired of pretense, he took a step back, lifted his helmet off. One small cut bled on his chin. "Stop teasing me, Hermia. What's wrong with you? We agreed—"

"Things have changed." She looked at him, a calm, unflinching look.

"Changed? How?"

"The god appeared. You saw him. We all heard him. Now the god decrees that the Oracle will be silent. There will be no words from him until a peace is made." She came forward and touched his face, wiping the blood from it with the edge of her sleeve, and he let her, staring at her in a disbelieving wonder that left Mirany cold.

"You would do this to me?"

"I must."

After a second he said, "I loved you, Hermia."

She didn't flinch. "I thought so, my lord."

"Our alliance—"

She smiled at him with perfect calm. "Our alliance is dissolved," she said.

The Eighth Offering

OF SILENCE

Men don't know what the stars are for.

Nor the rainbow, or the rose.

Last night I lay on my back in the desert and counted the stars. Each one is mine, a point of light, a reminder.

Each one was carefully considered; its color, its heat, the part it plays in the story. Even when I closed my eyes I could see them, because the stars are tiny and can fall into my eyes like dust.

I was so tired with the journey that I cried.

The Rain Queen sang me to sleep.

They Are Pursued by Dreams

They were three days into the mountains.

After the bird city the landscape had fragmented, become a broken, shattered uprearing of red rock, a rusty landscape. The redness came off on their hands as they climbed; they breathed it into their noses and mouths. Oblek's bald head was finger smudged; Alexos' tunic was filthy with smears.

But it was wonderfully cooler. Up here there were breezes, and as they clambered over the sharp scree that slid underfoot, headgear was pulled off and rolled into packs, and finally the Jackal hauled himself up to the top of one splintered cliff face and stood there, taking in great breaths of air.

He stared down over the desert. "I can see the Animals," he called. "Huge shapes, clear from up here."

Wedged in a chimney of rock, Oblek struggled and swore. "As long as they're not coming after us."

The Jackal's fair hair streamed in the high wind. "Nothing is coming after us," he said firmly. Seth glanced up, caught by something in his voice. The Fox looked, too, then saw Seth notice him and glanced away.

Alexos, who always climbed nimbly, was sitting cross-legged on the cliff, picking insects from his tunic. "Did you think Argelin would be coming?"

Seth went cold. "After the gold? How would he know the way?"

"I expect he has ways, Seth."

"No one. No people, no camels, no caravans, no ferocious birds." The Jackal turned away.

"We are all alone, at the ends of the earth."

It certainly felt like that. Pulling himself up beside the tomb thief, Seth rubbed his scraped hands together and looked down. The desert was a wasteland of palest gray; it stretched far away to the horizon, to a blue vagueness that might be the sea, or the sky, or the place where the two joined and the great serpent encircled the world, biting its own tail. And yes, he could see the Animals, and he drew a long breath of astonishment at them, for from up here the complexities of the shapes were amazing, sprawled over the sand, and there were other lines, hundreds of them, crisscrossing the desert, and vast scrawls that looked like words, miles wide. They had journeyed across a landscape of stories without being able to read any of them, or even known they were there.

"A book of the gods," Seth muttered.

The Jackal nodded, his long eyes narrowed against the glare. "Indeed. Over the pages of which we crawl like flies." He glanced up at Alexos. "Does he know what they say, I wonder?"

Seth was silent. Since the bird had come back to life, none of them had felt easy with Alexos, even though the boy was just the same, eager and curious, tiring himself out so that Oblek had to carry him on his back for miles. It was fear, he thought. Of what lived inside the boy. Of what it could do. In the Archon's Palace, or on the Island with its complex rituals, the god was contained, a being propitiated with gifts, controlled by rites, spoken with formally through the Oracle. But out here there were no rites and no rules of behavior. Out here the god was wild and free and dangerous and no one knew what he would do next. And the only way of talking with him was face-to-face.

"Ask him."

The Jackal gave his wry smile. "I confess to you, scribe, I dare not. Such beings are best left to your friend, the priestess Mirany. Gold is all that concerns me."

He turned south, gazing into the distance.

"What's that?" Seth pointed. A dry watercourse lay below them. It descended from the hills somewhere to the west, a dry crack, its ridged tributaries like veins in the land. It ran directly toward the sea.

"The Draxis. The river that once ran to the Port." He frowned down at it. "When the Archon Rasselon stole the golden apples, the Rain Queen dried the river."

"Your ancestor. So he was a thief, too, then?"

The Jackal gave him a cold look. "We're all thieves. Our crimes pursue us and our descendants. Even though we think we can flee them." He turned abruptly.

Seth stayed, watching the shadows lengthen.

Mirany. He wondered what was happening to her. Whether Pa and Telia were safe. He couldn't even ask Alexos, because of the reason why they were in danger. But the god would know anyway . . . wouldn't he, if he was a god? The old arguments circled in his mind. Weary, he turned away.

They camped under an overhang a little farther up. This high, the nights were very cold; there was little to make a fire from, but the Fox foraged and came back with branches from a dead tree; he was an expert fire maker and Seth was glad of him. They ate dried olives and drank some of the precious water; the last source was past; they had three days' supply left and the next water would be at the Well itself, if they ever found it.

The Jackal stretched his long legs. "Well," he said softly. "Perhaps we should know how far away we are from our goal, Lord Archon."

Alexos yawned. "I don't know. We'll find it when we find it."

Oblek grinned. The Jackal looked sourly at Seth. "And the keeper of the lost Sphere's secrets? What has he to say?"

"That we keep climbing toward the highest peak, the one with the cleft top."

"The one the sun goes inside," Oblek rumbled.

"Inside, or behind."

The musician sucked a sour olive. "There must be a great chasm. Burning. The sun descends into it and the god's horses drag it across the Underworld. That's right, old friend?"

"If you like, Oblek."

"But the sun sets in different places through the year. So

does the moon." The voice was the Fox's, dry and sharp, and Seth looked at him with surprise.

"Does it?"

The one-eyed thief spat. "That's a scribe for you! Never lifts his nose from his grubby scrolls."

"A very big chasm then." The Jackal looked at Oblek. "A split at the world's end."

The big man spat out a stone. "Say what you want to say, Lord Jackal."

The Jackal raised an eyebrow. He leaned elegantly against the rocks. "You are more perceptive than you seem, aren't you? And yet it seems hard to think of you as a musician."

"He's a good one," Seth muttered. Oblek looked surprised.

The Jackal nodded. "What I have not said, then, is that Fox and I are . . . touched . . . that you felt you needed to rescue us." He sipped water. "We would have escaped without you, of course, but your help was appreciated."

Oblek snorted. "Maybe we should have waited and watched how."

"You might have learned something."

"The way to be eaten with dignity."

The Jackal's long eyes were expressionless. "Do I possibly detect some doubt?"

"You slimy ungrateful scum. We should have let that overgrown gull peck your innards out." But Oblek's voice was mild, and Alexos was grinning.

Then Seth said, "Where are the stars?"

"Oh yes!" Alexos sat up. "My stars!"

"*My* stars." But the tomb thief pulled the pack over and took them out, unwrapping them both. Light streamed from them, white and blue, unearthly brilliance. Alexos reached over and touched one; the glimmer lit the edges of his face, making his eyes dark. "They are so beautiful!"

He looked up. "But there's a third. We have to find it."

"I agree with you. But if you think you're tossing these into any well," the Jackal said, wrapping them quickly, "then you're mistaken, Archon. These belong to me, and if we find no gold, they may be my only profit." He looked at the boy. "What exactly do you want them for?"

Alexos took a deep breath. He seemed reluctant. Finally he said, "The Well is guarded."

Silence. Then Fox muttered, "By what?"

"Terrible beings."

"Beings?"

"Supernatural creatures of great power."

Fox was swearing under his breath; Oblek said quietly, "Why didn't you tell us this before, old friend?"

Alexos lay down and pulled a blanket over himself. He tucked the edges in tidily. "I didn't want to scare you, Oblek."

Dismayed, they all watched him close his eyes.

The Jackal's voice was acid. "How very typical of a god."

That night Seth dreamed of the Rain Queen. She walked down between the rows of desks in the Office of Plans, and her dress dripped and splashed, and trickles of water ran away between the paving stones. She put her hand on the scroll he was working on, and her fingers were wet, bound with strips of seaweed, ringed with coral and gold, braceleted with the polished shells of cowries.

He looked up, holding the quill tight.

Her face was just like Mirany's. But her hair was long, and curled over her shoulders.

"I have work to do," he said quietly.

"Work you do not wish to accomplish." She caught hold of his wrist and forced him to stand. Her grip was icy and slippery. "Come with me."

They went out into the City, and up onto the battlements. Above them the stone Archons rose; the Rain Queen led him along the row to the statue of Rasselon, and they climbed the steps and stood on the knees of the great figure, its torso towering above them, its vast face and sculpted eyes looking toward the mountains.

"If he could weep," she whispered, "he would weep a river for his people."

"Stone can't weep."

"No?" She smiled. "I can make stone weep. I can squeeze and contract and shatter mountains. I can slip along the veins of the world, make the desert blossom, make dry land a garden. I can make springs rise in the wilderness. If you only ask me."

"Is my father safe?" he whispered. "Is Mirany safe?"

The Rain Queen put her finger on her lips and smiled, and his heart sank, because he knew she wouldn't tell him.

Instead she said, "Look at him. His flesh is gone to ice." For a horrible second he thought she meant Pa, and then he saw she was looking at Rasselon.

The statue glimmered. All at once it was nothing but ice, a frozen mass, honeycombed with holes and tunnels of melt-water, the whole thing collapsing slowly inward, crumpling, dripping, sliding, the fingers shrunk to stubs, the face slowly smoothing out to a featureless slab.

"Remorse is a mountain of glass," she whispered, her lips cool at his ear. "Slippery, impossible to climb. But at its heart is a star of fire."

And he saw it, deep within the figure, entombed in ice, a burning, brilliant point of red light. He put out his hand to it, but felt only the cold slippery surface of the Archon's body.

And the Archon's hand took his and held it tight.

The Jackal seemed to be dreaming, too. Watching the man's long body twitch, Oblek sucked a dry pebble and said, "Should we wake him?"

The Fox shrugged, wrapped in blankets. "Let him sleep. If he wakes in the middle of it, he remembers."

The musician nodded. "I had such nightmares, in the desert. Walked in delirium. Things crawled beside me, monsters, beasts, women I'd known, men I'd betrayed." He gave a wry grunt, feeding the fire with sticks. "Neither of us has lived a good life, Fox."

The red-haired man rubbed his face with one palm. "Few men do. But at least if you betray the living, they don't haunt you."

Oblek turned, curious. "And the dead do?"

"They do." He looked at the Jackal. "They haunt the chief. Too thin-skinned, these aristocrats. After the first few tombs most of us get used to it. The smell, the silence, the foul air, though that can make you see things, in the corners of your eye. Movements. Rustles. Mostly it's just a question of how to get the goods out, avoiding traps . . . hellish, some of them. I've seen a man cut in pieces by a rusty contraption that came spinning out of a wall. Right in front of me, he was."

He grinned and spat. "He had a fine burial. The chief was so furious he had the old Archon thrown out of the coffin and Melas put in it. Buried like a king. But him, he's never got used to it. Not the bodies, not that. It's the thieving, robbing the dead. It's as if when he decided to turn against his class, he deliberately made himself the lowest of the low, gave himself a name of a beast that everyone detests. As if he hates himself. So he gets nightmares."

"He sees them?" Oblek asked.

"Who knows? Rarely talks about it. He sees something. Calls them the Furies. Like those tin-winged beasts in the plays."

The fire crackled. As if he heard it, the Jackal murmured and rolled in his sleep.

The Fox frowned. "One day, he says, they'll catch up with him. Believe me, in that cage I thought they had."

The door opened; a servant came in with a tray and placed it on the small brass table. Behind her a soldier stood, spear at the ready.

Mirany jumped up. "Sophia! What's happening?"

The girl gave her a dumb, hopeless shrug.

"She can't talk to you. Orders." The soldier waved the girl out hurriedly.

Mirany glared. "This is an absolute disgrace! Don't you know who I *am*! I *demand* to see the Speaker—"

The door slammed. The key turned. She was raging at emptiness.

Sick at heart she sank onto the bed and stared at the window. Like the other, it was barred with planks of wood, nailed roughly across. Thin shafts of sunlight slanted in, and a trapped butterfly fluttered to find an exit. She pulled a shawl around her, miserable.

The Nine had been locked in their rooms for two days. The only time she had seen the others had been at the dawn Ritual, which had to go on, but then each of them was masked and guarded so closely that it was impossible to pass any message, or even whisper.

But Hermia's voice had been strong as she spoke the ritual words, as if that was the only way she could show them nothing had changed, that the Silence was unbroken.

Mirany wandered over to the tray. She didn't want to eat, but at least it was something to do. Boredom was killing her.

She took a piece of cheese and nibbled it. This couldn't go on. Argelin's fury at Hermia had been terrible; he had raged and cursed and had almost gone to strike her, but all the time Hermia had been calm. There would be no more words from the god, she had said, until a truce was called.

They were all agreed. They would all stand together.

Mirany wondered. Some of the girls would; others were weak. Chryse. What was Chryse doing, locked all alone in her room, without anyone to giggle with?

She tossed the cheese down, picked up the soft bread and broke it open.

A small piece of papyrus fell out.

Mirany stared at it in amazement, then grabbed it and unfolded it quickly.

MIRANY. HE'S TRYING TO DIVIDE US. HE'S ASKED ME TO BE SPEAKER. I TOLD HIM NOT ON HIS TERMS. HE SAID HERMIA WOULD HAVE AN ACCIDENT. HE'S SCARED OF LOSING EVERY-THING. DON'T TRUST HIM. BE STRONG, MIRANY. KEEP THE SILENCE. I'VE SENT TO JAMIL. HE'LL COME.

It was signed RHETIA.

Mirany read it twice. She didn't know if it was genuine, or some trick of Argelin's, but it sounded only too real. Rhetia was clever, and her slaves were loyal. But to refuse to be Speaker! Something she wanted so much! Mirany admired her then, though she'd always admired Rhetia, her strength, her assumption that she was always right. It must be useful to be so sure of yourself.

Footsteps. In the loggia.

Instantly Mirany crushed the message in her hands and shoved it into her underclothes. As she whirled around the door opened; Koret, the tall steward, came in and bowed.

"Lady Mirany."

Breathless, she said, "What? Are we free?"

He gave a covert glance behind him; she saw the terrace was crowded with an armed phalanx.

"I'm afraid not, lady. Lord Argelin wants to see you."

It was a mountain of ice, just as the Rain Queen had said. Seth and Alexos stared up at it, the smoothness of its sides, the sheer, unclimbable slopes. Hearing the others scramble behind, Alexos turned.

"Look at this! Look, Oblek!"

The Jackal pushed past them. Carefully picking his way forward, he climbed over the splintered shards of sharp material that jutted out, then he squatted, and looked at them intently.

"It looks like glass."

"Ice," Fox said, dubious.

Oblek shook his head. "We're not high enough."

The Jackal stared up. "This is not old. This is recent."

The whole landscape had been smashed, seared, melted and re-formed. Some tremendous heat had vitrified it, made jagged cliffs, torn great holes in the world. The face of the Mountains of the Moon had been pulverized and re-formed, and not of rock, but of some blackened and carbon-coated unbreakable mineral.

The Jackal knelt. He rubbed the black coating from the surface, smelled it, licked it. Then his long fingers explored the seams and fissures of the stuff, its curious facets, the shining planes. "Fox. Your knife, please."

The one-eyed thief chose the sharpest and most delicate weapon and held it out; the Jackal took it near the end of the blade and scratched the surface. No mark appeared; the bronze made no impact. Then he tried to prize out a piece, but the blade bent and the Fox fidgeted, so he withdrew it and handed it back without a word, straightening and rubbing his hands clean on his tunic.

"I told you. Glass." Oblek sounded sour. "And how in the god's name are we going to climb it?"

The Jackal looked sidelong at Seth. His eyes had a strange look in them, and his fair hair drifted in the upland breeze. "Congratulations," he said quietly.

"On what?"

"We are all very rich. We are wealthier men than the Emperor himself, though we can never spend a stater of it." He looked up at the sheer tilted mass of the mountain, and then, quickly, at Alexos. "Perhaps the god knows what I mean."

Alexos took a deep breath. He looked uneasy, Seth thought.

"Do you know?"

Alexos shrugged. "I know the mountain is very hard."

"Hard?" Oblek came and put an arm around him. "I could tell you that, Archon."

The truth came to Seth like a blow. "He means it's made of diamond, Oblek. A great solid diamond."

In the utter silence a faint wind flapped the Fox's striped robe.

There was nothing any of them could say.

If There Was No Oracle . . .

The Island was unrecognizable. A barricade had been
dragged to block the bridge, and the road had guards on it.
Every building in the precinct was barred, with soldiers at the
entrances; even the vast doors of the Temple had been forced
shut, something no one had seen within living memory.

No one walked or laughed in the gardens. The pool was
empty, its salt water unchanged for days so that a scum of oil
and petals lay on it. The servants seemed to have been moved
out; the terraces were deserted and in the hot air scarlet flowers hung thirsty and unwatered. Insects buzzed around her;
she brushed them off, glad of the welcome heat of the sunlight on her arms and face after days in the shuttered room.

The phalanx closed around her; they walked up the steps
to the highest terrace below the Temple, overlooking the Port.
It seemed as though Argelin had set up some sort of headquarters here; she saw him sitting under an awning in a
bronze chair belonging to Hermia, a desk in front of him

littered with plans. Men came and went, messengers racing, officers with reports.

While she waited, she glanced down at the Port.

Jamil's ships hung over their still reflections, waiting, out of range. He wouldn't wait much longer. They would be short of water and food, despite the raid. Soon there would be an all-out attack, and the Port would fall.

"Lady." The optio waved her forward.

Mirany straightened. She felt grubby, wished she'd put the white dress on, looked a bit more dignified. Her hair needed arranging, too. Nervous, she pushed it out of her eyes.

Argelin rose, looked at her, then waved the guards away. They withdrew to a discreet distance; he turned on the optio. "No one else. Until I say."

"General—"

"Whatever it is, deal with it yourself!"

He turned her roughly, and she pulled herself free. Then he walked to the balcony and stood looking down over the sea. Not knowing what else to do, she followed him.

"I should burn this place," he muttered.

Appalled, she stared at his back. He swung around. "If there was no Oracle and no Nine, *I* would be the one to be listened to."

"You can't burn the god."

"What use is a god if no one can hear him? I think I might do it, Lady Mirany."

"Even you . . . the people would rise up—"

"Oh, I'd blame it on Prince Jamil, of course. It might even help me. The people would tear his soldiers to pieces with their bare hands. Then, after the invasion is repulsed, a new Nine." He licked his lips. A fine sweat glistened on his forehead and beard.

"What's to stop me, Mirany?"

"The Archon—"

He laughed then, a harsh laugh. "The Archon is almost certainly dead by now and there will be no search for another. I will be Archon and general all in one, and yes, king."

"And Hermia?"

His face darkened. "She has condemned herself. I always thought she was strong; I knew there was something in her I could never reach, but this obstinacy, this sudden treachery surprises me. We worked so well together."

Mirany's arms were burning in the sun. She drew her mantle up, rigid with fear. He looked at her. "As for you and me, no love has been lost between us, has it, lady? At every turn you've been the one who hindered me. Now things have come to this. I need a Speaker I can trust."

"Do you?" she breathed.

He smiled smoothly. "You know I do. And I've chosen one."

She swallowed. Bewildered, she said, "You can't—" But he stopped her with a gesture. Then he pointed behind her. She turned.

Down the terrace a girl was sitting on the balustrade, a blond girl in a new pink dress, feeding the tame doves. She looked up and waved happily. "Oh Mirany! I knew you'd see sense!"

Mirany felt sick.

"Do you see?" Argelin said calmly, pouring wine from a gilt jug and adding a splash of water.

Numb, she nodded. He held out the cup, and she took it and drank thirstily, not even noticing.

"I need someone who will do exactly what I tell her, when I tell her, and maybe there she is. Pretty little Chryse. She didn't take much convincing, I have to say. Not the cleverest of girls, not like you, or the acid Lady Rhetia, but with a certain sly intelligence. She knows what is best for her. I'll have no trouble with her as Speaker."

Mirany put the cup down. "You think not?" she said quietly.

Argelin glanced over. "No."

"Then you'd be wrong." She smiled at him coldly. "I know Chryse better. She serves the winning side, whoever they are. If you lost the war, she'd betray you to Jamil without blinking. She'd tell him the Oracle demanded your death. Believe me."

The general drank. "He won't win."

"He has the Empire behind him. Defeat these ships and more will come. You can't keep them out. Only the god can end this, and Chryse doesn't hear the god."

"I don't want her to."

She nodded and took a big chance. "And you don't really want her as Speaker, either, do you? Even you don't trust her."

Annoyed, he clanged the goblet down onto the tray. A soldier glanced across, nervous. Argelin glared at her. "No. I don't. She's a self-serving little bitch. But you see, there is no one else. Unless, as I say, all the Nine perish in some unfortunate fire."

He wants it to be you, Mirany. He's trying to threaten you.

The voice was so unexpected she almost gasped with shock; and then relief flooded her.

Where have you been?

Busy. With eggs and diamonds and stars.

She turned, looking down over the blue sea. *What do I do? I can't let it be Chryse!*

Do you trust me, Mirany?

She nodded briefly.

Then do exactly what I say. Tell him you will be the new Speaker.

Her hands gripped the white marble of the balustrade. It was smooth and cool. The god's words felt like a great pain inside her; she thought of the oath they had all sworn on the bronze bowl, of Rhetia's scribbled letter. Be strong. Keep the Silence. They would think she had betrayed them.

I can't! I can't!

I can't force you, Mirany. I just want to see if you trust me.

"Well?" Argelin was watching her curiously. "You must know what I'm offering you."

"Why me? You said yourself—"

"Because I trust you not to order my death if it comes to that. Any of the others would. And because the others believe what you say, that you hear the god. That may or may not be true, but your pronouncements will have a certain . . . integrity."

He came and stood over her, tall. "You will be Speaker

and you will announce that the Archon is lost, that I am now king. The rest of the Nine will be unharmed, if you agree, though a new girl will be needed and I will select her. The Temple and the Island will not be burned, and the Oracle will remain pure. Hermia will be kept in safety. Should you make any proclamation that we have not agreed on beforehand, she will be killed and the Oracle will be destroyed. You understand?"

"She'd be a hostage? You'd do that, to her?"

Argelin's voice was harsh. "She would have done it to me."

"But you loved her."

His dark eyes glanced at her. "Perhaps I still do. Love is not easy to understand."

She certainly didn't understand it.

Was she betraying them? Was she saving them? She had no idea anymore. But there was only one voice that had ever mattered and that was the voice of the god, wherever it led.

She looked up, past Argelin, at Chryse.

"Send her back inside." Lifting her chin, she faced him. "From now on, I will be the Speaker."

Seth hung on the rope. His feet slipped and slithered on the glassy slope, though he'd taken his boots off to get a better grip. Above, the Jackal leaned back, amused. "Come on! I would have thought clawing your way up was what you did best!" Somewhere beyond, the Fox hauled and grunted a laugh, the rope taut around the pinnacle.

Seth swore. His hands were raw. He'd never be able to use a stylus again. Below, horribly far, Oblek was shouting encouragement at him, and inches from his face the sun glinted in beautiful, brilliant rainbows in the powdery heart of the diamond rock. He was climbing all he had ever desired in the world.

He made a last great effort, pushed off, hauled arm over arm. His muscles throbbed; his arms were jelly. Scrambling up the sheer cliff made his knees ache; he knew he could never take another step, and yet each one came, and finally the Jackal's long arm leaned over and grabbed him by the tunic, hauling him up in an ungainly sprawling heap.

"Good. Get the rope off," the thief said briskly. He looked over the edge. "You next, boy!"

Disbelieving, Seth shrugged out of the noose. "I nearly fell down there."

"Rubbish." Fox checked the knots, flung it over. "You did fairly well for a scribbler of tax bills."

Seth nursed his sore hands. For a moment he almost felt pleased at the praise; then a sudden fury came over him. *Tax bills*. When he was a quaestor he'd have such respect. . . . But he would never be a quaestor if Alexos went home.

The boy was climbing now. Easily and lightly he clambered up the diamond mountain, as Fox had done. None of them could climb like the Jackal, though; his meticulous ascent with the rope over his shoulder had been unbelievable, a finding of cracks and crannies that were barely visible, a reckless sprawling and dragging of his body up the overhangs and fissures of the vast cliff.

"Take your time." The Jackal leaned over. "Fox, get the

spare. This may not hold the big man." Fox rummaged in the sacks. He tossed out a knife, an empty flask.

For a second Seth was alone by the tethered rope. It jerked slightly as the boy climbed, a small, impatient juddering around the diamond spike that held it.

"Nearly there." The Jackal leaned over. "I've nearly got you."

Seth stooped. The knife lay at his feet; he scooped it up. Its blade gleamed; it was sharp. Fascinated, he brought it close to the rope.

Now.

He'd never get another chance like this. The handle was warm; it felt rough in his sore palms. Fox had his back to him; he gripped the weapon tight, thinking of Pa, of Telia. Where were they? If he could know they were safe, just know that!

Tell me that, he thought. *Tell me! Or I'll kill you.*

The only answer was silence.

Save yourself! Just tell me!

Nothing.

Slowly, his hand shaking with reluctance, praying for someone to see, yell at him, he brought the blade to the rope. It was worn, fraying. It would take so little.

"Seth!" The Jackal's quiet voice made him jump in terror. "*What are you doing?*"

The rope snapped with a whiplash that slapped him right across the chest; he was flung hard against the Jackal. The thief slithered; gasped, "Fox!" Then he went over the edge.

*　　*　　*

Chryse stared openmouthed. "It's not fair! It was going to be me."

Mirany wanted to slap her. "I can't believe you! To side with him!"

"Oh Mirany!" The blond girl stepped back. "Isn't that just what you're doing? Of course, I'd just have pretended to side with him, but I wouldn't have really meant it. I just wanted to get out of that wretched room. As soon as I was Speaker, I'd have made a big silence, just like Hermia. And I'd have tried on all her robes."

Suddenly Mirany felt giddy. It was as if she was staring down some vast precipice; she sank onto the stone bench. "Get me some water, Chryse."

Chryse pulled a face. "I suppose you think you can give me orders now—"

"Just get it!"

Wide-eyed, Chryse stared. Then she went.

Mirany looked down at the sea. *What's happening?*

I'm falling.

She could feel that. Emptiness below and above. One hand, gripping tight.

Hold me, Mirany! Gods can't fall, can they?

He sounded lost, terrified. His voice was so faint she barely heard it. She stretched her hand out quickly, over the marble balustrade. Gulls whirled about her. She held his hand; it was small, and gripped her tight. There was no weight but there was his fear, and she held on to it in the sudden storm of white birds that screamed and flew around her, of the papers whirling from Argelin's desk, the shouts, the flapping awning, Chryse's screech as she grabbed her windswept dress.

And out in the bay the ships rocked and tugged at their anchors, the elephants in their makeshift corrals on the beach trumpeting in terror.

"Don't fall!" she whispered. "If you fall, where will we all be?"

Seth dropped the knife and dived; as the Jackal clawed at rock he grabbed his arm, was almost pulled over the edge himself by the weight. Then the Fox had him around the waist, screaming curses in his ear.

Half over the cliff, Seth hung on. Below, the Jackal turned in space, with his other hand clinging on to Alexos. Far below, Oblek's terrified face was a blur of agony.

"Pull!" The Fox heaved back. Seth scrabbled, but the weight of the boy and the man seemed immense, as if the earth wanted them, as if it exerted a terrible power to drag them down.

"Help me!" Seth gasped.

Shouldn't a god be able to save himself?

And then something happened. Someone was there. A grip. It was light and strong and far away, but it took some of the pain out of his shoulders, and he dragged, and the Jackal's hand jerked, grabbed, had the rope. Slowly, as if out of some great abyss, they heaved the tomb thief up, and Seth leaned down his agonizingly stretched arm and grabbed Alexos, too, and in seconds the whole tangled mass of them were somehow over the rim and breathless, Alexos curled in a shuddering heap, the Jackal's hand bleeding, Seth trembling in every limb, icy with sweat.

The knife was lying by the edge. He stared at it.

Then he pushed his hair back with both hands, got up, and walked away. He felt sick and weak and yet there was something that he knew now, knew for certain.

There would be no quaestorship.

"It's not over, scribe." The Fox sounded dry. "We've got to get the big fellow up next."

Seth didn't answer. He raised his eyes and looked up at the mountain rising above him, its pulverized, scorched slopes, the great cleft at its peak, where high winds drifted a faint plume of snow crystals.

Close behind, the Jackal's voice said, "It seems I have to thank you again."

"You held on to the boy."

"Instinct. One can hardly let a god fall." After a second he said, "What happened?"

"Nothing. It snapped." Then, "Will you tell Oblek?"

"You must tell him."

Seth didn't answer. His gaze was intent, focused. "I see that now."

The Jackal sounded curious. "Up there? What can you see?"

Seth was hoarse with weariness, shuddering with cold and relief. He wrapped his arms around himself and turned. "I can see the star. The third star."

How Can You Say No to a God?

It was deep inside.

The star had smashed into the mountain and carved a great swathe through it, a collision that must have instantly vaporized rock, scorched a great wound that opened before them like a road, wide and smooth, still smoking.

It led them in. Wary, the Jackal stalked ahead, a tall shape in the bewilderment of half-seen images, of reflections, the smooth walls of the tunnel transparent, so that they could see ghosts of themselves, and boulders embedded in the crystal. Tiny insects were held in there, and seams of minerals, maybe even gold, because the Jackal stopped a long time at one, his hands flat against the sides, long eyes intent. Then he'd shrugged and walked on. "Too far in," he'd muttered, almost to himself.

Seth said, "You'll never get it out."

The tomb thief glanced at him thoughtfully. "Perhaps the Lady Mirany was right. Perhaps the gold was only ever an excuse. Fox has a pocketful of diamond chips instead."

Oblek carried Alexos. Since the fall the boy had seemed worn out and listless; now he clung contentedly on to the big man's back, one cheek against his bald head, hugging him around the neck. As they walked Oblek hummed, a small sound that murmured and reverberated.

The tunnel through the diamond world was silent. The walls were a million shades of blue, the blues of the sea and the sky, of eggshell and distant cloud, of lapis lazuli and sapphire, of the watery robe of the Rain Queen, its waves and monsoon and storms. The blue of a small toy cart Seth had made once for Telia. Of the robe Mirany had worn when she came out of the tomb.

It sloped upward, steeper, so that the Jackal had to lean back and give Oblek his hand, and the musician leered a grin, breathless with the weight of the boy. Holes swelled and grew, interconnected; they walked in a honeycomb of exploded hillside, a great rock sponge.

But the star was so small to have done all this, Seth thought.

It burned, inside the mountain. For hours now they had inched and scrambled toward it, and its color was red, a coppery hot molten heat. As they approached, the porous rock became purple, shades of violet, scarlet. He could feel heat on his face and hands, a fierce blaze holding him back. Now they'd come this close to it, how could they touch it? How could they bear that pain?

At the end of the tunnel the Jackal paused. A thousand glittering movements paused with him; they saw a small chamber, the size of a room, faceted, polished to a gem by the terrible forces of the star crash. And on the floor, glowing red as a cinder, the third star waited for them.

They had arranged her hair and now they brought her the robe. She had seen Hermia wear it many times. Now she would wear it.

She stood up, the dress of finest white pleated linen falling smooth. Numb, without emotion, she held out her arms.

The Rain Queen's robe was so heavy. It was blue and it swished like the sea, and the million crystal raindrops sewn on to its surface swung in unison, each with a rainbow in its heart.

She turned. The slave fastened it, not looking at her.

None of the slaves looked at her, or spoke.

That was part of the ritual, Koret had said. Full moon, high tide, and silence. Not to be looked at, not to eat, not to be spoken with. Twelve hours sleeping alone in the Temple. Bathed from head to foot in the three lustral enclosures, of sea water in the black basalt, fresh water in the rose-colored marble, distilled precious rainwater in the last, the gold bath, so small the water had barely reached to her chin.

Once Hermia had done all this. Where was she? What was she thinking now? Mirany shivered. The wrath of the Nine would be unbearable.

The anointing with nine oils, the nine rings, the nine frail collars of silver, she let them all happen to her. She smelled differently, her skin felt strange. "It's still me," she said desperately, a blurted thought, but there was no answer. There had been no answer since the small hand had slid out of hers. **Trust me,** he had said, but she was terrified now; she wanted to call out, "Stop! I've changed my mind!" If he didn't speak to her again, would she have to pretend all her life? Would she become just another Hermia?

She turned.

The dark eyes of the Speaker's mask looked across at her from its stand, the looped crystals, the feathers and lapis, the beautiful calm face, coiled serpents carved on its cheekbones. Small breezes stirred in its open mouth.

"I never thought it would be you who'd be the traitor, Mirany."

For a startled moment she thought the venomous whisper was the god's.

Until she turned to face Rhetia.

Mirany!

Seth turned.

Alexos had mumbled the word; now the boy opened his eyes, slid down unsteadily. Seeing them stare, he wiped his face sleepily with his hand. "We've got to hurry."

"Is she in trouble?"

As if he didn't hear, Alexos pointed to the star. "There it is, Lord Jackal. If you want it, pick it up."

The tomb thief said, "It's red hot, Archon. Even you can feel that."

"It won't hurt you. I promise."

The Jackal took a step up close. The fiery glow lit his

face as he bent down; they could see the heat in the air shimmer. The star was a coal, burning. He reached out, then drew back. "I'd rather keep my fingers," he said dryly. "I tend to find them useful."

Alexos turned. "You have to get it then, Seth."

Seth came up to the boy. But all he said was, "First, will you tell them, or will I?"

"No one need tell them." Alexos looked unhappy.

"Tell us what?" Oblek growled.

Seth scowled. But he clenched his hands and said, "Argelin made me an offer before we left. Of a quaestorship."

The Jackal didn't move, but an instant wariness slid into his eyes. "In return for what?"

"The way here. And for the Archon never to return."

For a second no one moved. Then Oblek drew the boy to him. "You treacherous scum. You accepted?"

Seth shrugged, weary. "You can't refuse the general."

The Jackal was watching him carefully. "We knew you'd been picked up. No other inducements? No threats?"

He licked dry lips. "My father. My sister."

They were silent. Then Oblek growled, "You should have let me kill Argelin, Archon."

Seth looked up, all the fear of weeks flooding him in an instant of agony. "Are they safe? Can you tell me if they're safe?"

Alexos looked at the floor. "If people knew everything, Seth, they'd have no use for gods. Besides, the Oracle is silent." He sounded sad.

"You knew, old friend?"

The boy looked up. "Mirany warned me."

That devastated Seth. He avoided Oblek's eyes, but the big man said, "Did you think about it?"

Seth looked at the Jackal. The thief's animal eyes watched him, but he said nothing.

"Yes. I thought. I held the knife over the rope. For a minute, I would have cut it. Then it snapped, and everything else snapped with it." He looked up, hot with shame and despair. "If you want to punish me, do it! If you want me to leave, I'll leave."

No one spoke. Till Alexos said patiently, "Oh Seth! They don't want that and neither do I. You know what to do. The Rain Queen explained."

Seth swallowed. Then he nodded, turned, and walked up to the star. The heat from it was appalling, the rock around it still sizzling. He bent and forced his fingers to close over it; he picked it up, and it was cold and pure in his hands. They all looked at its red fire.

"I will pay Argelin back," he whispered fiercely, "if he touches Telia."

"Would you prefer it was Chryse?" Mirany's brazen defiance surprised herself. She marched up to the tall girl. "Because that was the only choice. Chryse, who'd do everything he told her, who'd sell us all for a new bracelet or the latest shawl. Would you really prefer her?"

"Don't be ridiculous. You swore!"

"I swore to keep Silence. I'll keep that oath."

"How can you? He's got Hermia as a hostage. The Island

is heaped with dry tinder. If the ceremony doesn't go well, if the Oracle doesn't say he's to be king, I don't know what he'll do. I really think he'd destroy the precinct, Mirany! He doesn't care about the god's anger. The only person he ever cared about was Hermia."

She nodded, trying to think. "I know. I know!" She looked up. "What about Jamil? Can you still contact him, tell him what's happening?"

Rhetia scowled. "One of his conditions was that the Speaker should change. You've done that." She sounded disgusted.

Mirany was silent. Then she turned away and folded her arms, looking at herself in the long bronze mirror. Suddenly all she felt was astonishment. "Look at me. Mousy Mirany from Mylos. I can't recognize myself. I think if my father was here he wouldn't know me." She turned. "I don't want this, Rhetia, but the god told me to do it. *He told me*. How can you say no to the god?"

Her voice was choked; she didn't want to cry so she stopped abruptly.

Rhetia frowned. "You can't," she said harshly. "I suppose."

On the other side of the chamber the mountain was seamed with cracks; they climbed through one out into the night air. Seth looked upward. About a hundred feet above them the cleft pinnacle was white with frost; before it, was a steep slope of scree, dusted with snow. His breath made clouds in the air. He had never been so high, so bitterly cold.

"I know where we are!" Alexos' cry was a murmur of joy. "I've been here before!" He caught the big man's hand and dragged him up the unstable rocks. "This is it, Oblek! We're nearly there! I can hear the Well of Songs!"

"In that case, old friend, take care!" Oblek held the boy still. "Let me go first."

"I want you to, Oblek." Proudly, Alexos pushed the musician forward. "After all, I've brought you all this way."

"You've brought *me*!" Oblek began to climb, his ugly face wry. "I admit at some points I was a liability, but I've done some carrying myself, Archon."

"Of course you have. I couldn't have done it without you. All of you." And then Alexos stopped, his face in an instant a picture of bewilderment and dismay. "Oh! Wait! *Wait*."

They looked at him. "What?" the Jackal snapped.

"I've just realized . . . there are only three stars." He held out his hands and then crumpled onto the rocks, knees up. He looked as if he was going to cry. After a moment Oblek came back and put an arm around him. "Explain, little god."

Eyes dark with tears, Alexos sobbed. Then he gasped out hopeless words. "There are four of you, aren't there, so there'll be four guardians. And we've only got three stars!"

Oblek looked at the Jackal. The tall man crouched. His fingers drew the boy's hands down from his face.

"The stars are weapons?"

"Sort of." Alexos sniffed, tears running down his face. "But don't you see, one of you won't have one! One of you won't have anything at all!"

The Ninth Offering

OF A LIFE

A god is born, but doesn't die.

He changes shapes and bodies, moves from one mask to another.

Sometimes I am so quiet you would not know I was here; at other times I rage and thunder.

Gods are rivers, that flow into the sea and never end.

Stories, that begin and tangle and interweave and are all one.

The sun, that rises and sets and rises.

Which is why we come among you. To know what grief is. What love is.

He Leaves Himself Unarmed

The Speaker was always anointed and masked at the Caves of the Python.

Huge and dark, they pierced the low cliffs that had once been the banks of the river Draxis before it had dried. They were sacred places, never entered except at the time of a new Speaker or at the Speaker's death, and they led far back into darkness. In the entrance cavern, the largest of them, the god had been born, so the story went, millennia ago, the god of light and darkness, sun and shadow. For a thousand years the Rain Queen had worked on the living rock, water dripping and eroding it, wearing it away, until in the morning of the world it had cracked with a great crack, and the god had emerged in three forms, first as a scorpion, small and red, then as a snake, sinuous, a ripple of scales, and finally as a boy, beautiful, naked, wriggling his head and shoulders out, then heaving himself up and standing at the cave mouth. He called, and the sun rose, far over the sea, and he held out his arms to its heat and smiled. And behind him out of the crack climbed his shadow, tall and thin and without color, and it stood at his shoulder, silent.

The crack was still there. Small candles always burned around it; withered flowers were placed on it, brought by expectant mothers and given to the custodian of the shrine.

Now the Nine—or Eight of them—stood waiting in a circle around it, silent, masked, their calm metal faces smiling at each other, and behind each mask all their anger and bewilderment and disbelief. Chryse had her arms folded, and Rhetia stood behind her. One of the girls was new, but from out here Mirany hardly knew which one.

She walked slowly, because the robe was heavy.

It was night, and the moon was full. Its early splendor glinted in the crystal drops; they clicked and slid and clattered. The path up to the cave was lined with soldiers, all silent. Above, along the tops of the cliffs, watch fires burned, and the people waited. She had thought they would be fewer, that they wouldn't dare to come out from the relative safety of the Port walls, but there they were, quiet crowds of women, sailors, beggars, merchants, looking down as she walked. She could smell the rank stink of the elephants, sense their restlessness in the corrals close by on the beach, and beyond the reach of artillery, far out at sea, the lights of Jamil's ships besieged the world with a ring of glimmers.

Mirany pushed hair out of her eyes. Even curled and brushed into elaborate coils it was stubbornly coming loose. Her new sandals were stiff and the path was rough, slippery like scree. It twisted among stunted bushes of artemisia and gorse; a lizard slipped sinuously away, and beyond the crackle of the fires and the soft slap of waves, the night rasped with the song of cicadas. She thought of her first time as Bearer. It seemed so much longer than a few months ago.

"I've told you what I'll do," she whispered urgently. "Is that right? Is that what you want?"

He wasn't here.

He was far away, and not listening to her.

"You should be here. You should be everywhere!" She felt light-headed with hunger, worn with the weight of the robe. She slipped, and caught at a bush to steady herself; clouds of moths rose around her.

Argelin loomed out of the dark. He held out his hand.

She ignored it, straightened, and walked up into the cave.

A small fire burned in a brazier, but apart from that, the great cavern was dark. Breathless, she paused in the entrance, and looked back. Below lay the dry watercourse, cracked in the heat. Behind her Argelin whispered, his lips close to her ear, "Go in. Stand by the god's birthplace. And remember what I want. The fate of the Oracle lies with you."

It was so cold. He had never thought there could be so much cold. The very rock was frozen; as he scrambled up, his hands stuck to it, his knees were bruised by it. Above them the cave opened, a darkness at the top of the world, and he took a breath and looked around, at the Fox toiling at his left, at all the other peaks, white and unknown, stretching into the distance on each side. Far away, like a stater in the sky, the moon hung, perfectly round. It would be hanging like that over the Island, and the Port and the City. He wondered if Mirany was watching it now.

Ahead, like a black spider, the Jackal climbed easily. He wore no pack; all the gear had been left at the foot of the slope, because Alexos had said they should take nothing but themselves to the Well. No weapons. Only the stars.

As he climbed the last part of the slope he thought of what the Jackal had done. The thief had stood and looked at Seth. "Keep the red star. You need it."

"Two of them are mine," Seth had muttered sourly. "I paid two hundred and fifty staters for the first one."

"A good bargain." The tall man had nodded. "Now I have them. However, I think I feel generous. Fox!"

The Fox had thrown him the pack; out of it he took the first star and unwrapped it. Its white fire had dazzled them as he held it up. Then, lightly, he had thrown it to Oblek.

Caught off guard, the musician's nimble hands barely caught it. Then he said, "Why me?"

"You also need all the help you can get."

Oblek sneered. "And you don't?"

The tomb thief smiled, his animal eyes bright. Then he had taken out the second star, the blue one. He had looked over at the Fox.

"Don't fear for me, chief." The one-eyed man tapped the row of weapons thrust into his belt. "No beast or stinking demon gets the better of me."

"I fear, Fox, that even your knives won't cut what we have to face here. Besides, the boy says to leave them behind."

"That's right," Alexos said gravely. "You must, Fox."

"Do we listen to boys now?" the small man growled.

The Jackal shrugged. "We listen to the god."

The Fox had thrown all the knives down in disgust. Then the Jackal had held out the blue star.

"I can't take that! You're the boss."

"Then I give the orders. And I don't lead my men into anything I can't handle myself. Take it."

"Chief—"

"Take it. You can watch my back."

"That leaves you unarmed."

The Jackal folded his arms. "Of all of you," he said evenly, "I am the fittest, lithest, most intelligent, and most well bred. It's a logical choice."

"And the most pigheaded," Oblek had muttered.

But the Fox had taken the blue star.

And now Seth clambered upright, breathless, at the threshold of the cave. The four of them stood there, shoulder to shoulder, and Alexos pushed between and went a little ahead, two steps into the darkness.

Before them they saw the Well of Songs.

She looked down at the birthplace of the god.

There have always been cracks and passages in the earth, he had said to her once. **Gods move along them, up from the Underworld, from the streams and the darkness.**

Like the Oracle. Like the Well the Archon had set out to find.

This one was wide and jagged. She looked down at it and knelt, and bowed her forehead to the ground, the stiff robe rustling. "We will begin," she whispered.

Then she lifted her head and turned quickly. "But first, remove the weapons."

Uneasy, the soldiers glanced at Argelin.

Mirany kept her face calm. "This is a sacred place and a sacred time. It will not be polluted by instruments of death; it is a place of birth. Get them out of here."

Argelin gave a brusque jerk of his head. The soldiers dumped their spears hastily in a heap; the optio snatched them up and removed them. She turned, meeting his eyes. "And you, my Lord General."

He looked at her with rigid control; then he took the sword from his belt and threw it out of the cave. Behind him, like a small ripple, others did the same; she saw in the shadows the dignitaries from the City of the Dead, a few merchants, the most important moneylenders, his officers.

Witnesses, no doubt. Carefully chosen.

And Hermia was with them.

Mirany took a sudden startled breath.

Hermia wore black, a long robe of it. She had removed all her jewelry and undone her hair; she wore no kohl on her eyes and her lips were pale. But her eyes were alive with anger, and she stood tall, her intelligent face tightly controlled. Mirany felt a thrill of fear; sweat broke out on her back. The new Speaker was always masked by her predecessor; she had forgotten that.

And Hermia would kill her rather than do it.

She stood slowly.

This was it. The time had come and nothing had happened to save her. Was the god waiting to see if she trusted him? She turned and opened her arms, the droplets clattering. Drums and rattles began to beat softly, in some corner. She took a breath to speak the words of the Opening.

Instead, someone shouted.

Argelin turned, instantly alert. His guards closed around him.

One man appeared on the path to the cave. He was bearded and dressed in a red robe; he carried a heavy box, and before the men could grab him, he laid it down cautiously and scrambled up.

"A gift of truce."

"Truce?" Argelin stared. "From Jamil?"

"From my lord the Prince."

"How? There's no truce."

Mirany turned. "Yes there is, Lord General. As from now. During the Making of the Speaker, violence is forbidden." Before he could answer, she turned back. "Has your prince come? Is he here?"

"He waits below, lady."

"Then let him come up."

Ignoring Argelin's gasp of fury, she watched the Pearl Prince darken the entrance to the cave. His retinue followed, men clothed in cloth-of-gold and silks, and everywhere the gleam of pearls.

He bowed to her, and to the Nine. "I had your message. That the first of our Emperor's conditions was fulfilled. That the Speaker was renewed." His dark eyes watched her gravely. "This is so?"

"If the god wants it," she said quietly.

"Then if I witness this, there will be peace. Because the cause of the dispute was not trade, or my Lord Argelin's rule, but the pollution of the Oracle. The Oracle is for everyone. That is what we believe."

Mirany nodded. Without another word she began the prayer of Opening, and the voices of the Nine joined hesitantly with her. The moon was high now, its light filling the cave with a frosty luminescence, glinting on embedded crystals high in the walls, causing a faint mistiness to seem to rise from the great crack in the floor.

When the prayer was over, she stepped close to the brink of it and looked down.

Water.

Was that what she saw down there?

Was it water?

Steam rose from the Well, steps led down to it. It was huge, a sacred pool of hot, shimmering water, and statues stood waist high in it, and it was green and unknowably deep. In the cave walls around it, ferns grew, their fronds uncurling, and yellow-green algae powdered the glistening rock walls. Water steamed and condensed and dripped. Ancient wooden shapes, once carved, leaned from cracks; withered remnants of dessicated wreaths were on the side of the pool. And there were masks.

They hung on poles in the water, rotting faces that

watched the strangers. As the steam drifted, Seth saw their eyeholes and cheekbones were bark and wood, paper and silver, corroded copper, tainted bronze. The masks of all the Archons until Rasselon, until the Well had been lost.

It was a quiet place. Only irregular drips into the pool broke its silence.

They came farther in, warily. The warmth was wonderful; he unwound the rags from his face and breathed it in, felt it thaw his numbed limbs.

"What now?" he whispered.

The cave took his words; it rolled them and muttered them, made them come back at him from behind, a low sonorous rumble that caused a row of drops to vibrate and spatter. The Fox eyed the entrance nervously.

Alexos went forward. He put both hands on the lip of the great pool and leaned over, into its steams and heat. "It's been so long since I was here!" he whispered.

The Jackal came beside him. "Where are these fearsome guardians, Archon?"

The boy's face turned to them. To their surprise they saw tears in his eyes; as he turned back one rolled down his cheek and fell into the water. "Come and see, Seth, all of you."

Seth glanced at Oblek. He put his hands on the crumbling rock; it was worn smooth, oiled with iron red sediments. Then he looked down.

The water steamed. He saw its greenness open, as if the Archon's tear had opened a hole, a darkness swelling before the four of them, clearing the Well.

A face looked up at Seth. It was handsome and burned

by the sun, its eyes alert and amused, but it was a mask, and behind it darkness lurked, a terror, an emptiness. He jerked back instantly. The face was his own.

Oblek, rigid, was staring into the pool.

"What are these, Archon?" he breathed, his voice raw with horror.

"The guardians, Oblek."

"They've always been here?"

"Oh no. We brought them with us." The boy looked at the Fox's disgusted stare, at the Jackal, who was looking into the pool without a flicker.

The water heaved. It bubbled and surged. Seth jumped back, dragged Oblek away; Alexos leaped hastily up onto a rock ledge. Out of the green depths came a pair of hands, agile, ink stained, Seth's own hands. They grasped the brim and hauled, and out of the water came a creature that wore his own face like a mask, dripping with steaming water, plastered with weed.

Beside it rose a thing like Oblek, vast and bloated and murderous, and a Fox-masked creature, cruel and shifty. And last of all crawled a slender, tall shape, its long animal eyes cunning and cold, totally without mercy.

The Jackal stepped back.

Without a word, the four of them faced themselves.

Speaker to Speaker

They faced each other, Speaker and Speaker. Hermia carried the mask, its gold discs and ibis feathers draped over her arms, its perfect face with the incised cheekbones gazing fixedly at the shadows in the depths of the cave.

Mirany was very still. She knew suddenly that if Hermia put the mask on her, they would have changed places. She would have become false to the Oracle, a speaker of lies. *Help me*, she breathed. *Without you I'm just as bad as she is.*

But her words only returned to her, fractured and echoing, from ancient depths.

Hermia should have raised the mask. Instead she raised her voice.

"Before the new Speaker is masked, I have something to say."

The Nine tensed; Argelin looked furious. She raised a manicured finger and pointed it straight at him. "I denounce this man. This man has plotted to have the Archon murdered."

She turned, shouting it out, so that it rang in the caves, and the people heard it clearly out on the cliffs. "He bribed one of the Archon's companions to murder him. I saw and heard. I give witness before the god."

People were murmuring; outside, someone shouted. Here in the cave everyone stared at Argelin. The bodyguards glanced at one another, tense.

The general stood very still. Faint beads of sweat broke out on his face, but he stayed calm.

"The *ex*-Speaker is obviously overwrought," he murmured.

"This is a terrible accusation." Jamil came forward, and from the shadows behind him, Rhetia's voice. "If it's true, the god will take his revenge."

"Revenge?" Argelin smiled coldly. "For what? He can always find himself another body. Isn't that what gods do?" He eyed them all. "But the Speaker doesn't speak the truth. She only has her own voice. Isn't that the reason we're all here?"

He walked up to her, his voice low and mocking. "Even if it could be true, Hermia, what will any of you do about it? I rule. The army follows me. Every weapon is under my control. Look out there. Even now, my enemies are burning."

Jamil tensed. Then he turned, shoving men aside, and swore.

In the darkness of the harbor, bright flames flickered. Smoke rose against the moon. On the beach the elephants trumpeted wildly in panic.

Mirany put her hand to her lips. Fire ships!

"You've sent fire ships into my fleet! Are you crazy?" Jamil whirled, but Argelin's men grabbed him and his retinue instantly. The general smiled coldly. "Yes, my lord. *From up here, you can watch it burn.*"

How can you fight against yourself? Every move was countered, every punch blocked. The creature that was himself had Seth by both wrists; it wrenched him to the ground, clamping both hands over his mouth, smothering him, laughing at him. It had no being, was air and water, felt no pain. But it could kill him, and he yelled and screamed at it, struggled, kicked, bit. Somewhere in the cavern Oblek was wrestling with a vast drunken shadow, and the Fox circled warily around his own slyness. Only the Jackal and his reflection stood calm, eyeing each other. They might even have been talking.

Alexos jumped down and crouched by the pool. His fingers trailed in the water. "I should be in here, too," he said.

Far below, as if it peeped through a tiny hole, one giant eye looked up at him.

Jamil was pale with fury. "When the Emperor hears—"

"Your fleet can flee. If they have sense they will."

"They'll never leave me behind."

"Those ships are packed with pitch. The wind is driving them out to sea. They'll leave you, Pearl Prince, and I'll keep you as my hostage." Argelin faced the bigger man. "And if the Emperor wants his precious nephew back, he can make terms. With me, and with the god." He whirled around on

Hermia. "Now mask the new Speaker and be silent! Nothing you can say interests me anymore. Nothing!"

Hermia looked at Mirany, and then at the Nine. For a second, Mirany felt sorry for her. Then Hermia lifted her head and the mask, but instead of fitting it onto Mirany's face she fitted it onto her own, and spoke through it, and the voice that came out was running and liquid and strange. It said, "Indeed, my lord. Then you will not mind me speaking about your dream."

Argelin stared. Then he hissed, "Get that off her."

No one moved. Hermia raised her hand and touched his face. "Last night," she whispered, "you dreamed of the Rain Queen. You dreamed she caught hold of your hands like this. She caught hold of you and drew you down, under the waters. Oh, you fought, and you struggled and tried to scream, but she stopped your mouth with water, she choked your lungs and dragged you into the depths. She drowned you, my lord. And you woke wet with sweat, gasping. Knowing you were dead."

She reached out and kissed him. But only the icy mask touched his face.

Argelin was white.

Mirany felt something finger her ankle, cold. She glanced down, then gasped.

Water was welling from the crack in the rock.

The star was useless. A lump of cold rock. He shoved his reflection away and dragged it out, but what did he do with it? "Archon!" he screamed. "Help me!"

From the corner of his eye he saw the boy gazing into the Well. He held the star up. "Do I throw it? Is that it?"

His reflection laughed. "Throw it? When did you throw anything away? It's ruby, worth a fortune, Seth. Buy yourself with it."

"No—"

"Buy Pa and Telia! Buy Mirany!"

"It's not . . . I'm not—"

"You are. You know you are." It had his hand, was prizing the star away. "You know all about yourself. You would have killed the boy, if you could have got away with it. That knife, over that rope? You wanted it to snap. You wanted it to fray—"

"*No!*"

He shoved it aside. "Give me the star," it whispered, head on one side, the cocky way everyone always hated, and he knew they did, that was why he did it. "Give it to me."

Seth licked his lips. Then he nodded.

And he hurled the star at his own face. Like a flash it went through himself, a searing pain that made him cry out, as if he truly was that other, and then with a hiss the star splashed into the pool, was gone.

No one stood opposite him. He felt empty.

He felt as if he had thrown himself away.

Argelin grabbed the mask and tore it from Hermia. He was shaking with wrath. Her face was flushed; a light shone in her eyes.

He thrust the mask at Mirany. "Put it on."

She didn't move.

"Put it on!"

But Mirany ignored him. Turning to Hermia she said quietly, *"It's been so long since we were here, together, you and I."*

The Well surged and boiled. "Throw the stars in! Oblek!" Seth roared.

The musician and his image staggered close to the brink. With a vast effort one gave the other a great backhanded blow; the water bubbled and instantly Oblek was alone. He crumpled, then leered up at Seth in triumph. "Nobody gets the better of me," he gasped. "Not even my stinking wastrel self."

The Fox was in trouble. As his shadow held him down he yelled and screamed, squirming desperately. The blue star rolled from his pocket and Seth darted in and snatched it up; then he hurled it into the Well.

There was nothing but the Fox, sprawled on the wet rock.

"Now nothing remains but the final offering," Alexos said. He stood, and then leaped up onto the brim of the Well. *"You must take whom you choose, Rain Queen. You always make the choice. And I will never steal it from you, as I did once."*

Argelin whipped around. "Get the weapons. I'll end this here."

A soldier ran out.

Instantly Mirany looked at Hermia; the tall woman snatched the mask, raised it, and put it firmly and carefully onto Mirany's face, so that darkness came over her eyes; the cold bronze was icy against her cheekbones. She could feel the god inside her; his scorn welled up and overflowed, and despite the vow of Silence he spoke through her impatiently.

"Did you think you could kill me, Argelin? Did you think you could kill a god? I am alive, and I say this. You will not be king. You will never be king. Destroy my sanctuary and defile the Oracle, and you'll still hear me. I will speak in your dreams. Beware the one who will stand face-to-face with you. Who can withstand the scorpion that crawls within, or the snake that coils at his own heart?"

The Jackal folded his arms.

"Do you really expect me to fight you? I have no weapons against you."

His masked image smiled a cold smile; he knew it well. "The others behave crudely. You react differently, I expected that. You know me better."

The Jackal nodded. He stepped forward. "And they're afraid. But I am not afraid of you."

"You hate me. You hate yourself."

"I hate what Argelin has made me."

"No one made you into a thief except yourself."

Their voices were so alike, Seth barely knew which one spoke.

"You're a desert, a wilderness. I've descended into the

depths of you. I've dug into you through sand and barren-ness. I've found a desiccated corpse wrapped in golden trappings, with a fine voice and fair hair, pampered, and painted. Around it I've seen treasures piled, all of them rotting and settling, falling to pieces, except the hard bright gems, the gold."

"And I've seen the dead following you like rats. Their hatred was never as fearsome as mine. As yours."

He had no idea which was which. Both were real, both the same man, standing in the waist-deep steams of the Well. And the water surged and boiled as the stars erupted in its heart, and Alexos jumped down and said, "Quickly, Oblek. Help him. He can't escape on his own."

"Help him? Why should I help him?" Oblek was still. "He left us to die in the desert, Archon. Have you forgotten that?"

"And you want revenge? Take it now. Save him, Oblek. He'll never forgive you."

Seth gasped. The Jackal's reflection had caught hold of the tomb thief, had dragged him struggling toward the Well. They stood at its edge; then the image leaped up onto the brim.

"End it here," it said. "For both of us."

It reached out; slowly, the Jackal took its hand and stepped up. Close, face-to-face, they stood on the very brink of the Well.

Seth moved. With a sudden decision he hauled himself up on the lip of the Well. He shoved the reflected creature aside, grabbing the man's arm. "Don't listen to it! Stand still!"

The water was a mirage. The Well was empty, a pit.

It descended endlessly into the earth, and—so far below they were only pinpoints of light—the three stars still plummeted, and for a second he was dizzy with that fall, as if down there was something that dragged at him, something huge and terrible, beyond the circles of the world. Then, he screamed. The creature had leaped at his back; its fine fingers clawed him. Something stabbed him, once, twice. He staggered, stunned with pain.

The Jackal grabbed him, flung him at Oblek; Seth fell with a shaft of agony that shot through him like fire; as Oblek caught him he saw the Jackal strike.

He struck with contempt, and fury, a blow at his own being, wresting the diamond sliver from the thing's hands, flinging it into the pit.

The creature screeched. It crumpled into nothing, into a withered mask and dessicated bones, a whisper of fair hair that dissolved into dust. Then it fell.

The Jackal staggered.

For a moment he was white with fatigue, as if he would crumple, too, as if some terrible duel had ended and drained him dry. Fox held him tight, on the edge of the abyss.

Behind them, with a great hiss and roar, the Well of Songs overflowed.

"Archon!"

Almost lost in the steam, Oblek's yell cut Seth to the quick. He tried to move. Pain jabbed through him. His own blood clouded the water. As the blackness closed, it had Oblek's voice.

"Seth's dying!" it whispered.

* * *

Argelin turned. The optio ran in with an armful of weapons; instantly the general grabbed a sword and whirled back. Water was surging out of the ground; the cave was awash.

Rhetia gasped. "The cave's flooding! Where's it coming from?"

Someone sobbed. People backed to the entrance. The circle of the Nine broke up.

Argelin leveled the sword at Mirany's throat. His face was pale and fevered, his eyes cold glints. "I should have done this long ago. There will be no Archon anymore, and no Speaker. I'll burn the Oracle and kill anyone who objects!" His voice was taut with rage. "If you want silence, then you can have silence. Forever, and ever!"

He drew his arm back. The sword whipped, through moonlight.

Whom Shall I Speak Through Now?

"Oblek!"

A scream, out of ancient nightmare. For an instant it rooted them all in terror; then Alexos was on his knees by Seth, rocking, gasping.

"Help him!" The big man grabbed him. "Archon!"

The boy looked up at him, his beautiful face distorted with anguish.

"Whom shall I speak through now?" he whispered.

Mirany had no time to scream. The sword slashed; she knew its buckling agony, the burst of blood, but at the same time Hermia was there; Hermia was in front of her, the shudder was Hermia's, the cry was hers, the blood was hers.

The sword cut deep into the Speaker's breast; she fell with a tiny gasp. Chryse was screaming hysterically. Mirany scrambled up, her dress spattered. She was numb, barely knew that Rhetia had hold of her, was yelling,

"Out! All of you get out! Now!"

The cave was a river. It was gushing from the rocks, lifting the edges of Hermia's dress, swirling around Argelin's knees as he knelt beside her.

Frozen, Mirany and Rhetia watched him crumple, as if some terrible invisible force crushed him, his hands reaching out hesitantly to Hermia's face, her hair. When he touched her a shock went through him; they felt it.

"Hermia!" His voice was blank, disbelieving. "*Hermia!*"

The Speaker's eyes opened; she tried to catch at him, and he snatched her up. Blood streaked the rising water.

"Don't leave me," he whispered.

She breathed sounds, barely heard. "The Oracle . . . spare the Oracle."

He shook his head, in anguish. "You always cared more for the Oracle than me! Always!"

Frantically he wiped the blood away, making it worse, spreading it everywhere. "Why did you interfere? Why did you move? God knows I would never have hurt you—"

She smiled weakly. "I was the Rain Queen. Just for a moment . . . I spoke . . . her words. You heard me."

"I heard you."

"We should not have become enemies."

"We never were." He gathered her up and her eyes closed, her head slipping to one side. "Stay with me, Hermia. I need you!"

She whispered, "I can see . . . the garden."

Mirany swallowed. Beside her, Rhetia took a step back.

For a long moment Argelin seemed not to realize she was

dead. He held her as the waters rose, lifting her out of the surging flood. When he finally raised his face, Mirany saw he was fighting for control, a terrible, rigid control.

Unsteady with Hermia's weight, he staggered up, her long skirts dripping.

He looked at them over her body.

His agony was worse than any threat.

The water was cold. It dripped between his lips and he drank it, and it was sweet.

It filled him.

It was light, a golden liquid. He felt it fill him like strength, like music.

It sang in his heart, a song that he knew, that he'd always known, and had forgotten. A song Telia hummed sometimes, playing with her doll, on hot afternoons.

A song his mother had sung.

He opened his eyes. He was propped up, surrounded by blurred faces. Somewhere, the Jackal's voice sounded incredulous. "The bleeding has stopped."

Seth pulled himself upright. He was aching and sore and the sound of the song was in his ears. He said, "Someone died. Was it me? Was it Mirany? *What's happened?*"

"She's dead," the boy whispered.

They stared, stricken. Seth took a shuddering breath, numb, not believing what he'd heard.

"She can't be! Why did you let her die!" he raged, grabbing Alexos and wrenching him around. "Don't you care! Don't you care about her at all!"

Oblek said, "Leave him! He's brought you back from the dead!" But Alexos reached out and touched Seth with his frail hand, and it was like the touch of a leaf, so light, and for one unaccountable minute it was his mother's touch, long lost.

"It's not Mirany, Seth. It's Hermia. Hermia is dead and Mirany is the Speaker now. Just as you wanted it to be."

Stunned, Seth stared at him. Then he whispered, "You make it sound as though I made it happen."

The Jackal said calmly, "Whatever it is, we can't do anything. If you want to drink of this magic Well, Oblek, drink, before we drown."

The Well surged.

Backing, they saw the water was black, as if nothing was there, as if a steaming nothingness was pouring out, a wide pool of darkness, and as Seth felt it surge around his feet, the Jackal yanked him up. "Can you walk?"

"I'm fine."

The tomb thief looked shaken. "You should be dead."

Alexos said, "Drink it, Oblek! All of you! Quickly!"

Part of the side wall collapsed; a great gush of darkness roared out. It was hot around their ankles; in seconds it had risen to a raging outpouring, sweeping stones aside, cascading out of the cave mouth. Hastily Oblek bent and scooped up some in his hands; nothing was there, but he drank and drank, and Alexos sniffed and watched him, and then with one of those sudden changes of mood that turned Seth to ice, the boy was laughing. "Does it taste nice?"

Oblek swallowed. "Foul as sulfur. Will it really give me songs?"

"As many as you can sing, Oblek." He smiled, proud. "Just like you used to."

To Seth's amazement the Fox was drinking, too, gulping handfuls as if he could never get enough of the black water; it ran from his fingers.

"You, too, Lord Jackal."

The thief eyed the cauldron of darkness warily. "I don't trust magic, Archon."

"It's not magic." Alexos caught his arm, pulled him to the brim. "Please. We've come all this way and you must be thirsty."

The tall man looked down at the boy. "I am thirsty," he said quietly.

"Then don't hesitate. Or it will be too late."

The Jackal turned. He dipped his fine hands in and drank delicately. But he had time for only one mouthful. Then the earth shuddered; the cave shook.

He jerked back. "Move!" he yelled. "Now!"

The earth shuddered. Everyone had fled; now Argelin waded to the cave mouth. He yelled, "Bring them!" The guards struggled back, water to their waists.

"Up here. Quickly." Mirany tugged the Speaker's mask off and pulled Rhetia after her up onto a higher ledge at the back of the cave. Already the water was too deep to get to the entrance. Across the torrent the soldiers looked at them hopelessly. "Jump in!" one yelled. "We'll get you out!"

"He's right. There's no choice." Rhetia moved; Mirany held her tight. "Look. Look outside."

The Draxis was rising. It was welling out of the earth, snapping brittle fences, ravaging waste fields of dried-up lemons and olives. A raging torrent, it foamed and bubbled, pouring from somewhere far upstream, and a thousand things were carried along in it, buildings and stones and birds and dead rats, and she saw it thicken and fill its ancient watercourse, foaming into the sea, a great dark wash of sediment clouding the pure blue ocean.

Argelin backed away from it but it surged around him, over him. He gave a gasp of terror, then yelled, "No! I won't let her go!" But the water had fingers; it dragged Hermia from his arms, pulled her deep, took her far into the depths.

"Leave her with me!" he screamed. "Leave her!"

But all around him the Rain Queen's fury surged.

"He'll be swept away!" Mirany gasped. She could feel the water's anger, its pent-up vengeance. But Jamil had yelled, and now in reply a strange trumpeting thudded the earth, and she saw the elephants had broken free and were strung out in a great linked line, trunk to tail. The first knelt; Jamil grabbed Argelin and thrust him toward the beast. Then they were aloft, the great animal's strength holding itself steady.

Argelin looked back, into the cave. The soldiers were scrambling out.

"We're trapped," Rhetia hissed, "and he knows it. He's leaving us here."

"More than that." Mirany had understood that look, seen how he called up to the cliff top, one savage command.

Then the elephants lumbered away.

•   •   •

Water hit them like a wall. Hot and steaming, it gushed out of the cave and swept them along with it, until Oblek grabbed an outcrop of rock and hauled himself up to the cleft pinnacle of the mountain top, reaching down and plucking the Archon out of the flood with one mighty jerk. The boy whooped with delight, dangling above the waters. Seth and Fox climbed out and the Jackal came after them; on top of the rocks they sat shivering, staring in disbelief at the river that had come from nowhere.

"We did it!" Alexos cried happily. "We brought the river back! Isn't it beautiful, Oblek?"

The big man grinned. "A miracle, old friend."

It roared down the mountain. Stones and boulders were rolled in it, a red flood, and already they could see it surging far below, out into the dry watercourse of the Draxis, raging toward the sea. Downstream the waters would crash like a wall, Seth thought, sweeping away dead trees until the thunder of their coming would bring everyone in the Port running out of their houses. Because the god's act was a danger and a wonder, and to some it brought life, and to others death. To Hermia. And was Mirany really the Speaker now?

The Jackal was standing, staring east. Far off, the sky was alight, streaked with pink. As the sun rose, the desert flushed with splendor, the new water glinting, a streak of fire fingering out, filling tributaries, streambeds, drowning flat cracked slabs of scorched rock.

Seth stood next to him. "It'll be chaos down there," he whispered.

*   *   *

"We'll drown," Rhetia breathed.

Mirany scrambled back from the black torrent. "Where are you?" she gasped. "Come quickly!"

His answer was pleased and happy.

We have drunk from the Well of Songs.

"And the river?"

The golden apples are returned. It seems the Rain Queen has forgiven us.

For a moment, even as the water came above her waist, she laughed, knowing the god's voice was back with her. Until she saw that Rhetia had heard it, too, saw her wide-eyed stare into the back of the cave.

He was standing in the shadows. He was tall and thin, his hair white, his skin drained of color. He held out his narrow hand and beckoned them quickly. *"Mirany. Come with me. Hurry."*

Mirany pushed Rhetia. "Move!"

"Is he—?"

"Just hurry!"

The cave ledge led back, into darkness. The Speaker's mask under her arm, Mirany waded after Kreon, seeing his silhouette flicker in front of her. Once she slipped and went under with a choked scream, because the water was black and steamed, as if it had surged from somewhere incredibly deep. Ahead, Rhetia was chest deep, breathless. Then, above the great crack, Kreon stopped. "This is the only way out."

Rhetia could still manage to snort with scorn. "Down! Are you crazy?"

"The caves lead to tunnels that link with the tombs. This whole area is a honeycomb, centuries old. The water will not fill them." He looked at them sadly. "You have to come with me now, Mirany. It's the only safe place until the Archon returns. Argelin has killed the Speaker, and the god's wrath will fall on him. Nothing will be the same."

"But Mirany's the Speaker. Why should we skulk in the tombs?"

"There's nowhere else." He looked beyond her. "Do you see?"

Smoke was rising from the Island. In the dawn light it was a black column, and it went straight up, like the smoke from a pyre.

"He's done it." Rhetia gasped as the water reached her face. *"He's destroyed the Oracle!"*

The sun was rising; its light touched the cave wall above them. Kreon looked away quickly. "We must go."

The crack was deeply drowned. He lowered himself in, took a deep breath and was gone, the blackness covering him.

Rhetia said, "Good luck. Jump with me."

Over the sea, over the surge of the new river, the sun was rising. Its light flooded Mirany's eyes.

Hermia was dead and she was Speaker. But a Speaker in the darkness, exiled, outlawed.

"They'll be back," she whispered.

Rhetia shrugged. "What can they do? A boy and a fat musician and a scribe."

"And a jackal." Mirany looked down at the mask, its empty eyes filling with water, the darkness pouring through its open mouth. "They can defeat Argelin. For Hermia's sake."

Rhetia grabbed her. "Hermia wouldn't want him defeated. That's the worst thing."

Mirany slipped, losing balance. Then she raised her head and spoke to the sun.

"Don't be long. Things will be terrible now."

She took a deep breath.

Together, they jumped.

Turn the page for a preview of the next electrifying book in

The Oracle Prophecies:

Day of the Scarab

She Hears the Thunder
of the Rain Queen

She could only squeeze in if she went sideways. Even then the axle stuck out through the wooden wheel, and she had to hold her breath and drag herself past it, her infuriating black veil snagging on the wall.

But behind the cart there was a space.

Once in, Mirany reached up and caught hold of the boards; putting her foot on the axle, she pulled herself carefully higher and peered over the top.

The cart was piled with oranges. Their smell was mouthwatering, a sharp juicy sweetness that made her hunger worse and her dry lips sore. She hadn't eaten a whole orange for weeks. Maybe she could have sneaked one out, but three of Argelin's guards were sitting in the dust of the square, gambling, and the risk was too great.

Dice rattled.

Mirany bit the nail of her thumb, then noticed and stopped herself. It was a habit she'd had when she was small;

lately it had come back. There was still no sign of Rhetia. Where was she? An hour must have passed since the time they'd arranged to meet, when the afternoon gong had chimed from the City. Now the hottest part of the day held the Port silent. The market had closed and everyone was indoors. Only stray dogs snoozed in the baking streets.

What is she up to? Do you think she's been caught?

She asked out of habit, but there was no answer. Maybe there never would be an answer again.

And where are you, Bright One? she thought angrily. *Where are you when I need you!*

The piazza was high in the fullers' quarter. Rhetia had chosen it because it had five different exits, and the streets around were a maze of doorways and alleys and steps hung with drying cloth. At this hour it should be deserted.

But it wasn't.

There were more soldiers across by the shuttered wine shop. And as she watched in dismay, an entire phalanx of Argelin's new mercenaries marched in, pale-skinned men who dressed in foreign clothes and spoke some guttural language. Their bronze greaves and corselets and spears glittered in the sunlight.

Something was going on.

Crouched, her bent knees aching, she watched the men halt in the center of the square, below the statue of the Rain Queen.

The officer yelled a curt command; the column fell out, mopped sweat from their faces, brought up mules, unpacked equipment. Echoes rang in the enclosed space. All around them, from the white buildings, the sun's wrath blazed.

Mirany sucked her parched lip. If she could work back under the shadow of that striped awning, she might make the nearest alleyway, and slip away without attracting more than a few glances.

But if they stopped her . . .

And what if Rhetia turned up?

A commotion jerked her head around. A man had come running out of one of the buildings, a small, oldish man. He was shouting in alarm and holding his hands above his head, racing straight at the soldiers.

Instantly the nearest one grabbed a spear and swung; the old man stumbled over it, then fell with a painful thump.

The mercenaries laughed. One made some comment.

The man was pleading with them; he scrambled onto his knees, and Mirany heard his breathless, barely intelligible gasps. "You mustn't do this. Lords, please! This is a terrible thing. This is a desecration."

They probably couldn't understand a word he said. Almost casually, one of them gave him a kick in the chest that took the breath straight out of him; then they turned back to their task.

In sudden horror Mirany realized what they were doing.

Ropes and tackle were being dragged from mules. Efficiently the fair-haired men swung weighted loops; the ropes soared up and around the shoulders of the Rain Queen, her neck, her outstretched arm.

"No!" Mirany breathed.

The statue was vast, higher than the houses. It had been

carved from a single piece of sea green stone, a veined agate. Ancient beyond memory, the calm face of the Rain Queen had looked out over the Port for centuries, over the white houses to the endless azure semicircle of the sea. In the thousand pleated creases of her dress crystals glinted, embedded by the sculptor, and the blue lapis lazuli of the collar she wore glimmered with linked scorpions of gold, and scarabs of coral and amber. She held out one hand, and in her fingers a bronze bowl burned in the sun. Once a fountain had cascaded from it, splashing, diamond bright, into a white marble shell at her feet. But during the drought the fountain had been dry, and even now, when the river ran again, it had not been restored. Lizards basked in the hot curve of the shell, among rubbish and a broken pot.

Ropes rattled.

Mirany gripped her hands into fists. *Do something!* she demanded.

But the god did not answer. He had not answered for two months. And in that time her world had fallen apart.

Suddenly the gambling soldiers were scrambling up, thrusting dice into helmets, grabbing spears. Even before they could get themselves in order, the first rank of the bodyguard rode into the square.

Mirany ducked lower, hissing one of Oblek's worst swear words.

Among the armed men was a litter. She stared at it grimly. Litters were no longer allowed in the Port, except for this one. It had no flimsy curtains, but stiff blinds of papyrus, reinforced, she'd heard, with metal against any sudden knife-thrust. Instead of windows, small slits were dark; eyes moved behind them. And she knew whose.

Since the destruction of the Oracle, Argelin rarely rode out openly. He traveled enclosed, protected by armed riders. He needed to. Every statue of the god and the Rain Queen in the Port was being systematically destroyed by his men, every image confiscated and smashed. Instead, paintings of Argelin decorated walls and squares; vast statues of him were hastily being constructed. All day she'd seen them—Argelin seated, his hands on his knees; Argelin standing astride, grasping a spear; Argelin in a war chariot striking down his enemies, his deeds written in hieroglyphs on shining new obelisks and pylons.

There had been unrest. But then the longships of Argelin's new army had arrived, and terror had cowed people. After the chaotic riot in the harbor last month, when fifty men had been rounded up and beheaded, and their wives sold to slave traders, the general had become a figure of hatred and dread.

And if he found out she was still alive . . .

She smelled a heady jasmine scent, and glanced around anxiously. In the wall behind her was a small door; now it was ajar, an eye peeping out at her through the dark slit.

"Please," she breathed. "Let me come in."

A pause. Then the door opened.

Instantly she slid inside. The bolt clicked behind her. The darkness smelled of cats and incense; she sensed a woman near in the dark passageway. A hand caught hers, and led her up some twisting stairs. Cobwebs hung against her face, and under her feet sandy dust crackled. Mirany guessed this was some sort of storage cellar, little used now that there was nothing to store. She wrapped the black veil hastily around her face and shoulders, so that only her eyes showed. There was no knowing who these people were.

A curtain was pulled aside.

She climbed into a sunlit room, its shabby walls patterned with bright rays that streamed through latticed shutters. It was full of women. They turned to look at her briefly, then clustered again about the windows, as if unwilling to miss a moment of what was happening outside.

The girl who had brought her in was little more than Mirany's age, her face painted with kohl and rouge, her dark hair tangled and unkempt. A small toddler clutched at her skirt.

"You shouldn't have been out there," she said quietly.

Mirany nodded. "What's happening?"

"They're going to destroy the statue, what else?"

Mirany glanced around. The room had couches, frail hangings. Three cats slept in the sun. There was an image of the Rain Queen in one corner; small sticks of sandalwood burned before it. The girl shook her head. "He's insane," she whispered.

As Mirany moved to the window, the women edged back. They were mostly young, garishly made up, flimsily dressed. All at once she realized what sort of house this was, and blushed under the veil.

Then she saw Argelin.

He had climbed out of the litter and was looking up at

the statue. She had not seen him since Hermia's death, and was shocked at the change in him. His beard was still sharply razored, his breastplate glinting bronze, but the eyes that stared up at the Rain Queen had sunk and seemed duller; his face was haggard, its expression a cold loathing.

He stepped back, gave a curt command.

The men hauled on the ropes. Around Mirany, hands went to lips; someone breathed a prayer. The Rain Queen swayed. Very slightly, her hand moved against the sky, her remote face shifted in the sunlight. Dust fell from her ledges and shoulders; one of her fingers cracked where the rope held it, and a knuckle of marble, big as a man's hand, crashed to the ground.

There were people in the square now. They had emerged from the houses, gathered in the shade. They were silent and ominous; Argelin snapped something and the soldiers formed a hasty double formation around the work, facing out, spears crossed. The old man sat stunned in the dust; he seemed unable to believe what was happening. He had probably known the statue all his life, Mirany thought, and the fountain too.

In her mind she said grimly, *Gods are supposed to see what happens on earth. You must be able to see this.* Do something.

As if in answer, a gong chimed. All the women looked to the right.

"Who is it?" one breathed.

A procession was entering the square from the archway down to the harbor. Mirany pushed to the front. "Officials."

"From the Emperor?"

"From the City of the Dead."

She recognized them easily. The Chief Embalmer in white, the Overseer of the Tombs, five of the top scribes, the Archon's steward, the Mistress of the Sacred Cats.

"They'll stop him." One of the older women folded her arms. "They have to. He just can't go on pulling down everything."

"He can do what he likes," the girl next to Mirany said quietly. "He killed the Speaker. The god has cursed him, and all of us with him."

Mirany edged the shutter open slightly. The dignitaries came forward. Just below the window, Argelin turned to face them. After a moment all of them bowed, the embalmer's white robe sweeping the dust, the bareheaded scribes sweating.

"What's this?" Argelin sounded more amused than annoyed.

The Chief Embalmer licked dry lips. He was a fleshy man, his thick fingers heavy with rings.

"Lord General . . . ," he said hesitantly.

Argelin smiled a smile like steel. "Lord *King*."

A fraction of silence. Then, "If you wish it, sir."

Argelin stepped forward. "I more than wish it. I have ordered it. You saw me crowned, Parmenio."

Mirany had heard about that. Kreon had brought news down into the tombs that Argelin had crowned himself king with the silver diadem from the god's statue in the Temple. She remembered how appalled Rhetia had been. And how furious.

The Chief Embalmer had an attendant with a feathered fan. Argelin waved the boy away. He backed quickly as his master stammered, "Lord King. Yes. Indeed. But I . . . we . . . the servants of the dead. There is something we wish to say."

He had nerve, Mirany thought. Now he extended a plump hand, and a slave came forward with a casket. The embalmer opened it.

The women gasped as one.

Even from here the contents blazed. Diamonds, almost certainly. Their brilliance threw tiny rainbows across Argelin's face. His eyes narrowed, but he showed no surprise. The embalmer took a small scroll out and his gilded fingers held it tight. "Lord King." His voice was high with tension. "Your actions are your own. But we cannot stand by and see them without pleading with you . . . without supplicating you . . . to show mercy, and desist." He gave a nod; at once the officials knelt, clumsy in their cumbersome robes, the Mistress of the Cats in her whiskered mask, the scribes in saffron and red. They bowed their foreheads to the ground.

The crowd murmured.

Argelin watched, unmoved.

"For a mortal to make war against the gods is to invite disaster," the embalmer went on. "You will bring the god's wrath and the Rain Queen's anger on all of us, on the people, on the slaves and the children. We, the officers of the Land Below, beg you to spare this last image. There has been enough terror. You are too generous, too wise to refuse us. In return, accept this token of the people's gratitude."

Terrified, the slave laid the casket at Argelin's feet. The general looked down at it. When he raised his face, Mirany saw his eyes were cold.

"What about my anger, old man? What about my wrath?" Like a striking snake, Argelin reached out and grabbed the embalmer by the neck of his robe, heaving the fat man's sweating face close to his. "This Rain Queen of yours took Hermia's body out of my arms, blinded me into murder. I swore I would tear down every image of her for that, and I'll do it. And I defy you, and the stinking dead, and the god himself, to stop me!"

Viciously he kicked the casket over. Diamonds hissed out. He ground them into the sand with his boot heel.

"My lord," the embalmer gasped, "think again. When the Archon returns—"

"*I am the Archon.* I am the Oracle, and the Nine, and the god himself. Get that into your head, Parmenio, and make the City understand it, too. Because when I've finished with the Port, I'll be coming to you, and if I want the riches of the tombs, I'll take them, with my own hands."

There was a terrible silence.

And then a shriek. It was so eerie and unexpected that even Argelin's head shot up; he turned, and the soldiers gripped weapons.

On all the housetops around the square, the town baboons sat watching. As if the noise had wakened them from their siesta, the monkeys stared down, desert wind ruffling their fur. Mothers held babies; the males prowled, anxious. Another screeched, then another, and suddenly the whole square was a cacophony of panic, the animals rising and beating their chests, grabbing jutting stone and jabbering furiously, their white teeth wide.

Out at sea, thunder rumbled.

Argelin dropped the Chief Embalmer. The man staggered, said, "Lord King, she will send plagues—"

"Enough!" Without another word Argelin turned on his heel. He gave one yell; the mercenaries took up the ropes. The pandemonium the baboons were making must have been terrifying and strange to them, but they ignored it, their hands grasping the rough thick cables.

"Hear me, Rainwoman!" Argelin yelled. "Take this for your worship!"

He jumped back.

The soldiers heaved.

With a crack like lightning, the statue snapped. Black fissures shot up from its base; the sea green dress shattered. Fingers and curls of hair and an ear rained down. Rocking as the soldiers heaved and yelled and heaved again, the Rain Queen toppled. She jolted forward, her calm face fragmenting, and for a moment Mirany was sure the goddess would turn her head and shimmer into life, that she would shrivel Argelin with one touch of her crystal fingertip. Instead, with a shudder that shook the house and the world, she fell, and all that crashed into the stones was a mass of agate, a heaped tumble of broken slivers and glistening shards.

Dust rose in a great cloud, billowing in through the windows. The girls coughed, covered their faces. Objects fell from shelves. A baby woke and screamed.

Slowly, the huddled monkeys fell silent.

The officials stared, appalled.

After a moment, his boots crushing rubble, Argelin crunched over to the broken face. It lay on its side, one eye and half a nose, and as they watched he crouched and laid his hand almost tenderly along the cracked brow.

"So, lady," he whispered, "destroy me now, if you can. Do your worst. Because we are enemies, you and I."

Crystals glinted all around her. In the corners of her eyes.

Argelin snatched his hand away. He turned his palm up, and behind the window shutter Mirany drew in her breath, because in all the blazing heat, his skin was wet.

And in her ear a breathless voice said, **Look at him, Mirany. Does he really think he's me.**

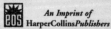